USA TODAY bestselling author **Jules Bennett** has published over sixty books and never tires of writing happy endings. Writing strong heroines and alpha heroes is Jules' favourite way to spend her workdays. Jules hosts weekly contests on her Facebook fan page and loves chatting with readers on Twitter, Facebook and via email through her website. Stay up-to-date by signing up for her newsletter at julesbennett.com

Joanne Rock credits her decision to write romance after a book she picked up during a flight delay engrossed her so thoroughly that she didn't mind at all when her flight was delayed two more times. Giving her readers the chance to escape into another world has motivated her to write over eighty books for a variety of Mills & Boon series.

Discover more at millsandboon.co.uk

FAKE ENGAGEMENT, NASHVILLE STYLE

JULES BENNETT

A NINE-MONTH TEMPTATION

JOANNE ROCK

MILLS & BOON

First Published in Great Britain 2021
by Mills & Boon, an imprint of HarperCollins*Publishers* Ltd
1 London Bridge Street, London, SE1 9GF

www.harpercollins.co.uk

HarperCollins*Publishers*
1st Floor, Watermarque Building,
Ringsend Road, Dublin 4, Ireland

Fake Engagement, Nashville Style © 2021 Jules Bennett
A Nine-Month Temptation © 2021 Joanne Rock

ISBN: 978-0-263-28293-1

0521

MIX
Paper from
responsible sources
FSC™ C007454

Printed and bound in Spain
by CPI, Barcelona

FAKE ENGAGEMENT, NASHVILLE STYLE

JULES BENNETT

In remembrance of Mistie, who always had a love for writing and hoped to have her work published one day. Our book chats and your infectious laugh are truly missed.

One

"You've got another visitor."

Luke glanced up from his computer at the desk where he'd been hiding for most of the evening. "Tell her I'm busy," Luke told his bodyguard.

Normally he loved being out with his customers at his rooftop bar, The Cheshire, but not since that damn magazine article had thrust him into the spotlight.

Meet Luke Sutherland: Tennessee's Most Eligible Bachelor

That term, along with a photo of him in a pair of jeans with his dress shirt completely unbuttoned, had attracted every woman in the state—and some men, too—like some type of magnet.

Jake stepped farther into the room. "Uh, sir. It's Cassandra Taylor."

Cassandra Taylor?

That was a name he hadn't heard in years, but one he'd certainly thought of often enough.

All of that long black hair that he used to glide through his fingers and over his body. Her sweet smile that turned him on before she could even say a word. And the way he'd confided in her... He'd loved her once—she'd been his best friend.

Unfortunately, marriage hadn't been in the cards for him, not even to his best friend. Their paths had been destined for different directions and he'd let her go.

It had been the right choice.

So what was she doing back now after all this time? Surely she hadn't seen the article and now thought they had another chance at being together? That shot had been ruined when she'd left town nearly eight years ago with barely a goodbye. Oh, his brothers had blamed him at the time, and perhaps a portion of the blame did fall on his shoulders—he hadn't gone after her. But she hadn't stuck around to see if things could be worked out, either.

They'd both let go, and there was no going back after that.

"Tell her I'm busy, then," he repeated, almost wishing the uninvited guest had been a stranger.

Jake, his bodyguard and a top bouncer who had been with Luke since the opening of his first bar, knew full well the impact Cassandra had had on Luke's life. Luke continued to stare across his desk, but Jake didn't move.

"Is there a problem?" Luke asked.

"Let her in. She came a long way after all this time."

Luke leaned back in his leather chair and rested his elbows on the chair's arms. "When did you take her side?"

Jake laughed. "Her side? Sir, it's been years and I think you know where my loyalties lie, but you two have a history. She's not like those other women who have seen the article and are vying for the role of Mrs. Luke Sutherland. I doubt Cassandra is looking for a ring on her finger from you."

Luke swallowed. Maybe she wasn't, but he'd been prepared to put that ring on her finger when she left. Well, in theory. He'd had the ring, but somehow he'd never found the right moment to propose. And then she was gone. His brothers had ridiculed him—hell, he'd blasted himself on more than one occasion—but she hadn't even given him a chance to tell his side or explain his motives. Obviously, a marriage between them would have been doomed from the start.

If she'd been able to walk away so easily, then it was best he had never proposed. He'd been hurt, he'd been angry—maybe a part of him still was—but he wasn't the same naive guy he'd once been. Now he was glad he hadn't settled down. He loved the life he'd created and venturing back to his past wouldn't do anyone any good.

"Stop thinking so hard," Jake growled. "You know if you turn her away you're only going to be wracking your brain over what she might have wanted."

Damn it. Jake was right. That didn't make the fact that she was back any easier to digest. Apparently, she could still get to him after all this time. Or, maybe if he saw her, perhaps she wouldn't have any effect on him. She'd likely changed just as much as he had over such a long stretch of time.

There was only one way to find out.

Luke sat up and rested his arms on his desk. The decision volleyed back and forth in his mind. He had no clue what to expect. He hadn't seen Cassandra in years, save for the time he'd looked her up on social media a couple of years ago. He'd found her still single and still just as sexy as ever.

But his curiosity got the better of him.

With a deep sigh and some serious concerns, Luke nodded. "Fine. Bring her in."

As Jake left the office, Luke wondered what the hell he'd just done. Why would he purposely agree to see her again? They'd parted ways and agreed that was it. Yet now she was back. He didn't know why, but he had to assume her abrupt reappearance had to do with *Country Beat*'s article on him.

He'd been doing just fine with his bars in Beaumont Bay and Nashville. He'd been contemplating expanding to other cities. Maybe Chicago or Atlanta. He wasn't sure, but his life was always in forward motion. The only time he'd ever considered slowing down had been when he was with Cassandra, and look how that had turned out. Now, having any woman in his life would only hinder his career. He loved the country-music industry, loved the bar-and-restaurant lifestyle and loved combining the two. He didn't want to change any of it, not for anyone.

Luke got to his feet, then cursed himself. Should he

be standing, as if he was anticipating her arrival? Or should he sit and try to appear relaxed? Sitting might be a jerk move, but he wanted her to know he wasn't affected by this visit. He could be casual with her, just like he would be with any other visitor.

Hell. She hadn't even gotten through the door yet and he was already tied up in knots. How would he feel coming face-to-face with her? A chunk of time had settled between them and the weight of that firmly took root in his chest. There was a heaviness he couldn't explain, but he didn't have time to try to.

All thoughts vanished as Cassandra Taylor stepped into the opening of his office and met his gaze. Luke realized he should've remained seated because she nearly knocked the breath out of him.

There was something so familiar about her, and yet so new. That confidence, with the straight shoulders, the tipped chin and the determined eye contact, was certainly new. But the curves, the dark hair falling over her shoulders and the slight smirk on her lips brought memories rushing back.

Despite her familiar beauty and new confidence, she was still the one who'd walked away and Luke had no desire to revisit the past. So he shoved away those emotions and memories. He'd gotten this far by living in the moment and taking control of his own destiny. Nobody and nothing would ever change that again.

"Cassandra."

The door to the bar slid shut behind her and she jerked around to see that she'd been closed in.

"An automatic door. That's fancy," she muttered as

she turned back to face him. "I appreciate you seeing me without notice."

She took a step inside and then another until she stood just on the other side of his desk. He could reach out and touch her. He could see those navy flecks in her deep blue eyes.

He'd only had a two-minute heads-up, but he certainly hadn't expected this onslaught of emotions to come flooding to the forefront of his mind...and his body.

"Luke."

Oh, damn. His name sliding through her lips had him recalling starry nights and heated moments. No matter why she was here, he'd get her in and out. No way could he get caught up in her like he had in the past. He was perfectly fine remaining single... Wait. Was that why she was here? She'd seen that article and now she wanted to come back and secure her original role as his woman?

No way. That was a hard no.

Agreeing to see Cassandra Taylor had been a mistake. Somehow, he knew this moment would no doubt change his life forever.

Nerves curled into spirals in Cassandra's belly. She'd given herself a pep talk the entire drive here—all three hours. Luke was just a man and she was just a woman. There was no reason she couldn't approach him about her critical need. They were different people now.

When she'd left their relationship years ago, she'd done so because she'd had to guard her heart. Staying would only have caused more pain. Luke had been so set on moving ahead in his career and seemed perfectly content keeping her tucked in a corner, always assuming she'd be content to stay there. While she'd been proud of all he'd accomplished, she'd also wanted to be by his side. She'd wanted them to grow together…and she'd learned too late that they'd had two different visions of what they'd wanted out of life.

So she'd walked away, made a successful career for herself and absolutely loved the life she'd created in Lexington, Kentucky.

So why the hell was she so shaky now that she was back?

When Luke's intense stare became too much, Cassandra pulled together all her courage and forced herself not to turn and walk out. She stood her ground.

Clearly, he wasn't going to say anything, even though she'd called him by name to snap him out of whatever trance that had overtaken him. Although, he was likely waiting on her to explain why she'd shown up, out of the blue, after not a word in eight years.

"Your bar is amazing and Jake seems…intimidating," she began, not wanting to jump right into the real topic. "You've done really well for yourself."

"Jake does his job skillfully." Luke shifted his stance and rested his hands on his narrow hips. "But did you come all the way here to tell me what I already know?"

Okay, well, obviously his ego was still intact and he wasn't in the mood for the small talk she had rehearsed to lead up to her real reason for coming back.

Pulling in a deep breath, Cassandra jumped right in.

"No," she replied. "I came here to tell you I need a favor."

Luke stared another moment before that rich, familiar laugh filled the spacious office. Unable to stand still, Cassandra moved around and glanced at the black-and-white images on the walls. Pictures of Luke and his brothers. The Sutherland men were all handsome and powerful, and she had loved each of them like family... but none like Luke. Gavin, Cash, and Will had all been like her own brothers. She'd missed them when she'd left town without looking back.

But Luke... He'd left her bitter and angry. He'd strung her along, allowing her to think they'd spend their lives together, when he only cared about the next bar he could open or how quickly he could book the next big star so he could have bragging rights.

So she'd left.

Cassandra had gathered up the pieces of her shattered heart and continued on with her own dreams. She'd gotten along just fine in her career as a wedding coordinator, despite being jealous with each "I do" she helped create. And now that she'd branched out and opened her own company, she needed something amazing to make her stand out in a saturated industry. She needed a celebrity wedding.

And that's where the favor she was after came in. That's why she'd set aside her pride, and her carefully repaired heart, and driven the three hours to Beaumont Bay to put herself in front of Luke.

"I know Will is getting married." Cassandra turned from the images to face Luke once again. He still hadn't moved, but those eyes remained on her. "That's what I'm here about."

"Sorry, darlin', but he's already got a bride."

Cassandra sighed. "Obviously. I'm aware his bride is Hannah Banks. I want to be their wedding coordinator and you're going to get that job for me."

Silence settled between them and her heart pounded so loud, she could hear the rhythmic thump in her ears.

"You came all the way here to make that demand?" Luke circled the desk to stand right in front of her. "You could have called."

Oh, mercy. He smelled too damn good and seemed broader, stronger, sexier than ever. Maybe a phone call would have been better.

No matter. She was immune to his charms now. She'd known when she'd decided to ask for this favor that Luke would be handsome and successful. He'd been both of those things when she'd left. The hurt he'd left her with had trumped any physical attraction.

"Would you have taken my call?" she asked.

Luke shrugged. "Sure, why not? We've both moved on."

His eyes dropped to her lips and that flair of arousal shot up again. She'd only been in the office for all of two minutes and already she wanted him. Maybe it was the memories creeping up. She had to keep reminding herself to stay in the present and focus on the real reason for her visit back to the Bay. Luke owed her for the years she'd spent with him, when she'd waited on him to commit, and all the hurt he'd caused in the end. Cassandra was ready to cash in his debt.

And yet, who could blame her for getting sidetracked by Luke Sutherland? Even if they hadn't had an intimate past, the man would have demanded attention, with his dark gaze, his strong jawline, and those broad shoulders. When he crossed his arms and widened his stance, Cassandra swallowed the lump of arousal in her throat.

The man knew exactly what he was doing to her. How dare he stand there and look so, so…

Ugh. Frustration was taking hold of her.

A shrink would have a field day in her head, considering her past heartbreak when it came to a man who'd refused to marry her, along with her current line of work helping happy couples walk down the aisle. Maybe she was just a hopeless romantic who still believed in the miracle of happy endings.

Just because things hadn't worked out for her didn't mean she didn't believe in love. She saw the reality of it every day as a wedding coordinator. Maybe one day she would find the man she was meant to be with.

Once upon a time, she'd thought for sure that man was Luke. Now she was glad she hadn't hung around any longer waiting for him. She'd seen that *Country Beat* article. Apparently, he still wasn't in the market for a wife.

"What makes you think I have any pull with Hannah?" he asked, jerking her attention to his low, gravelly tone. "She's a superstar. She's got her own entourage of people. I'm sure she has found her own wedding coordinator since they want to do something quick and small."

Cassandra smiled. "Do you think I would have come all this way if I hadn't done my research? She has no coordinator as of yesterday, which is why you need to get on the phone now and make an appointment with her for me."

The muscles in Luke's jaw clenched as he continued to stare at her. Cassandra really didn't want to pull the past into this moment, but she would do it if she needed to. She wasn't leaving this office without an appointment.

"What makes you think you'll get the job?" he asked.

"You get me the in-person meeting and I'll get the job."

Luke rested his hip on the edge of his desk and seemed to study her…and he also seemed to be considering her idea.

"Why is this job so important for you?" he asked.

"I started my own company," she told him. "It's only six months old. I worked for Brides and Belles for almost eight years and it was time to go out on my own. I need a celebrity wedding to push my business and put my name at the top of other celebrity lists."

Even if that meant swallowing her pride and begging.

Again, Luke landed that intense stare on her and she forced herself to remain calm and not fidget. He *had* to agree to this. He absolutely had to. Launching her own service, Be My Guest, had taken most of her savings and every ounce of her courage. She would fight with everything in her being to make this next career move a huge success…even if that meant putting her heart and sanity on the line once again and facing Luke Sutherland.

"I'll help you."

Cassandra nearly threw her arms around him, but

then remembered touching him would be a terrible idea. Still, she couldn't stop the smile from spreading across her face.

She'd always believed in love, always wanted to see other couples be happy and help them create the most perfect day. She'd even envisioned her own perfect day with Luke way back when. But now...well, now she wouldn't allow herself to even mentally walk down the aisle—not until she found a man worthy of her. Now, all her energy was on making Be My Guest a success. And Luke was helping her do it.

"Luke, you don't even—"

"On one condition," he added, straightening and leveling his gaze on her.

Her excitement was short-lived as she heard his stern tone. "A condition?"

"You will help me in return."

He circled around the other side of the desk and pulled a magazine from a drawer. He slapped the magazine on the desktop, the harsh sound echoing throughout the office, and angled the article for her to see.

"That is ruining my life." He pointed to the open pages. "I'll get you that appointment if you pretend to be my very doting, very public fiancée until Will's wedding is over."

Cassandra waited for the punch line of this sick joke. She'd waited so long for him to ask her to marry him. He'd been working toward opening his first bar, and she'd been trying to break in to planning weddings. But the longer she'd waited, the more he'd become involved in his work. One bar turned into another and he'd reached a point where he'd been too busy for her. Between bar openings, hiring of employees, and finding bands and artists to keep the stages full and the customers coming back, a solid wedge had formed between them. And, one day, Cassandra had realized she would never be able to compete for his affection.

The realization had stung because she'd supported him, had wanted him to fulfill his dreams as she chased her own. Unfortunately, he chased them so far, he forgot to take her along.

And now he was asking her to fake the one thing he'd never been willing to give her?

"You're not serious," she finally said, anger bubbling deep within her.

His stern face and steady stare told her he was quite serious. Now she just had to think about how badly she wanted this job. Planning a celebrity wedding would be invaluable. It would open doors she wouldn't be able to get close to on her own. She'd been willing to see Luke again, to put her pride on the line, to beg. But he was asking for much more than that.

"Is there any other way around this?" she asked hopefully.

"Not if you want that appointment."

"What all would this pretending entail?" she asked, still quite skeptical and not at all amused.

Was she seriously considering this craziness? Pretending to be engaged would require much more emotional work than she'd been willing to do when she first came in here. She actually hadn't even thought that Luke would require something in return, but he hadn't become a successful businessman by giving everything away.

Luke shrugged. "A few social-media posts, public appearances. You'd need to be here a few nights with me so everything seems authentic. Some PDA wouldn't hurt, either."

Public displays of affection? They wouldn't hurt? Kissing, touching, *pretending* would hurt. There was no way she could be in that type of situation and not recall everything she'd once dreamed of having with him and ultimately lost.

Damn it, he'd gotten shrewd since she'd left...

Okay, fine. She wanted this wedding. So she could play the game. She'd loved him once, so pretending to love him shouldn't be difficult. At least now, she knew how things would end. There wouldn't be naive stars in her eyes. She wouldn't lose her heart this time and she would stay in control. Besides, she'd be too busy planning the celebrity wedding of the year to get wrapped up with her ex, right?

"Fine." She moved closer to him and held out her hand. "It's a deal. And after the wedding, we're over. For good this time."

"Sounds good to me."

He took her hand and her heart began pounding. Her stomach knotted once again, and she knew in that instant that she was in trouble.

Playing her ex's pretend fiancée.

What the hell had she just gotten herself into?

Two

His brothers would no doubt give him hell over this, but the deal was done. Luke now had something he'd never wanted—a fiancée. Oh, when he and Cassandra had been together before, he'd bought the ring as a stepping stone, but he had never gotten up the courage to take that final step and actually propose. He just hadn't been sure, and then she'd left and he knew not asking her had been the right decision.

And now she was back and he was giving her everything she'd wanted before that he couldn't give. Well, pretending they had what she'd wanted. The entire situation was too ironic. Luke couldn't even wrap his mind around where the hell he'd come up with the idea, where the hell he'd lost control. Cassandra had swept in and presented her demands, and he'd been caught off guard so completely that he'd reacted without thinking.

Luke eased back in his leather desk chair and stared at the door that had slid closed after Cassandra's departure. She'd made one hell of an impact in such a short time, but Luke refused to admit he was anything but immune at this point. He'd been in love with her at one time, yes, but he hadn't been ready for a walk down the aisle. He still wasn't. She'd always wanted more than he could give.

Now, well… Who knew why he'd caved in to her demands. Or why he'd asked her to pretend to be his fiancée. True, he'd wanted the swarm of women to ease up ever since that damn article had been released. But, on the other hand, maybe he was trying to prove to himself that he had gotten over her, that she was nothing more than a memory from his past.

He sent Jake a text, asking him to find out where Cassandra was staying, how long she planned to be in town and everything else about her that he could find. Luke wanted to know all he could about his *fiancée*.

Within minutes, Luke's bodyguard informed him that she was staying just one floor below his bar, in the penthouse suite of The Beaumont. Fantastic. She was practically within touching distance. He sent a message to her room to be at The Cheshire tomorrow evening to play the role of his doting girlfriend.

And once everyone's initial shock wore off, they could discuss when and how to announce their…

Luke swallowed and pushed aside his frustrations.

Their engagement.

* * *

"Thank you so much for agreeing to meet with me."

Cassandra stepped inside Hannah Banks's lakeside three-story mansion and couldn't believe she was actually here. She'd listened to Hannah's music for years and the superstar was just as stunning in person as she was on television. Her smile seemed genuine and all the makeup and bling seemed to suit her over-the-top personality.

"Of course." Hannah closed the door and turned to face Cassandra and Luke. "I'm thrilled someone who knows Will is interested in taking part in our special day. I've been so swamped with work and with the new record, I haven't been able to zero in on anyone who really sees my vision. I know I want something quaint and quick, but I didn't think planning this would be so difficult."

There wasn't a doubt in Cassandra's mind that she would land this job. This would be her biggest undertaking, but the most rewarding and the most thrilling of her entire career.

"Sorry. I start chatting and can't stop. Come on out to the patio," Hannah stated as she started down a hallway leading to the back of the house. "I've got some drinks and Will is out there. I think he's on the phone, but he needs to finish up. I swear that man is always working."

"That's what we Sutherlands do," Luke chimed in. "I'm sure he'll be excited to take a break and discuss flowers and seating charts."

Cassandra smacked his abs as they walked through the home. "Hush. The groom should be part of the special day just as much as the bride."

"I agree." Hannah approached the patio doors and gestured for Cassandra and Luke to go first. "Looks like he's off the phone now."

Luke placed his hand on Cassandra's back and ushered her outside. Just that simple, dominating gesture had her shivering…and pulling away. She didn't want him to touch her. Not because she didn't enjoy it—she did, too much—but because she didn't want to get used to his strength or his affection. She didn't *want* to enjoy this.

True, they were going to pretend to be engaged, but they didn't have to start the show just yet. She wasn't sure what Luke was going to tell his brothers or his parents, but now wasn't the time to get in to that. First things first—land this dream job.

They hadn't exactly discussed when the faux engagement would begin, though he'd sent a message to her room that she should be at his bar tonight posing as his girlfriend.

Nothing like being summoned for affection. All of this was just as romantic and warm as the ending of their first go-round.

For now, though, she wasn't going to be overly doting on her ex. They would just have to speak in private later about the exact details of their in-public relationship.

"Will," Hannah said as she came around the furniture to stand beside her fiancé. "You know Cassandra."

Will's smile widened as he closed the gap between them and pulled her in for an embrace. She hadn't seen him in years, and he was still just as kind and handsome as she remembered. All of the Sutherland men were known for their Southern manners and sexy good looks, and a couple of the brothers had a reputation with the ladies, Gavin in particular. She wondered if he'd ever settled down or want some family life.

She'd wondered about all of them over the years and if the brothers had remained as close as they had been when she was around. Being an only child, Cassandra had always envied the bond these brothers shared. She'd been welcomed into the Sutherland fold just as if she'd always belonged there.

A twinge pinged at her heart and she had to ignore the yearning. This was not meant to be her family. That had been decided long ago and there was no turning back now.

"So great to see you again," Will said as he eased back. "You look great and you have a brand-new business. Sounds like life is treating you well."

Cassandra shifted her portfolio under her other arm and nodded as she stepped back. "I'm doing quite well. It seems so strange to be back in Beaumont Bay. It's grown even more since I left."

The shops, the bars, the homes—everything seemed to be on a bigger, grander scale than she remembered. Then again, the celebrities that had moved to this area had definitely made upgrades and they had certain expectations. Nashville was no longer the hottest spot or where the high-society folks went to play. There was no city that could compare to the nightlife and homes in Beaumont Bay around the lake and up into the hills.

"Please, sit." Hannah gestured to the large sectional. "Can I get you something to drink?"

"I'm fine, thank you."

Cassandra took a seat and the fact that Luke sat right next to her did nothing to help squash those growing nerves. They hadn't even gotten to the point of pretending to be a couple and he was already getting under her skin.

For now, she had a deal to seal and nothing else could bother her or get inside her head.

"I can't wait to see what you brought," Hannah said, beaming. "I have a few ideas of my own, but I haven't found anyone who shares the same vision."

"Well, I'm sure you will love what I've come up with and everything is negotiable. This is your wedding and I insist that all my clients be happy."

Cassandra placed the portfolio in her lap and flipped open the cover. She turned to show Will and Hannah, who were sitting across from her on another matching outdoor sofa. The glass table between them provided a perfect area to spread out the images and samples Cassandra had brought with her.

"The most important thing is for you both to enjoy your day and feel as if everything is flawless," Cassandra went on. "You should have no worries except how long you want to hold that kiss after you say 'I do.'"

Will laughed. "Oh, that will be all up to me."

Hannah elbowed him in the side and Cassandra saw how these two were made for each other. The way they looked into one another's eyes had her heart melting. She loved working with a couple in love, and sometimes, there were people that Cassandra could tell would actually make their marriage work. She could already see that Will and Hannah would definitely have their happily-ever-after.

"That is just about the only area I don't get involved in," Cassandra assured them. "I would like to start with the general overview. After doing some research, I understand the importance of privacy and I don't blame you one bit. I know Will values family, so I'm thinking something small, private yet stunning. I've drawn up two options for you to look at."

Cassandra slid easily into work mode. This was what she lived for, what kept her smiling and moving forward. Just because she'd lost the man she thought had been the love of her life didn't mean she'd stopped being a hopeless romantic. Seeing people found their soul mates, and knowing she had a part in making their dreams come true really was the best part of her life. She never felt like this was work; she was living out her own dream…even though she was going home alone at night after seeing happy couples getting started on their lives together.

As she flipped through the sample portfolio, Cassandra managed to push aside the fact that Luke was still sitting right next to her with his hip resting against hers.

Her emotions, their past, their current situation— none of those things mattered right now. All that mattered was wowing Hannah and Will with her ideas. Luke sat silently, but she knew he was listening and taking everything in.

She would have been fine had he not tagged along. She didn't trust him. She didn't want to spend more time with him than absolutely necessary. Considering this was his brother's wedding and the meeting had been set up through Luke, she supposed he deemed himself a vital part today.

"I'm amazed," Hannah finally said. She glanced to Will. "What do you think, babe? Which one of these sample ideas do you love?"

Will shook his head. "This is all pretty overwhelming."

Cassandra laughed. "It is at first, but we take everything one step at a time, and I won't pressure you or bombard you with questions or decision-making. This should be a fun process as we lead up to the big day. Even though we will be working at lightning speed, I will take the brunt of the stress. That's my job."

Hannah glanced back to the portfolio and flipped through again, pausing on the outdoor option with a sunset backdrop. Secretly, this was Cassandra's favorite, too, but she never offered her opinion unless asked.

"I've always dreamed of something outdoors," Hannah murmured. "The other designers I talked with urged me indoors in case of weather or for privacy, but I'd love to be out in the open."

Cassandra nodded. "We will take extra precautions with security, and as for the weather, we have beautiful tents that can be set up with chandeliers and draped in flowers so you won't even realize you're under a tent. But I always go in hopeful for a perfect outdoor wedding, so we won't think rain just yet."

Hannah smiled and tapped her polished red nail on the design. "This is what I want," she declared, looking back to Cassandra. "And I want you to be the one to make this happen."

A burst of elation and a swell of pride overcame her. Cassandra had believed she could get this wedding. That's why she'd dealt with the devil to get the meeting.

With a smile, Cassandra reached out her hand to Hannah. "I cannot wait to get started, and I promise you will be the happiest, most beautiful couple. This will be the wedding of the year."

Will sighed. "How hard is this going to hit my budget?"

Hannah elbowed him once again in his side. "*Our* budget, and I don't care. We're only getting married once."

He wrapped his arm around her shoulders and pulled her closer to his side. "You better only marry once. I'm it for you."

Luke got to his feet. "Okay, so if they're going to start this lovey-dovey stuff, I'm out of here."

Will glanced over to his brother. "Don't be jealous."

"Jealous?" Luke laughed. "I'm not jealous. Between you and Cash, something is in the water around here."

Cassandra had seen the news that their other brother, Cash, had gotten engaged during one of his concerts. The online photos she'd seen had been so damn romantic—the way he'd pulled his fiancée onto the stage and dropped the ring out of his guitar before proposing to a screaming crowd. Cassandra wouldn't be above asking to plan that epic wedding, too.

Will and Hannah stood, so Cassandra gathered her

portfolio and also rose. She tucked it beneath her arm and glanced to Luke, whose eyes were locked onto hers.

"I'd say we're ready to go," she told him, then turned back to Will and Hannah. "I will be emailing you a detailed timeline. I don't want you all to be in the dark, even though some of the items are all on me. I would like to get together again in a couple days, or when it's good for you two, so we can get some of the larger things decided and pinned down since the wedding is in seven weeks."

Hannah nodded. "I'm free Wednesday morning, if that's okay? Do you want to meet here again?"

"Perfect." Cassandra pulled out her cell and made a note of the appointment. "I can't tell you how thrilling this is for me. I absolutely love your music."

Hannah beamed and smoothed her hair behind her ear. "That's so nice to hear. I'll be sure to get you some VIP tickets to my next concert. Where do you live?"

"I live in Kentucky, actually."

"Oh, well, I'll be doing a couple of shows there. We'll work something out."

Cassandra couldn't believe how perfect this day had gone. Hannah Banks was just as sweet in private as she'd seemed in public. This wedding would be such a fun and a rewarding event to work on. And hopefully Cassandra would be so busy with this project, she wouldn't have too much time to devote to her "fiancé."

Once they were back in Luke's truck, he pulled out of Hannah's drive. Cassandra smoothed her hair over one shoulder and adjusted her sunglasses against the bright sky.

"You're really good at your job," he said.

Cassandra glanced over to Luke, who was keeping his eyes on the road. "You sound surprised."

"Not surprised at all, actually," he admitted. "I knew you'd be amazing at this. I've just never seen you in your element before."

A little taken aback by his admission, Cassandra smiled. "Well, thanks. I love my job and I always think that if you're doing what you love, then it never feels like work."

"I agree. Owning bars was always my goal. I love the atmosphere, the people... Well, I did love the people until I was bombarded with women ready for me to make them Mrs. Sutherland."

A burst of jealousy surged through her, but that was ridiculous. She had no claim to Luke and it wasn't like the man hadn't dated over the years. Maybe he'd even had a serious relationship. None of that was her business or concern, which was why she shouldn't be thinking of it.

When Luke pulled in front of The Beaumont, where she had rented the penthouse for the next few months, he killed the engine and stepped out. Before she could get her own door, Luke had opened it and reached his hand inside.

Cassandra shifted her gaze to his and found that intense stare looking back at her. She slid her hand into his and there was no ignoring the familiar jolt that had always aroused her. Apparently, now was no different than eight years ago.

When she stepped out of the truck, he didn't move

back, and instead he caged her against the opening and smiled.

"What are you doing?" she murmured as their bodies pressed together. Instant bursts of arousal coursed through her and she cursed herself for allowing herself to feel such worthless emotions.

"Practicing."

And that was all the warning she got before his mouth descended onto hers.

Three

What the hell was he doing?

Well, he knew what he was doing. He was finally kissing Cassandra after an entire day of fantasizing about it. But what was he thinking? There were no cameras around, no one to care that he was kissing his ex.

No, this kiss was purely selfish and completely wrong…and also so damn perfect. He was supposed to be proving the point that he was over her and had absolutely no interest. Yet here he was, wondering what else remained the same…because his reaction to kissing sure as hell had.

Cassandra sighed into him, her body practically melting against his. Luke shored up every ounce of resolve not to touch her anywhere else. Gripping her waist would be so easy, but he'd already lost his mind and kissed her.

She pressed a hand to his chest and leaned away. "Luke."

Muttering a curse beneath his breath, he took a step back and kept his eyes locked on her. She blinked up at him and licked her lips, clearly waiting for an explanation.

"I figured we should get the first kiss out of the way," he explained.

"We've shared thousands of kisses."

As if he needed the reminder. Luke was well aware of his experience with Cassandra and that's why he couldn't stop himself. Okay, so, fine. They'd kissed and he'd liked it. But now it was out of his system...right? He could ignore his sexual desires.

Luke berated himself. He was a damn fool for coming up with this plan—for kissing her, and for asking her to pretend to be his fiancée—but now he was in it. At least his wild idea would calm the masses after that article.

"I didn't want our first kiss in eight years to be in front of people," he told her. "Just in case things were awkward."

Cassandra laughed. "Awkward? Luke, every bit of this is awkward, but I want this wedding and now that I have it, I'll hold up my end of the deal. But no more kissing when we don't have to. No touching, no nothing."

Oh, but he wanted to...and he likely would ask her again when they were alone because she'd melted against him and clearly craved that physical connection, just as he did.

Did she expect him to deny them both when it was clear she enjoyed it just as much? Had she not melted against him and returned that kiss with just as much desire and passion as he was feeling?

"What time do you want me at The Cheshire tonight?" she asked.

Considering her penthouse was just below his rooftop bar, he fully planned on picking her up and taking her with him.

"I'll get you at seven and we'll have dinner before we head to the bar."

"Dinner?" she asked, quirking an eyebrow.

Luke couldn't help but smile. "All part of the ruse, Cass."

Her lids lowered a fraction and he realized he'd used her nickname. It suited the girl he used to know, but *Cassandra* definitely fit the woman he'd seen working her wedding magic earlier today. There was a new side to her now—an intriguing side that he had to ignore. Just because they had a past and now a faux relationship didn't mean he needed to dig deeper into her life and find out all that had happened since she'd left.

Once he'd picked up the pieces of his heart and concentrated on what he could actually control, Luke had found he was a happy man. He didn't need love, or whatever that emotion was people claimed to feel. He didn't need marriage. This chapter of his life right now was the happiest he'd ever been, so there was absolutely no need to look elsewhere to fill voids that weren't there.

He'd filled all of those voids with a hefty bank account and loyal friends.

"Fine," she conceded. "I'll be ready at seven."

Luke stepped out of the way and let her pass. He watched as she went through the glass doors into the hotel and felt a little twinge of pain when she didn't look back. It was quite the parallel to when she'd left years ago and hadn't even given him a second glance.

A few hours without being around Cassandra had helped Luke get his head on straight before seeing her again tonight. There was no room in his life for him to get caught up in her again.

When she'd left town eight years ago, he hadn't been quite ready to propose. He'd had too much tied up in all of his start-up businesses. And then when she'd left, Luke figured he was better off without her. He'd been such a fool, but not anymore.

That was all in the past, and he'd certainly learned from his mistakes. He'd never let anyone get that close to him again and he'd managed to build the life and career he'd dreamed of for so long. He couldn't be totally upset about how things had turned out.

Obviously, he and Cassandra weren't meant to be and that had just taken some time to sink in.

Luke pulled in a breath and stepped off the elevator at the penthouse level. There was only one door, but Luke knew the chime sounded inside her room because the private elevator indicated when there was a guest. Just as he started to knock, the door flung open and Luke nearly gasped, but managed to suppress his reaction…barely.

She stood before him in hip-hugging black leather pants, a pair of black heels and a dark red halter with a very low scoop neck that left nothing to the imagination and showed off all of that mocha skin he craved to touch.

Gone was the professional woman from earlier who'd been wearing a sundress and classy sandals with minimal makeup. Now, those red lips and dark eyes tempted him in a whole new way. He wanted to lean in and see how much he could mess that up, but he remained still.

What the hell game was she playing?

She was still smiling that almost innocent smile and she had that perkiness about her that just drew people in. Cassandra was like a magnetic force…and he re fused to be drawn in.

"This outfit will certainly get attention."

Cassandra held out her arms and did a slow spin. "That was the whole idea, right?" she asked as she came back around. "You wanted people to notice you're taken."

Yeah, he did, but at what expense? Because he still needed to be able to work and to function. With this damn outfit, he'd be lucky if he could string two coherent sentences together.

From the smirk on her face, she knew exactly the effect she had on him and she was loving every minute of it. She was a vixen. That's exactly what Cassandra Taylor was, and he had nobody to blame but himself. Maybe he should have just stuck with the women bombarding him for dates and marriage. At least he could control that situation, even if he'd found it annoying and overwhelming.

"Let's head on up," he told her as he stepped aside so she could come out into the hallway. "I've had the chef prepare our dinner and it's ready in the private back VIP room."

"Don't you have customers there?" she asked.

"Only a few and that's the point." He punched the elevator button and waited. "We want to be seen, but not seeming to be throwing it in their faces. It will look even more authentic if people think we're to trying to keep this quiet."

They stepped onto the elevator. Luke was glad they were only going up one floor because he was too tempted to push the stop button and practice those kisses again. There was no way in hell she was immune to this sexual tension. It was as if she'd chose this outfit and that sultry lipstick to torment him even further.

"A secret fake engagement," she murmured. "Sounds like a lot of work."

"That's the price you agreed to pay," he reminded her.

Though at this point, he felt like he was paying a greater price.

Luke had to shift his focus to something else. Maybe to the fact that he'd let her go once and she blamed him for their breakup. If he kept telling himself that this was the same woman who'd broken him so many years ago, that should be more than enough to make him see that he'd been lucky to have her step away from his life. He'd refused to beg back then and he wouldn't be doing any begging now, no matter how much he'd enjoyed that damn kiss.

As they stepped into the rooftop bar, Cassandra glanced around. He let her walk on ahead, as she clearly wanted to see the space. She'd only been here once before, when she'd first come by his office to ask her favor. Luke waited as she walked through and glanced around at the high-top tables for mingling, the low leather sofas for cozying, the stage where there were nightly performances, and the long bar that was home to the best bartender in all of Tennessee.

Luke was proud of everything he'd accomplished. True, he'd lost Cassandra in the process, but that was all in the past and she'd made that choice clear. This bar, and his others, were his present and future. His work ers were like family and he had his brothers. With Will and Cash's fiancées, he was gaining two new sisters. His life was full.

So why did he still feel a hole that he couldn't quite explain?

A few customers were hanging out at the high-top tables, where there were no seats. He found that some people wanted to stand and some preferred more intimacy, which was why he'd installed the outdoor sofas and the small tables with club chairs. His goal from day one had been to create an atmosphere where everyone could feel comfortable and offer his customers a place to come and enjoy the amazing music he prided himself on offering.

In a few hours, especially once the band showed up,

this rooftop would be flooded with patrons. The food and drinks would be passed around and that's when Luke truly loved his job—he loved getting to know the people of the town and the surrounding areas.

"This is really amazing," Cassandra said as she came back to him. "I'd seen pictures online, but was too focused yesterday to pay too much attention. Everything is truly stunning, from the atmosphere to the views."

The views were indeed breathtaking and one of the main reasons he'd chosen to open a rooftop bar. Seeing the city lights of Beaumont Bay and the homes in the distance that surrounded the lake, nestled between mountain peaks like a big city, was definitely unique. This area was undeniably the place to be, and over the past few years, the Bay had really blown up with the arrival of real-estate moguls, high-rollers, artists and country-music transplants, who all wanted even better nightlife and larger homes than they had in Nashville.

"Are you ready for dinner?" he asked.

Cassandra nodded and crossed back to him. With his hand on the small of her back, Luke led her to the private VIP area that was in the back behind one-way-mirrored walls. They slid open and shut as soon as they were inside.

"Swanky like your office with all these hidden walls," she murmured. "Maybe I should've dressed up a little more."

His hand slid around to the dip in her waist as he eased her against his side and leaned down to whisper in her ear.

"This is more than sexy enough."

Her body shivered beneath his touch and that's precisely the reaction he wanted her to have. He wanted her to remember all the amazing times they'd had together, both in public and in private.

While he'd moved on successfully and happily, maybe there was a thread of payback in this plan that he hadn't realized until now. He didn't want to be an ass, but there was nothing wrong with showing her exactly what she'd missed out on by leaving.

Luke didn't give her time to reply as he ushered her over to the corner booth where he'd had their meal set up. Luke hoped her tastes hadn't changed too much over the years because he'd gone with her favorites from the main restaurant downstairs.

Once Cassandra was seated, Luke slid in beside her and purposely eased his thigh right alongside hers. She wasn't immune to him, like she wanted to be. She wouldn't have melted against him with that kiss if she had been. Besides, it was just a simple touch, right?

"You're practically on my lap," she muttered as she glanced between them and then up to his face.

Luke smiled. "I feel like you're not taking your role as doting fiancée seriously."

"I feel like you're purposely being difficult."

He shrugged. "Too late to back out. We had an agreement."

Her eyes narrowed and Luke ignored her anger. There was a fine line between anger and arousal, and right now, he was on one side and she was on the other. He knew just where to touch her, just what to say, to pull her over to his side…or, at the very least, to meet him in the middle.

Yet here he was, trying to play all noble, as if he didn't want to strip her down and see if they were just as good together as they'd been before. There wasn't a doubt in Luke's mind that they would be just as hot, if not hotter.

Damn, he could use a physical release, but he wasn't going to go that far…not with Cassandra. He wasn't a masochist. He wouldn't be hurt by her again. And despite how they'd ended, he still respected women and would never be such a jerk.

Cassandra turned her focus back to the table. "So what are we having? I'm starving."

That was one thing he remembered. She'd always had a hearty appetite, and he had really loved that about her. She wasn't one to shy away from what she wanted, or worry about carbs and all that. Cassandra had so much confidence, she had such a love for life… He'd naively thought they could have some grand dynasty with his businesses.

Looking back, maybe he had been selfish, maybe he hadn't seen how important her own goals had been because he'd been so busy with his own. He hadn't thought she would just up and leave him, though. That harsh action on her part had proven they weren't meant to be together. If they were, she would have stayed, or they would have found a way back to each other…and not in some warped fake manner.

"I had them prepare bacon-wrapped sliders, some crab cakes and there is some grilled asparagus."

She started removing the domed lids and she literally moaned right there. Moaned. As if he needed another reaction from her to turn him on.

"Eat as much as you want. I had a late lunch and I'm fine with beer."

She reached for a slider and set it on her plate. "What beers do you have on tap? Local ones, I presume."

"I try to support local as much as possible, but I also keep up with the demand of more well-known brands, too. There is a demographic that doesn't like the IPA or craft beers and prefers the more traditional."

"Give me your favorite local draft," she told him with a smile.

Luke jerked slightly. "I didn't think you liked beer."

Cassandra shrugged and her smile widened. "There's quite a bit you don't know about me now. I'm not the same girl I used to be."

Clearly, she wasn't. With that revelation, a part of him wanted to uncover all the ways she'd changed. First off, she drank beer, which was surprising. She'd never liked any type of alcohol before, always saying it tasted bitter.

"Do you prefer a fruity beer or something stout?" he asked.

"Surprise me," she countered with that saucy, flirty grin.

Now that was the old Cassandra he knew. She used to love surprises and he had always enjoyed giving them. Spontaneity had been one of the main components of their relationship. They'd been happy once. Hell, he'd been happy up until the moment she'd left. He hadn't seen that coming and the bitterness had consumed him for much too long after she'd gone.

Now she was back and he hadn't even realized he wanted the chance to prove he was over her, but he was getting the opportunity. He'd prove that he'd been just fine without her, and would continue to be fine without her. And if he got a sliver of payback at the same time, then so be it.

Luke glanced to his VIP-room bartender and that's all it took for Miles to come over and promptly take their orders. After deciding on a couple of flights for Cassandra to try, Luke ordered his favorite pilsner.

Just as the drinks arrived, Cassandra let out a gasp and grabbed her cell. Luke glanced over to see her fingers flying over the screen, and she kept muttering.

Intrigued, Luke curled his hands around his chilled stein and watched her. She continued to talk to herself, something about catering and seating charts.

After several minutes, she slid her phone back into her purse and turned toward him.

"So, tell me what we have here," she said as she gestured toward the flights.

Luke laughed. "What was all that about?"

"What?"

"The phone, the self-chatter. Do you do that often?"

"Oh, um, yes." She shrugged and turned back to survey the flights. She chose the palest first. "When I think of something for work, I need to get it into my notes or I'll completely forget it. There's too much swirling around in my mind for me to possibly remember everything I have going on."

"And something inspired you from being here and ordering beer?" he asked.

Cassandra threw him a glance. "I get inspiration from everywhere."

Interesting. He wanted to dig deeper into that mind of hers. He wanted to know what made her think of his brother's wedding while they were on a pretend date. Did she ever insert elements into others' weddings that she wanted in her own? Did she even want to get married anymore?

Why was his mind even wandering to those questions? He didn't care about her personal life. The only reason he'd come up with this fake engagement was to get some relief from the women bombarding him since he'd been named the most eligible bachelor in the area. Working had become difficult when all he'd been able to do was pose for selfies, have phone numbers slipped into his pockets, and get propositioned. While that was all great as an ego boost, he really did need to focus on work, and he sure as hell wasn't looking to add a Mrs. to his Mr.

A flash of red hair and a tight dress caught the corner of his eye and Luke glanced around for a split second before dread settled in his gut. Quickly, he slid his arm along the back of the booth behind Cassandra. She turned to him, her eyes darting to his mouth as he leaned in closer.

"What—?"

His lips covered hers, and once again, she seemed to fall right in tune with him as she met his kiss with a demand of her own. The passion was instant and strong, which was why he knew if they attempted a temporary fling, it might be dangerous, but they would both thoroughly enjoy themselves.

Cassandra's hand slid along his thigh as she eased closer and opened her lips for him. She might tell him that she'd changed over the years, but this was still the same passionate woman he'd enjoyed years ago.

Luke tipped his head and reached up, cupping her jaw and seeking more. Damn, the woman could kiss, and there wasn't a thing in this world that could make him stop…

"She's gone, sir."

Except the sound of his bodyguard.

Luke broke the kiss and turned his focus to Jake, who merely nodded and then slipped away.

"What—what was that?" Cassandra panted.

"A woman was walking this way with her eyes on me," Luke murmured, still trying to catch his own breath.

Cassandra smoothed her hair away from her face. "Oh, right. Our *relationship*."

Yeah, exactly. She'd forgotten about the ruse and for a brief moment, so had he. Those kisses, all two that they'd shared so far, were already getting to him…

How in the hell was he supposed to keep pretending? Every single part of him wanted her, wanted more than this farce. True, he'd set the terms, but he needed a redo and he needed to add in a hell of a lot more than kisses here and there.

"I'm going to need a heads-up before you come in for the attack next time," she murmured.

With his arm still behind her back, Luke shifted his body to angle more toward her.

"Attack?" he whispered. "You were more than a willing participant, in both instances."

Cassandra pursed her lips. "So what? You're a good kisser. That doesn't mean I don't need a second to process before it happens."

"Fine," he conceded. "What word do you want me to say before I kiss you?"

She seemed to think for a half second before a grin spread across her face. That grin should've scared the hell out of him because the woman looked like she was about to make him regret that question.

"Sorry."

Luke blinked. "Excuse me."

"I'd like you to say 'sorry' before you kiss me next time."

Of all the things he thought she'd say, "sorry" certainly wasn't one of them.

"Why would I do that?" he asked.

"Because you asked what I wanted and that's it." She scooted away just a fraction and took a drink of the next beer in her sample lineup. "This is delicious. I definitely love this one the best so far. It's smooth, but still full of flavor."

As he sat and listened to her discuss her beer, he realized that he'd lost control here—she'd just successfully laid down another rule. Damn it. He really wasn't sure he was going to come out the other side of this unscathed.

Unless he set a few rules of his own.

Four

Cassandra maneuvered through her computer-generated layout, still not happy with the arrangement of the decor. Even though this was Plan B, in case of inclement weather, it had to be just as perfect as the main plan.

She stood up from the desk in her penthouse and stretched her arms over her head. She'd gotten in late last night after spending several hours at The Cheshire with Luke. She couldn't deny that she'd had a great time and had seen him in his element. People loved him, especially the ladies.

Cassandra also couldn't deny the surge of jealousy that had stayed with her all night. Too many women had tried to slip Luke their numbers or get their picture with the Most Eligible Bachelor. No way did Cassandra dare walk away from him, or she'd never hear the end of how she hadn't kept up her side of the bargain. She'd stuck by his side all night, just like any devoted fiancée would have.

Luke had kept his arm around her waist most of the night and one time even slid his hand into hers, but there had been no more kisses. Maybe because he didn't want to use the code word, but she smiled every time she thought about him having to apologize before kissing her next time.

Cassandra went to the minibar and poured a glass of pinot, then turned back to the balcony doors and stared out at the sunset. This was such a gorgeous view and she felt comfortable here, even though this was all temporary. For the next few months, this was going to be her home.

She wasn't sure if she'd settled in so easily because she'd grown up in Beaumont Bay, or if seeing Luke and Will had pulled her back to the good times in her past. She wasn't sure what would happen once she saw the entire Sutherland crew. They'd been like family to her, but she had to expect the flood of memories—she just hoped she didn't get too swept up in the ambiance of the wedding and the tight bond of the brothers and their parents.

Travis and Dana Sutherland were the quintessential couple who worked hard to show their children how to make their way through life. Travis was the most popular real-estate mogul in Beaumont Bay and the surrounding area. He'd hoped one of his sons would take him up on the idea of joining the family business, but all four boys had loved music in one way or another.

Cassandra knew they each had gone in that direction in their own way.

Cassandra took a sip of her wine and reminded herself once again that she was only back here on business…and those kisses were just business, too. All part of the temporary arrangement to get the boost she needed as she set off on her own in a high-profile industry.

This would all work out and the sacrifice to her sanity would be worth it. Besides, it wasn't like she didn't enjoy kissing Luke. The man was impossible to ignore and she couldn't deny her attraction to him. But attraction didn't mean she had to take action. She could kiss him, hold hands, even snuggle a little, and still remain emotionally detached.

Right? She just couldn't get too wrapped up in the Sutherland family because they had been so damn difficult to leave the first time. She'd missed them so much and had felt like she'd broken many relationships, not just the one with Luke.

With another sip of wine, Cassandra turned to the piano next to the wall of windows overlooking the city. She couldn't believe it when she'd come into the penthouse and spotted this beauty. About seven years ago she'd taken up the hobby of playing, needing something to occupy her time when she wasn't working. Coming home to an empty space after being in a relationship for so long had been way too quiet, way too lonely. It had started taking a mental toll on her, so she'd taken up the piano and fallen in love.

It had taken her a long time to get over the heartache of Luke Sutherland. Learning the piano had been so relaxing, giving her a creative outlet that only she knew about. That way there was no criticism, no right or wrong way. She just enjoyed herself, and over the years she'd actually gotten pretty good.

Cassandra set her glass of wine on the top of the piano and took a seat at the white bench. She lifted the piano lid and stared down at the ebony and ivory keys before delicately placing her fingertips over them. Instantly, she closed her eyes as her hands traveled, a familiar tune filling the open space, immediately soothing her soul.

When she finished with one song, she eased right into another, humming along as she allowed the music to whisk her away. Cassandra didn't know how long she played—all she knew was she needed the mental break and nothing relaxed her like the piano.

She played the final note of the song, then pulled in a deep breath and opened her eyes. Movement from her peripheral vision had her jerking around on the bench.

"Sorry, just me."

Cassandra came to her feet, her heart beating fast. "What the hell are you doing in here? How did you get in?"

"I buzzed for you to let me in," Luke explained. "I heard the piano, so I guess you didn't hear me. When did you learn to play? That was amazing."

Crossing her arms over her chest, Cassandra narrowed her eyes. "Answer my question first. How did you get in here?"

He just stared at her like she was silly for asking.

He might be powerful and own the bar space and be chummy with the owners and managers of The Beaumont, but that didn't mean he could do whatever he wanted.

This nonchalant manner of his had to go…and so did his line of thinking.

"You can't just let yourself in," she scolded. "What if I'd just gotten out of the shower?"

His eyes traveled over her body and she realized she'd said the exact wrong thing. No doubt that would have made him even more excited.

"I've seen all you have," he reminded her. "And I didn't mean to creep you out by letting myself in. I just assumed you couldn't hear me."

"Well, I still deserve respect and privacy," she retorted. "We're just pretending, remember? I need my own space, Luke. What are you doing here, anyway?"

He shook his head. "I answered your question, now answer mine. When did you learn to play like that?"

"When you crushed my heart and I moved away. I needed something to occupy my time so I picked up a hobby."

Luke's lips thinned as the muscles in his jaw ticked. He took a step toward her, and then another, until all that was between them was the piano bench.

Cassandra held her ground and never looked away from that expressive stare that had her pinned and mesmerized. She'd always loved his dark eyes, which were framed by even darker lashes. Now he also had a close-cropped beard that only added to his sexy, rugged allure. He looked nothing like the billionaire he'd come to be and maybe that's why she was having such a difficult time focusing. She kept seeing the young man he used to be, but she was also fascinated by the man he'd become.

"Crushed your heart?" he repeated. "Maybe you don't remember exactly how things went down."

Seriously? Was he honestly trying to play the victim here?

Cassandra reached for her glass of wine and took a sip, realizing it had gotten warm. She was definitely going to need to refresh her glass.

"I'm not rehashing the past." She turned and headed toward the bar in the corner, putting some much-needed distance between them. "That's not why I came back to town and what's done is done."

She refilled her glass and turned back to face him. Thankfully, the bar top now separated them. "Now, what are you doing here?" she asked again.

"I wanted to know if you would like to come up tonight," he told her. "I have a new band that sounds amazing and I think they're really going to hit it big. They have some interest from Nashville and I invited Will tonight to listen to them and hopefully offer them a deal."

Luke seemed pretty excited about this group, which made her smile. Despite how they'd parted years ago, and their current turmoil, Luke had really grown something remarkable with his businesses. She had to admit a sliver of her was jealous, but that was ridiculous. How could she be jealous of a thing? Of course, he was proud of all he'd accomplished, and he should be. Being jealous at this stage in the game was both childish and un-reasonable.

Besides, she'd moved on, as well, so anything she felt now was just residual and had no place in the present.

"That sounds like fun, but I really need to work so I can be prepared when I meet with Hannah again."

Luke leaned against the glossy bar top, flattening his palms on the marble. "You were so damn prepared when we were there last, you were all but ordained to do the ceremony yourself."

Cassandra pursed her lips and thought. "You know, that's not a bad idea."

"I'm being serious. You can come up for a bit to make an appearance. It's important."

Cassandra sighed. "And your work is more important than mine?"

Maybe nothing had changed after all. Still battling over careers and emotions, just like old times. At least now she knew the outcome and wouldn't be blindsided.

Luke growled and eased around the bar to stand right next to her. She shifted her body so she could gaze up into those captivating eyes. He'd always been able to persuade her with just a look, but she was in charge now and no sexy glance or cute words or even toe-curling kisses could get her to give in. This wedding was too important to her and would most certainly be career-changing, which was precisely what she needed for her brand-new company.

"Just for an hour," he commanded. "You can stay for an hour."

Cassandra wanted to give in. She wanted to go hang

out and have a drink and listen to music and unwind, but that wouldn't help her try to figure out the details for Hannah and Will's big day. They'd entrusted her to make this the best day of their lives and not even Cassandra's attraction to Luke Sutherland would make her lose sight of that responsibility.

"As much as it sounds like fun, I can't."

Luke continued to stare until she realized he was leaning in closer...and closer still.

"Wh-what are you doing?" she murmured.

His hand slid along her jawline and Cassandra couldn't help herself as she leaned into his touch. Then when his thumb raked over her bottom lip, she closed her eyes and instinctively touched the tip of her tongue to his skin.

"I'm just getting to know you again," he answered, his voice husky from arousal.

More like trying to seduce her again...and, damn it, it was working.

"There's no need for that." She pulled in a shaky breath and willed herself not to lean in and kiss him. "You know me well enough to pull off this fake engagement."

The back of his fingertips feathered over her jawline, along the column of her neck and down to the V of her shirt before he pulled away slowly, methodically.

"Maybe I still find you attractive," he countered. "Maybe I'm done denying my wants...and your wants."

She stared up into his eyes. "You have to deny everything. What we're doing is nothing more than a temporary sham."

"Perhaps," he agreed, then leaned in closer until his mouth was a breath from hers. "Or maybe while we're together, we should explore this."

"This?"

His warm breath tickled her face and she wished he'd just close that distance and put her out of her misery. She could finish this and take what she wanted, but considering she was telling him this wasn't a great idea, she'd just be contradicting herself.

"We're adults, Cass. We're still drawn to each other. There's nothing wrong with acting on that and realizing exactly what this is…and what it isn't."

She blinked up at him and forced herself to take a step back before she lost her mind and gave in to everything he was offering—gave in to everything her body so desired.

"There's everything wrong with it," she countered. "I can't get wrapped up in you any more than I already have."

His eyes held hers for a second before he nodded. "Then I'll let you get back to work."

Without another word, he turned and let himself out. Cassandra stared at the door long after he was gone, wondering how the hell he'd been inside her penthouse for so short a time, yet had made such a sizable impact on her every thought.

She also wondered what had made him leave and finally accept her rejection. Had she wounded his pride? Did he finally see that pushing forward on some temporary fling was a terrible idea?

One thing was certain—Cassandra knew Luke well

enough to know that once he set his mind to something, he wasn't about to give up…and that meant he would be back. He would try to convince her they could still be good together.

She had to be ready to resist.

Five

She was a damn fool. When she should have been in her penthouse working on the wedding, Cassandra found herself hanging out in the back of the crowd, listening to the new band Luke had introduced thirty minutes ago.

He'd been right. The band was amazing and no doubt they'd be a hit one day soon.

Luke had also been right that she should be here. Enjoying music at his bar was better than worrying and second-guessing herself with her work.

Maybe it was the almost kiss. Maybe it was the way he'd stroked her jawline. Or perhaps the way he'd looked at her, as if he actually needed her in the most primal way.

No matter what had gotten her up to the rooftop, she couldn't deny that memories were intertwining with present emotions and she had no idea how she was going to handle all of it.

After he'd left, she'd taken a few minutes to battle with herself over what to do, but she couldn't stay in that penthouse with her thoughts and her sexual frustrations.

Cassandra had changed clothes, thrown her hair into a messy bun, added some mascara and gloss, and found herself up at The Cheshire.

As she glanced around the crowd, she noted many people smiling, drinking, nodding their heads to the catchy beat of the music. She saw Will back in the corner with Hannah tucked in at his side.

Cassandra made her way over and realized Cash and Gavin were seated on the couch across from Will and Hannah. Well, the entire Sutherland clan was here, and she assumed the lady between Gavin and Cash was Cash's fiancée, Presley.

Maybe she shouldn't have started walking that way, but it was too late to turn around because Will caught her eye and immediately waved her over. That motion caught the attention of everyone else and they all turned to see who was coming.

With a smile in place, Cassandra maneuvered through the crowd. Will came to his feet when she got to the sofa.

"Luke didn't tell us you'd be here." He greeted her with a hug. "Have a seat."

"I told him I was working, but I wanted to take a break." Cassandra eased down onto the couch where Will had vacated his seat. He went to sit on the other side of Hannah.

"So, how is everything coming along?" Hannah

asked with a gleam in her eye. "You don't know how excited I am."

Not nearly as excited as Cassandra was as she worked on this once-in-a-lifetime dream wedding.

"It's all she's talked about," Will stated. "You've created a bridezilla."

Hannah laughed as she slapped his chest before turning her attention back to Cassandra. "I'm not a bridezilla. I'm just so thrilled that someone knew my vision better than I could ever explain."

Cassandra smiled and then turned her attention to the other sofa, where Cash was staring at her.

"Hey, Cash," she greeted. "It's been a long time."

"It has, and apparently things have picked right back up where you all left off." He continued to stare at her with an unsettling gaze. "Rumor is you and Luke are engaged."

"What?"

"You are?"

Will and Hannah had spoken up at the same time. Cassandra's breath caught in her throat and she wished like hell Luke would've given her a heads-up as to what he'd told—or not told—his brothers. Then again, he'd been busy sneaking into her penthouse and trying to seduce her.

"That's what I saw online," Cash laughed. "So who knows."

Why hadn't she and Luke discussed what they'd tell his brothers? Or why hadn't he addressed this with them to begin with? Now she was stuck in an awkward spot. Did she go along with this or deny it?

But their whole plan had been to pretend to be engaged, right? So she went with it.

"Actually, we are," Cassandra announced. "It's new—you can ask Luke about all the details, but we didn't say anything because we really didn't want to take away from Hannah and Will, or Cash and Presley."

"Nothing would take away from any of that," Hannah exclaimed. "I can't believe you guys didn't say anything when you were at the house. This is so exciting."

Well, Cassandra wouldn't quite put that bold label on the moment, but she was on shaky ground here and really wished they could talk about something else.

"Where's your ring?" Will asked, his eyes darting to her left hand. "Don't let Luke skimp on that. He's frugal, but come on."

"That last one he picked out wasn't as big as what he could afford now," Cash joked.

"The last one?" Cassandra asked. If she thought her nerves were shot before, that was nothing compared to the effect of this bombshell.

Cash nodded. "When you two were together before. He'd asked Mom to help him look for one in his price range. He ended up with a pearl with diamonds or something like that. Do you remember, Will? It wasn't traditional."

Cassandra's heart pounded. Luke had gotten her a ring before? Why had he never said anything? He knew she wanted to marry him, that she'd left because he wouldn't do just that. How could he let her walk away without a word? What the hell? He couldn't have come to her and told her what he'd planned—that he had a *ring*?

She had so many questions, but asking them would only result in thrusting her back into the past and nothing good would come from that.

Besides, the more she tossed this new fact around in her head, the angrier she became…which wasn't good for either of them. She wasn't in town to analyze everything that had gone wrong in the past. Too many years had passed, and quite honestly, she wasn't the same woman anymore, and it was obvious Luke wasn't the same guy. The man she'd fallen in love with would never play games. He would have been totally transparent and open. So what had happened?

"Oh, yeah. He'd put all his money into starting the bars," Will replied, pulling her from her thoughts. "We gave him hell over such a small ring, but he refused to take money from anyone."

As the brothers went back and forth about the ring and what ancestor the piece belonged to, Cassandra scanned the rooftop area as her mind raced. Through the variety of people mingling, drinking and dancing to the music, she finally spotted her faux fiancé.

Luke smiled and nodded as two twentysomething ladies were talking to him. One of the women placed her hand on his arm and threw her head back in a dramatic, nearly pathetic laugh for attention. Jealousy hit Cassandra hard, so she excused herself from the group and made her way through the crowd.

She had no idea why this whole scene pissed her off, but if they were going to fake a relationship, then that's what they needed to do. Aside from the women hanging on him—oh, and now trying to get a selfie

with him—Cassandra was still reeling from the revelation that Luke had gotten a ring for her when they'd
been together.

Without even an "excuse me," Cassandra slid between the women and her "fiancé." With her arm
around his waist, she glanced up at him, loving that
surprised look on his face.

"Hey, babe," she greeted. "Sorry I kept you waiting."

"I thought you had to work," he stated, clearly
shocked she was here.

She smiled, though she gritted her teeth to keep from
lashing out…which was ridiculous. She had no reason
to be jealous. None. Luke was a sexy, successful man
and Cassandra knew full well he'd been with women
since they'd ended things. But having the fact shoved
in her face didn't sit so well with her.

"Nothing is more important than spending time with
my fiancé," she declared, purposely pouring on the fake
affection.

"Wait," one of the ladies said. "You're engaged?"

Cassandra glanced to them, pretending she'd just
realized they were so close. She really should earn an
award for her acting skills.

"Oh, how rude of me." She extended her hand. "I'm
Cassandra Taylor, Luke's fiancée. And you two are
friends of Lukie's?"

Lukie?

She hadn't meant to sound that fake, but she also
knew that nickname would tick off Luke, so she
couldn't help but be a little giddy. Okay, fine. She was
petty. This whole situation had obviously caused her

to override her common sense, but she couldn't rein it back in at this point.

"We actually just met," one of the women said. "We didn't know he was engaged."

"It's still fairly new," Cassandra explained. "We dated years ago and I just got back into town and we realized we couldn't live without each other."

Luke's arm slid around her and his hand came to rest on the curve of her hip.

"So, you see, ladies, that's why I couldn't do the selfie," he told them. "I have nothing but respect for my girl here."

His girl. At one time she'd loved when he called her that. And there was still a sliver of excitement and a little arousal that slid through her at the declaration.

She really should have just stayed in her penthouse. Then she wouldn't have been in the company of the Sutherland brothers' crew, learned about the ring, or gotten jealous over two very young women talking to Luke.

This was what he did, though. He mingled, chatted with the customers, flirted. He was just being typical charming Luke. How could she fault him for being in his natural state?

"If you'll excuse us, ladies. Please, continue to enjoy the show and the drinks."

Luke smiled to the duo and eased Cassandra away. She kept her arm around him as he guided her toward the back hallway behind the bar. He tapped in the code and the wall door slid open to reveal his hidden office.

She had too many questions, not to mention the un-

wanted possessiveness she'd felt when she obviously
had no real claim on Luke. There was nothing other than
a superficial business deal going on between them and
she would do well to remember that from here on out.

The wall slid closed after they stepped inside and
Luke came to stand in front of her. He shoved his hands
in the pockets of his jeans and stared down at her as if
waiting on some explanation.

The silence curled around them, the force of it almost magnetic as she found herself taking a step toward
him. She really didn't know where to start, but he finally broke the tension and saved her from opening up.

"What happened to work?" he asked.

"I needed a break."

"I heard you say that before, but what's the real reason?"

She had needed a break. She also wanted to see
the bar and enjoy the atmosphere and the band, and
maybe she wanted to see Luke again in his element.
She couldn't just turn off her attraction, nor could she
turn off her curiosity.

Cassandra pulled in a shaky breath and stepped back,
away from those intense eyes and that powerful stare.

"We need to get our story straight because your
brother just asked about our engagement, which he
read about online."

"Which one?" he asked.

Cassandra stared. "Which one what?"

"Which brother?"

"Cash." She shoved her hair behind her ears and
laughed. "Does it matter? Now your family and your
soon-to-be sisters-in-law believe we're engaged. When

they started talking about my bare ring finger, I had to excuse myself."

Luke continued to study her for another minute, then he shrugged. "Then we'll find you a ring."

"Just like that? We're going to move to that level?" she asked. "At what point do we stop? Are we going to have to actually get married? Maybe you should suggest a double wedding with Will."

Luke laughed as he took a step toward her and reached for her shoulders. "Take a breath and calm down."

Calm down? How could she? She was still reeling from the realization that at one point in time, Luke had thought about asking her to marry him. Or, he at least had gone to the trouble of getting the ring. Maybe he'd changed his mind or maybe he'd been waiting for a right time that never came—she didn't know. At this point, bringing it up wouldn't solve their issue at hand, and she didn't want to dig back into a host of feelings that had taken a great deal of effort to bury.

"We'll get a ring," Luke told her in that low, slow drawl of his. "We'll pretend to be engaged, but right now the focus will be on Will and Hannah. Maybe we'll flash your hand in a few of our social-media posts, but we don't need to do anything more."

Cassandra shook her head. "I wasn't prepared to be blindsided like that and then when those girls…"

Damn it. She hadn't meant to let that part slip. There was no reason she should let other women bother her. They were faking this relationship because of the women who'd been pestering him. He'd wanted this engagement to deter unwanted attention.

"Don't tell me you were jealous," he said, smirking.

Cassandra tipped up her chin. "That would be ridiculous. I can't be jealous over something that's not even real or a man who isn't even mine."

Those hands slid over her shoulders and the rough pads of his thumbs grazed the side of her neck, then he tipped back her head just slightly as he stepped closer to her.

Cassandra's breath held as her heart beat faster, and nerves curled low in her belly as she waited for him to say something...or to close this gap and kiss her. Not that she *wanted* him to kiss her. There was no need since there was no audience, right?

"You're jealous," he murmured.

"I want you to stay in the role we discussed," she snapped, refusing to let him see just how right he was. "How can we convince people we're in love if you're laughing and chatting it up with other women?"

His lips quirked. "You want to be convincing?"

"We have no choice."

"Sorry."

"What?"

He didn't say another word before his mouth descended onto her lips...and that's when she realized he'd used her code word. Cassandra's knees weakened and she gripped his wrists to hold herself up.

Damn him for still being able to make her weak in the knees.

Luke claimed her with a powerful kiss and everything about him was so familiar, yet so new. How could this be the same man she loved so long ago? Now he was so much more—sexier, bolder and much more in control than she remembered.

Before she could stop herself—a theme with her as of late—Cassandra wrapped her arms around his waist and aligned their hips. She wanted to feel him, all of him. If he was going to be so demanding with this kiss, then so was she. There was a fire burning inside her. As cli\-chéd and silly as that sounded, she didn't know another way to describe what she was feeling. She was hot...too hot. She needed something more—she needed Luke.

Maybe coming back had been a mistake, but she was here now and would have to face her past *and* present feelings at some point.

He released her face and gripped her hips as he spun her around. Cassandra found herself being lifted and then set down onto something sturdy—a desk, maybe?

Luke settled between her spread knees and she arched against his touch. When he nipped at her bot\-tom lip and broke the kiss, she stared up at him as she tried to catch her breath.

"What are we doing?" he muttered, gazing down with hunger in his eyes.

"Ignoring the red flags," she panted.

"This isn't right." But he didn't step back. "Why is this wrong when it feels too damn good?"

Cassandra braced her hands behind her as she watched various complex emotions play over his face.

"This was never our problem, Luke. Sex with you was the easy part."

He laughed. "Easy. Hell, honey, none of this is easy."

Cassandra closed her eyes and tried to focus on calming her breathing and her nerves. No matter how much she wanted him, having an intimate relationship right now would just mess things up...and not only her business, but also her heart.

Cassandra eased off the desk, causing Luke to take another step back. He continued to study her and she could tell by that familiar look in his eyes that he was turned on and just as ravenous for her as she was for him.

But...she'd been right. Sex had always been the easy part of their relationship. Communication had been their downfall—clearly, considering she'd just found out tonight he'd had an engagement ring for her eight years ago.

"We need to figure out what we're telling your family," Cassandra repeated. "If you want to pretend with them, fine. If you want to tell them the truth, that's fine. But we need to be on the same page."

Luke raked a hand through his messy hair and sighed. "I can't lie to them. I wouldn't do that and I wouldn't ask you to. I know how close you were with them once."

From the moment Cassandra had met Luke, she'd thought of Gavin, Will, and Cash as the brothers she'd never had. She'd grown up an only child with a single father. He'd been her only family, and when he passed away after a stroke when she'd been only twenty-three, she'd instantly taken even more to the Sutherlands. Travis and Dana had welcomed her with open arms and treated her like the daughter they'd never had. Losing them had been another blow when she'd left town. She hadn't just left Luke—she'd left her second family.

Starting over hadn't been easy and it hadn't been fast, but she'd made a life for herself in Lexington. That was yet another reason why she couldn't get wrapped up with Luke now. There was no way in hell she could go back to what it had been like at that point in time. She wasn't so sure she could recover from another broken heart.

"I'll tell them tonight once we close," Luke decided. "Do you want to hang around? No touching, no kissing. Just hang around here for a while."

Cassandra tipped up her head. "Why?"

He shrugged again in that casual manner he always had. Sometimes she couldn't tell if he really didn't care, or if he just kept his emotions guarded.

"Because I like having you here," he finally admitted. "It's nice having you back in town and we can at least be friendly after everything, right?"

Friends. Sure. That sounded logical, didn't it?

Then again, she'd never kissed her friends like that and she sure as hell had never wanted to rip off her friends' clothes.

"I'll stay," she told him with a smile. "So long as you buy my drinks."

Luke's quirky grin widened. "Anything you want."

And that was the most loaded statement she'd heard since she hit Beaumont Bay.

Six

"You're a damn fool."

Will's outburst was no surprise to Luke. All of the brothers had been taken with Cassandra from the beginning, years ago. They'd all been stunned when she had left town and fully blamed Luke. They'd said he was so wrapped up in his business that he'd let her go without a fight. He'd told them at the time that if she wanted to go, then she wasn't the woman for him. If she could walk away so easily, then they weren't meant to be. Why should he have to choose between the personal and the professional? At the time, he'd thought he could have both.

And that's how he'd ended up alone, with the most successful bars in Tennessee.

Now that Luke had explained the current deal he and

Cassandra had set up, all of his brothers glared at him. Gavin relaxed back on one of the sofas, Will leaned against the railing and Cash sat on a high stool nursing a beer. All sets of eyes were directly on Luke and he wished he would've sent this news out in a text instead of waiting for the bar to close to tell them in person.

"What did you expect me to do?" he asked, defending himself. "Cassandra needed help and so did I. It was a perfect setup."

"You think I wouldn't have given Cassandra a chance to talk with Hannah?" Will asked. "It would have all worked out without you going to such extremes and practically blackmailing her."

Luke couldn't have been so sure, and he'd needed Cassandra to play his devoted girlfriend. So far, the ruse was working and social media was exploding with "Lassandra" hashtags and posts. And with a few exceptions, women were now leaving him alone.

But he hadn't blackmailed Cassandra into anything. She could have turned him down and walked away. They were both using each other to get what they wanted and that's what was called a win-win.

"So how long are you two planning on playing this charade?" Cash asked.

Luke sighed. "Until Will's wedding. We'll go our separate ways then."

"Just like that?" Gavin chimed in with a disapproving grunt. "That seems cold. I mean, I'm a lawyer and that's even heartless to me."

Cold and heartless, those were the very last things Luke felt when it came to Cassandra. And he was positive once Will's wedding rolled around in just under two months, he and Cassandra would be more than ready to get back to their own lives.

"Do you feel nothing seeing her again after all this time?" Will asked. "I can't imagine losing Hannah and then seeing her again years later and trying to pretend like everything is normal. She's not some old classmate, Luke. She was the woman you wanted to spend your life with at one time."

"We're two different people now," Luke argued. He shook his head and got to his feet. "Listen, Cassandra and I have this under control. Okay? I just didn't want to lie to you guys, but you have to keep up the charade."

"Do you think this is fair to Cassandra?"

Luke turned to Cash and glared. "Are you being serious right now? She came to me and needed my help."

"You could've helped her without asking for something in return," Cash claimed.

Luke raked a hand through his hair and seriously wished like hell he would've just texted this whole thing and then he could've ignored their opinions.

"It's done now and I just need you guys to go along with this until after Will's wedding. Is that asking too much?"

His brothers continued to stare at him with their judgmental gazes. Luke was tired from the late hours he'd been keeping. He'd been staying until close for the last couple of weeks because there were so many new artists performing and he wanted to be there to support the folks he had booked. He always wanted them to feel welcome in his establishment.

But even when he was home, Luke's thoughts kept turning to Cassandra. He couldn't help but relive their time together from years ago and compare that woman to the woman he knew now. There were certainly similarities, but there were also some changes he couldn't help but hone in on.

Her determination, the strong will, that sassy walk, and her quick wit—maybe all of those things came with life experience, or maybe she'd been that amazing all along. Maybe he'd been so wrapped up in his own world that he'd totally missed the fact that he wasn't even trying to combine business and pleasure until it was too late.

"I'll go along with this ridiculous charade, but if you hurt Cassandra again—"

"Wait," Luke said, cutting off Gavin. "What do you mean if I hurt Cassandra again? She's the one who left the first time."

"Because you were putting her behind everything else in your life," Gavin retorted. "I can't believe she waited as long as she did before giving up on you."

Luke rarely got pissed with his brothers, but right now he didn't like how they were Team Cassandra and not seeing his point of view at all here.

"I'm not asking for opinions, I'm only asking that you keep the secret."

He met each of his brothers' gazes until they all nodded in agreement. Luke hated feeling like he'd just been put through a mental battle that he wasn't quite sure he'd won. Now that he'd talked to his brothers, he needed to have a conversation with his parents, and that was going to be equally as enjoyable.

"I'm heading home," he told them. "Be sure to take the service elevator when you leave. I'll come in early tomorrow and clean up whatever mess you heathens have made."

Without waiting for a reply, Luke excused himself and headed toward his private elevator. Every part of him wanted to stop off at the penthouse, but normal people were likely sleeping right now.

Odd that his first reaction when he was troubled was wanting to reach for Cassandra. That had been the case at one time in his life, but not now. She was nothing more than the one who got away and the one who was now his temporary, very fake fiancée.

"What do you think?"

Cassandra glanced at the spread of floral options and sketches and could tell by Hannah's exasperated tone that she was confused. Knowing when it was time to take a little control out of the bride's hands, Cassandra pulled her three favorites for the venue and slid the others to the side.

"Okay, so I'm going to give you my own personal opinion," Cassandra began. "And I'm only doing this because from what we've chosen so far, I'm confident I know your tastes."

After two weeks of working diligently on the wedding, Hannah had also been recording her new album and doing interviews, which had taken her out of town for a few days. So when she was home, Cassandra had to take every moment she could and yet still make their meetings seem like a zero-stress environment.

"I trust your judgment," Hannah stated. "In fact, I'd love to take the pressure off me for just a moment and talk about you."

"Me?"

Hannah's smile widened. "Yes. I'm aware that you and Luke used to be involved and Will told me the other evening that you two are engaged, but not really engaged."

Cringing, Cassandra nodded. "It's complicated."

Hannah got to her feet, then walked over to the wet bar in the corner of her sitting room and grabbed two glasses. After pouring mimosas, Hannah came back over to the sofa and handed one of the glasses to Cassandra.

"Thank you." Cassandra smiled and took the drink. "I'm not sure this will even help at this point."

"So I'm just trying to understand." Hannah took a sip and eased back into her seat. "And, please, tell me if I overstep here."

Cassandra couldn't help but laugh. "I'm planning the wedding of my favorite singer and I'm in her house and she wants to offer advice. I promise—you're not overstepping."

Hannah laughed, too. "Well, thank you, but I'm just a regular person with honest feelings. Which makes me wonder how you're dealing with all of this. From what Will told me, you and Luke ended things a long time ago. But still, is this all weird or are you okay?"

Nobody had asked her about her feelings on this bizarre setup. And, honestly, Cassandra hadn't even taken the time to think of them herself. She'd gotten wrapped up in this whirlwind of a dream job, then a fake engagement, and now being splashed all over social media as "Lassandra." All in a few weeks' time.

"I'm fine," Cassandra assured Hannah. "It's strange being back here with Luke, but familiar at the same time, if that makes sense."

"If you don't mind my asking, what happened the first time? I mean, you are an amazing woman and Luke is such a great guy."

Cassandra took a moment to gather her thoughts as she took a sip of her mimosa. "Luke is a great guy, but we just weren't great together. Well, we were…until the day we weren't. Does that make any sense?"

Hannah pursed her lips. "About as much sense as the fake engagement."

"Pretty much." Cassandra sighed and glanced down to the stack of three options for the floral arrangements. "Okay, let's circle back to your wedding. Fall is such a gorgeous time in Tennessee, so I really don't think you can go wrong with any of these options."

Cassandra splayed them all out onto the glass table in front of the sofa and waited while Hannah glanced over each one.

"They're all so perfect," Hannah muttered. "I feel like Hallie should be here to help me decide. Sometimes she knows what I like before I do."

"I imagine that's just one of the perks of having a twin."

Hannah nodded. "There are many, that's for sure.

But, since she's not here, tell me which one you would choose."

"It's not my wedding."

Hannah shrugged. "Pretend it is. What would you choose if you were me?"

Even though she loved them all, Cassandra pointed to the images of the greenery with varieties of white blooms.

"This one," she told Hannah. "I love the simplicity, especially with it being an outdoor wedding. Around the lake and being in the fall, I think the delicate green and white will be timeless. Plus, it will carry over so nicely to the reception at The Cheshire and the decor Luke already has in place."

"And do you love the idea of the lakeside gazebo ceremony?" Hannah asked.

Cassandra smiled and nodded. "I've always wanted an outdoor fall wedding. When I get to plan those, it's like a little piece of me gets even more excited. I treat all my brides equally, but this time of year and especially being by the lake surrounded by colorful mountains… Well, this is just going to be absolutely breathtaking."

Cassandra stared down at the graphic and sighed. "The way the greenery is draped around the posts and the cream flowers are intermingled, and then the sprays nestled around the base of the stage…it's just so roman- tic and dreamy. I can see the bridesmaids in their dusty pink, holding their tight bouquets of cream buds and greenery sprays, the taupe chair covers all adorned with a simple floral arrangement on each one, the cream-colored petals sprinkled down the aisle between the VIP guests."

"You make things sound so perfect," Hannah stated. "I think you've talked me in to this one."

Cassandra blinked and glanced at the option she'd just described. "Are you positive? This is your wedding, not mine."

"You'll be planning yours soon enough," Hannah replied with a smile.

A little stunned at the statement, Cassandra shook her head. "Oh, I'm not so sure about that. I think I'd have to have a man in my life before I'd be ready to choose between lilies or hydrangea."

"You have a man in your life." Hannah patted Cassandra's knee and grinned. "You may be pretending, but who knows. Maybe the old sparks are still there?"

If by sparks she meant sexual attraction, that was a definite yes. Who knew how things would be between them now? She could only assume the sex would still be great, if not greater than it had been before.

Damn it. She'd tried not to let her mind go there, but now she couldn't help herself. Intimacy with Luke had been off the charts. He'd always known just how to touch her, exactly how to make her feel amazing. He'd been such a giving lover and their intimacy was something she'd never been able to find with anyone else since…and she'd tried. Mercy she'd tried, but all that her trying had done was lead to dreams that involved Luke in a very erotic manner that only left her satisfied in her sleep. Which was something she'd never admit to anyone, ever.

"You're smiling."

Hannah's statement pulled Cassandra from her fantasy as it was just starting to get out of control. And, damn it, she hadn't realized she'd been smiling.

"Maybe there's something left over after all?" Hannah asked with a teasing grin. She took a sip of her mimosa then set the glass on the table. "Teasing aside, if there's something you want, maybe you should go after it. I know Will and I danced around each other because we didn't think being together was right for our careers, but there's so much more than what brings in a paycheck. Had we only focused on that, all of this that is so real between us could have been lost. We have to take charge of our own happiness sometimes instead of waiting for someone else to give it to us."

As much as Cassandra loved getting advice from Hannah, and this was solid, sound advice, things just weren't going to magically turn from pretend to real. They'd had their chance once and now they were both happy in their lives and their careers. They'd made their own paths and just because they'd been thrust into a situation that kept bringing up their past didn't mean they had to pick up where they'd left off.

Besides, he'd had his opportunity and he'd blown it. Luke had chosen his business ventures over her. Why shouldn't she chase her own dreams and be successful? She'd taken time to build and grow her career, create a foundation for herself in the wedding industry, and she wasn't about to let Luke derail her now that she was branching out on her own and making a name for herself.

"I think you've got too much wedding and floating hearts on your mind," Cassandra joked. "Let's focus on your love life. It's less complicated."

"Love doesn't have to be complicated," Hannah replied, then laughed. "I think that's in one of my songs."

Yeah, well, songs and real life didn't always go hand-in-hand. Cassandra was truly happy with where she was on her journey. She didn't need love or a man to complete her. Fulfilling other people's happily-ever-after dreams was more than enough for her.

So why did she have a yawning ache in her chest that told her she was only lying to herself?

Seven

Luke glanced again at the headline on the social-media page and he still couldn't pinpoint his emotions.

Another Sutherland Brother to be Married

He leaned back in his leather desk chair and sighed. Luke didn't want to be married, not now or ever. At one time, back when Cass was in his life the first time, he'd been working toward asking her. He'd been laying a firm foundation for their lives, but she'd seen that as him pushing her aside and putting his work first. She'd crushed his soul when she'd left without seeing that everything he did was for her.

He'd never let himself get that attached to anyone

ever again and he wasn't in any need for such nonsense now, either.

The glaring headline was like a sucker punch to the gut. This particular article had a photo of him and Cassandra, one that she'd posted on her social-media account just this morning. She'd taken the selfie a few days ago when she'd popped into the bar. It was a quick picture of him kissing her on the cheek, her smile wide and quite convincing. No sooner had the photo been taken than she'd rushed back out the door to do more wedding planning.

And maybe that's what irked him. The way this arrangement seemed like a business deal rather than... What? This *was* a business deal. They had nothing else between them other than this agreed-upon charade, which was precisely the way he wanted things.

So why did he still get an unsettling ache inside each time he saw something new in the press?

He clicked on another article about them and cringed at the headline on this one.

Another Sutherland Engaged...but Where's the Ring?

The piece went on to joke that maybe he was giving Cassandra one of his bars instead of the gift of a rock on her hand. This wasn't the first time a ring had been hinted at, and honestly, after a few weeks of this game he really should've gotten her one.

But thinking of getting her a ring only brought back

the memory of the time he actually had bought a ring. He'd scraped his own money together to buy something he thought she'd love. He'd been working on getting two of his bars up and open and he'd wanted to do it all on his own with the wise investments he'd made and a few loans.

He still had that damn ring. When she'd left, he hadn't been in the mindset to do anything with it, then when he'd attempted to get back to his life and start again without her, he hadn't wanted to return it. When he'd asked his mother for help choosing the ring, Luke had no clue when he would eventually give it to Cassandra. He wasn't ready then, but he assumed the day would come when they'd get married. The timing had never felt just right and then she was gone.

For reasons he couldn't explain, he'd hung on to the piece as some crazy symbol of what he'd let slip away. Every time he saw the velvet box in his safe, he was reminded of how far he'd come, that if he wanted something, to go for it.

So many thoughts swirled around in his head and before he could talk himself out of this terrible idea, he opened his messages and sent one to Cassandra. He held his breath waiting for her reply, but once it arrived, Luke got to his feet. He'd put a plan into motion and now he would have to see how it all played out.

Cassandra stepped off the private elevator of The Cheshire and scanned the crowd. Another night with a packed house of VIP guests and many from the high society of Beaumont Bay. People were laughing, drinking and chatting, and the band was getting set up. Cassandra noted the band tonight was made up of two young women who looked nervous yet excited. They kept smiling at each other as they stood just off the stage. Luke came into view as he approached them. Cassandra eased a little closer and overheard him giving them a speech.

"You guys will be fine," he told them. "I wouldn't have invited you here if I didn't think you were awesome. You both need a boost of confidence and this is where you'll get it. You know I only have the best artists on my stage."

"That's why we're so nervous," one of the girls laughed. "But thank you. This has been one of our dreams, to play The Cheshire stage."

"Once people hear you, you guys will be booked solid and I'll be begging to get back on your busy schedule," Luke stated. "The crowd is ready. Are you guys?"

The girls glanced at each other and nodded.

"I'll go introduce you," he said.

Cassandra moved to the bar as Luke took the stage. As always, the moment he grabbed the mic, the crowd started cheering. Luke Sutherland was a natural charmer and he could hold anyone captive…and she was no exception.

He'd texted her earlier and asked her to come up this evening because there was another impressive new band and because he had something to show her. Intrigued by his message, she'd agreed. Then she'd had a hell of a time trying to get her focus back on Hannah's wedding.

Between Hannah being gushy with her ideas about love yesterday during their meeting and then Luke texting her tonight, Cassandra's thoughts were all over the place. Not to mention that she had weddings she was working on remotely, and was planning ahead for the brides who had come to her looking to book for a year or more out. Cassandra's stress level was higher than she'd ever let it get before.

She wished she could just jump straight to the end of this journey and go back to her life in Lexington. Her new business would surely take off and she could focus on that and future brides instead of Luke.

"Gin and tonic with extra lime?"

Cassandra turned to the bartender—Miles, she believed his name was—and smiled.

"You remembered."

"That's part of the job," he replied. "But I also couldn't forget the future Mrs. Sutherland's order."

Future Mrs. Sutherland…that would be her. Well, it *would* be her, if all of this was real.

The lump in her throat stopped Cassandra from saying anything else. She hadn't thought of herself as the future Mrs. Sutherland in a long, long time. Not since she'd had the naive notion that she might actually hold that title one day.

"Here you go," Miles stated as he slid her drink across the bar top on a leather coaster imprinted with the bar logo. "Let me know if I can get you anything else."

He moved on to the next customer as Cassandra nodded her thanks and picked up her tumbler.

"Glad you could make it."

She jumped and turned to see Luke right behind her.

The band started up, playing something fast and peppy, getting the crowd excited. The drumbeat seemed to match the rhythm of her heart.

"You intrigued me," she admitted, then took a sip of her drink.

"Extra lime?" he asked, nodding to her glass.

"You have a good memory."

His gaze ran over her face, and he seemed to be studying her or trying to gauge what to say next. The rooftop bar might be packed, but she didn't notice anyone else except for Luke. He took a step closer and reached up to smooth a strand of hair away from her cheek. He took a little extra time in trailing a fingertip along her jaw.

"Come to my office."

He hadn't exactly whispered, since the area was too loud, but he didn't shout, which made the command seem intimate. Cassandra nodded and when he reached for her, she held her breath.

Luke's arm slid around her waist as he led her behind the bar and to the private hallway to his office. The door slid open and then closed as they stepped in. Once they were alone, the music was drowned out, and Cassandra was glad she held her drink so her hands had something to do.

Why was she so nervous? Or was it not nervousness, but…arousal?

She was such a mess, she couldn't even figure out her own thoughts right now. After a quick sip, she moved farther into the office and leaned against the edge of a leather club chair.

"So what is this mystery you called me up here for?"

Still standing across the room, Luke sighed and crossed his arms over his chest. His eyes remained locked on hers and a muscle ticked in his jaw.

"It's come to my attention that you still don't have a ring," he began. "We need to fix that."

Confused, Cassandra shook her head. "I thought we discussed just telling everyone we were going to choose one later."

"Considering we've been engaged for a few weeks now, I'd say that's long enough."

Luke walked to his desk and opened the drawer. Cassandra turned to face him and watched as he pulled out a velvet box.

"Luke, I don't think—"

His eyes met hers. "You will wear a ring. My ring."

He circled back around the desk and came to stand before her. When he lifted the lid, Cassandra gasped at the simple gold band with a pearl in the middle, encircled by tiny diamonds.

"I remembered you used to always wear this little pair of pearl earrings so I wanted to get something that you'd like," he told her. "I saw this and thought it suited you."

She stared at the stunning ring for another moment before looking back up to him. Had he actually gone somewhere and picked out this ring for her, or was this the original ring she'd heard about from his brothers? There was so much to interpret in this moment and Cassandra was terrified to delve deeper into all the questions she had. She was even more afraid of what the answers would be.

"I can't... This is... Luke..."

"I'm glad you're speechless," he laughed. "That means you like it."

She continued to stare, unsure of what to say or what to do. She hadn't wanted him to present her with a ring—that would make all of this a little too real. Even though years had passed since she'd dreamed of this moment with him, having him give her a ring now only thrust her mentally back to a time she'd tried to forget.

"I don't think this is a good idea," she insisted.

Luke reached for her drink and set it on his desk, then turned back and that damn ring glinted in the light. It was so beautiful, yet simple, and something she would have chosen herself. He'd done such a beautiful job and she still had those pearl earrings he'd mentioned.

"When did you go get a ring, anyway?" she asked.

"That's not important and this *is* a good idea," he countered. "We're playing the role of being engaged and I don't half-ass anything."

When he slid the ring from the slot in the box, she held her breath. Luke pocketed the box before reaching for her hand. Without a word, without getting down on one knee, without any fanfare or romantic gestures one should have with an engagement, he eased the ring onto her finger.

Definitely not how she'd thought her engagement would go. The ring felt so foreign, nearly as much as this crazy gesture. There was something almost cold and sterile about this moment. A shiver crept through her and she couldn't suppress it.

"You okay?"

Cassandra continued to stare at the ring on her finger and felt the burn in her throat. Emotions were welling up, yet she couldn't afford to cry now. Never in her life had she thought she'd get upset when a man put a ring on her finger, but…well, this wasn't exactly the moment she had dreamed of her whole life.

She was in the business of romance and milestones, memorable moments. She rejoiced in happy couples and shared their wedding journeys with them. Yet she couldn't even be excited about her own moment because nothing was real…except that shattered heart she'd thought shc'd mcnded.

"Fine," she lied, taking her gaze off the ring and putting it back onto her official fake fiancé. "But at the end of all this you will get the ring back."

"If that's what you want."

"It is," she commanded. There was no way she wanted any type of souvenir from her time here in Beaumont Bay unless it was a favor from Will and Hannah's wedding.

"We really should have done this before now," Luke told her. "We can play it off by saying that we didn't want to overshadow Cash's or Will's engagements. We should definitely post more photos, but we shouldn't be obvious about it. Let the media draw their own conclusions and keep the mystery behind the ring."

The ring. Something so small and simple, yet it held so much importance in her life right now. Why couldn't he have gotten her something big and gaudy? Something flashy for the world to see from a distance?

No, he'd gotten her something delicate and soft, something that truly summed up her style, a piece she would be sorry to give back. Because just like their arrangement, this engagement, and the ring, would all vanish in a short time.

"Whatever you want," she murmured.

Luke stepped forward, closing the gap between them. He took her left hand in his and held it up, but his eyes remained on hers.

"This is what we agreed on," he murmured. "You're mine."

"For now."

"For now," he agreed.

He tugged her gently until she fell against his chest and he released her hand to wrap his arm behind her back. Cassandra's hands flattened against his chest. The warm scent of his cologne wafted around her. The strength of his body aroused her even more. The familiarity was present, but there was still something about him that was new, thrilling, exciting. She wanted more, even though she shouldn't because he clearly still wasn't ready for any commitment. Hell, he'd been voted the most eligible bachelor and had women flocking around him and he wasn't interested. He was still just as married to his job as he'd ever been…possibly more.

"What are you doing?"

"What we both want. And I'm not apologizing."

He leaned in closer and Cassandra eased back her head slightly. "Is this a bad idea?"

"Maybe," he allowed. "But we still both want the same thing."

"We shouldn't want more," she murmured, but there was no conviction in her tone and she knew as well as he did that her words were in vain. "Desire isn't something I can fight. It never has been with you."

And maybe having him put that damn ring on her finger had her thoughts a little more jumbled than usual, because she was actually considering letting him do whatever he wanted—what she wanted.

"I don't want to fight," he told her. "I'm just tired of pretending I don't want you."

He wanted her.

She'd known, but hearing the words said aloud had even more knots forming in her stomach. Maybe coming back here had been a mistake. Maybe she should've contacted Will directly and simply asked about being his wedding planner.

But no. She'd come straight to the one man she should have kept her distance from. After all these years, though, she thought she'd be fine seeing him again. She thought they'd put enough of a gap between them that the past wouldn't interfere with her future plans.

She'd been wrong.

"This isn't a real relationship," she explained. "We can't complicate things with…"

"Sex."

There it was. The word they'd danced around for a while, and now it was out in the open and hovering between them.

"Why can't we?" he asked, his mouth hovering just a breath from hers. "Are you going to tell me you don't wonder if we're even better than we were? Are you going to tell me you don't want this just as much as I do?"

She needed distance. She couldn't think with him touching her, not with that strength he possessed and that heavy-lidded stare he owned.

Cassandra eased from his embrace and took a few steps away, taking in a deep breath to calm her shaky nerves and get control over herself.

"My wants are irrelevant," she stated when she turned back to face him. "And so are yours for that matter."

Luke continued to stare at her, and it was the silence between them that had her questioning herself yet again. Why wasn't she taking what he offered? He'd been right in saying they both wanted this. She couldn't even lie to herself, let alone him, because she did want him. Part of her wondered if they'd be even better than before, while the other part wondered if she'd get lost in the lust and passion and forget that this was all a fake, temporary relationship.

"I should go," she told him.

"You don't want to."

Cassandra shrugged—there was reason not to be honest. "Like I said, that doesn't matter. I didn't come here for a fling and that's all this would be. I have no room in my life for anything more."

At least not with the man who'd shattered her heart years ago.

Luke said nothing and Cassandra couldn't take the

tension, or the desire emanating from him, for another second. She went to the door and tapped the security panel to slide open the wall. Immediately, the blaring music surrounded her. Happy customers were all still milling about while singing along and drinking. Everyone continued on about their lives as if hers hadn't just taken a drastic turn.

How was she going to get through the next few weeks before the wedding? She would have to stay busy. She would have to focus on work and not the fact that she still wanted the hell out of her ex-lover turned fake fiancé.

He'd wanted a fling and she couldn't deny she wanted him, too. But at what cost? Because no matter how much they enjoyed themselves, even that small bit of happiness would be ripped away in the end, and Cassandra didn't want any more heartache where Luke was concerned.

Eight

Luke called himself all kinds of a fool for the way he'd treated Cassandra. She deserved better than his pushy assumptions and now he had to do something to make up for his actions.

He hadn't seen or spoken to her in a few days and he knew from talking with Will that Cassandra and Hannah were busy planning all things wedding. She was here for a job, not to be harassed by him. She'd come to him for help and he'd turned the tables on her by asking for something of his own. He'd wanted to prove to himself that he could be close to her and be completely unaffected. Then he'd wondered if he should take advantage of this prime opportunity for a little payback.

But that was a jerk move. How could he be cruel when Cass's leaving long ago had obviously been the best thing for both of them? They were now successful in their own ways and had built happy lives, right?

Yeah, he owed her a damn big apology and he was going to do that right now. He shot off a quick text that he had a surprise for her and he would pick her up at noon.

Luke rested his arms on the railing of his balcony off his master suite and stared at his cell screen. Immediately, he saw she was typing a response. He thought for sure she would tell him no, or to go to hell...both of which he deserved.

I'm busy right now. Make it one.

That extra hour was even better. Now Luke could plan appropriately. His mind traveled back to the twentysomething guy he'd once been who'd wanted to give her the world. So much had changed in both of their lives and he found there was still a sliver of him that missed what they used to share. Not just the intimacy, but their friendship. He hadn't even realized how much of a void her leaving had left until she'd returned.

Luke pushed off the railing and pocketed his phone. He'd made sure to let the managers of his bars know exactly where he'd be today in case of an emergency, but he had such competent employees, he didn't worry one bit. They could certainly all manage without him for one day.

He didn't recall the last time he'd taken an entire day off, but if anything warranted some time away, Cassandra sure as hell did.

With a little burst of hope and excitement, Luke put his plan in motion and started counting down the hours until he could see Cassandra again.

With a quick click of her mouse, Cassandra sent the rush order to the florist for all of the fresh blooms the local florist would need to create a masterpiece for Hannah and Will's perfect day.

The penthouse echoed with the buzz at her door. She got up from where she was sitting at the corner desk and smoothed a hand down her pants. She'd been told to wear pants and boots, and to be comfortable. Now she was intrigued, and wondered if they were going hiking or if there was something else on Luke's mind that she didn't know about. He'd been cryptic with his texts when she tried to get him to tell her what was going on.

Cassandra blew out a breath and headed toward the door. She would have to face him at some time, and if they were going out, that was the best option. Staying in or being alone with him wouldn't be smart at this point. She'd been dreaming of him these last few nights and all that did was leave her aching and wanting.

She had to shove aside all of that nonsense and focus on the job. There was no reason she couldn't be friendly, though, right?

Cassandra flicked the lock on the door and opened it to reveal Luke standing there holding a large gift bag.

With a laugh, Cassandra eased back to let him inside. "It's not my birthday, so what's the bag all about?"

Luke stepped into the penthouse and set down the

bag at her feet. He stood straight up and pointed to the tissue-filled gift.

"I wanted to bring you something to start off my apology, but flowers are overrated and I had no clue what to do." He let out a laugh and raked a hand over the afternoon scruff on his jawline. "I figure you're a wedding planner, so a planner would be useful. Then the lady at the store said you can't have a planner without special markers, then she showed me this whole display of sticker things on a wall."

Cassandra watched as he fumbled over his words and sought some attempt at an apology. She crossed her arms and simply waited for him to finish.

"So I had no clue what the hell you had or didn't have, so I just told the lady to give me everything from that wall of stickers. Well, I didn't have her give me the baby or expecting-mother packs because, well... for obvious reasons."

Cassandra didn't know whether to hug him for being so damn adorable, or inform him that planners and stickers weren't quite the type of planning she did for a career.

But she absolutely loved the gift. She loved the gesture. She really hadn't expected anything so sweet from him. Not only had he done something thoughtful, but he'd also shown his vulnerable side. Never once in all the time she'd known him had she ever seen Luke admit he didn't know something, or venture into a territory that wasn't in his wheelhouse. The fact that he'd gone into a store and stepped outside his obvious comfort zone all to show he was sorry...

And other than that one kiss, he'd never told her he was sorry for anything. Who was this new Luke and why was he being so damn perfect? She didn't want to find him even more charming and adorable than usual. She could handle the sexy Luke, but the tender side... She wasn't so sure what to do with that.

Cassandra bent down, pulled out the tissue paper and laughed at the sight of what was inside. "You really did go all out, didn't you?"

"Considering I was a jerk the other night for propositioning you into a fake engagement..." He raked a hand over his hair and sighed. "I know you wanted marriage when we were together before, so that wasn't fair."

Cassandra stood straight up and met his gaze. There was something there beyond the apology she could clearly see. It was that other emotion she couldn't quite put a label on.

"No, it wasn't," she agreed. "But this is where we are now."

"I can't help but think there's something to explore here."

His statement shocked her and immediately her heart kicked up. "What?" she whispered.

With a shrug, he took a slight step forward. "I don't know, Cass. I just can't help but feel that pull. It's strong, it's completely physical, but it's there and damn difficult to ignore."

In addition to that fast heartbeat, now she had a quiver of nerves curling in her belly. She'd obviously had those same feelings since she'd come back to Beaumont Bay, but now that they were out in the open, she didn't know what to say.

"I'm not trying to make you uncomfortable," he added. "And I don't know what the hell I want, but you deserved an apology and I plan on making it up to you."

Then Luke gestured toward the door, and suddenly, the moment was gone. "Ready to go?" he asked.

Just like that, he'd swept in here with the most adorable gift, given her a heartfelt apology, and admitted he wanted to explore something more. Damn if she wasn't in trouble here and she had no way out. The only way to go was forward and she hoped she didn't get crushed in the process.

Cassandra pushed aside her fears because there was nothing she could do about them now. "Are you going to give me a hint as to what we're doing?"

"Not one."

She couldn't help but laugh as she went to get her purse.

"You won't need that," he told her.

She froze and glanced over her shoulder. "No? Now I'm really intrigued."

Cassandra grabbed her room key from her purse and slid it into her back pocket. Nerves curled through her belly at the anticipation of what Luke had in mind. This was the Luke she remembered—always doing sweet things. Granted, the passionate Luke from the other night was also familiar and damn difficult to turn away.

He'd admitted he wanted something physical. Could it really be that simple between them? After all the drama they'd been through, she really didn't know.

But they did have a deal between them and she planned to hold up her end. A few more pictures on social media to keep this farce going wouldn't hurt. Which reminded her to also grab her cell.

"I'm ready," she told him after she'd gotten her phone. "Should we do a selfie now or is there something more exhilarating that will be a better backdrop than my hotel living room?"

Luke smiled, and damn it, he was irresistible...yet somehow she'd resisted him. She'd pushed him away, but since then, their attraction and sexual tension was all she'd thought of.

Cassandra wanted to rewind to the other night and just let go. What would have happened if she'd shoved aside those red flags waving around inside her head? Where would they be now if they'd just let this fling happen? They were adults; they weren't the naive couple they used to be. Her eyes were wide open now...and she wasn't sure she could keep resisting him.

"I have something more exciting planned," he assured her. "Unless you want a quick kiss selfie?"

He waggled his eyebrows at her, still with that naughty smile in place. Cassandra crossed to him and smacked his chest.

"Nice try," she told him. "I'll wait to see what you have planned."

"Does that mean no kiss?" he joked.

"Not right now. I'd like to see what you have in store and how we can spin it to our social media. That is the whole reason for this date, I assume?"

Luke's smile faltered slightly. "When I planned this,

I hadn't given social media or other women a single thought. I just wanted to take a breather from everything and I figured you needed a break, too. And I wanted to see you smile."

Oh, hell. When he said things like that, she couldn't remember why she was ignoring her own desires. The man wasn't just sexy and successful—he was kind and generous…and he clearly wanted her.

She had to get out of here or she would forget all the reasons she couldn't get entangled with Luke Sutherland again. The bomb his brothers had dropped about Luke having a ring for her years ago had taken root in her mind and she thought about it every time her gaze caught the current band on her finger. Layer all of that information with her current emotions and she was a walking wreck.

"Everything okay?"

Luke's question pulled her back to the present and Cassandra pasted on a smile. "Perfectly fine. I'm ready for more of my surprise. You know I love them."

She bent down and slid the tissue paper back inside the gift bag, then took the heavy bag to the small dining table just off the living room. She still couldn't believe he'd done all of that for her. Just that gesture alone had her heart softening. She couldn't imagine how she'd feel at the end of this day. Maybe she would completely succumb to his charms and her needs.

Nine

Luke hadn't known what Cassandra's reaction would be, but he smiled when he saw her face light up as he turned onto the lane that led to his barn and pasture. He'd called ahead and had his stable hand get two of the stallions ready.

"Who owns all of this?" Cassandra asked as she looked out onto the fields lined with white fencing and horses dotting the horizon.

"I do."

Her attention jerked to him. "You own all this land?"

Luke pulled up to the stable and killed the engine, then turned to face her. Her shocked expression had him laughing and swelling with pride.

"Did you think I just tended bar and partied all day and night?"

Cassandra stared for a moment before shrugging and turning back to the acreage. "I never thought about it. I mean, I just assumed if you owned all of those businesses, then you were married to those. How do you have time to come out here?"

"It's just like anything else. I make time. And as much as I love my bars and all the people I meet, there are times when I need to get away."

That was something that had changed since she'd left. He'd never made time for anything else other than work before that point. But he'd learned the benefit of taking a break, and now, he was taking time for her. Their outing had nothing to do with the fake relationship. There was no one around to care or see.

Cassandra smiled. "You always loved riding."

"If I recall, so did you."

She looked back at him with a sweetness in her smile and a softness in her eyes. "We always said we'd have a horse farm outside Beaumont Bay where we could escape. Looks like you did everything you wanted."

Back then they'd discussed many dreams for the future. But he hadn't been ready to put that ring on her finger and she'd wanted nothing more. He'd gone on to fulfill his every career goal. Wasn't that what he'd wanted? He had the social scene and nightlife in Beaumont Bay, he had his businesses, plus a place to go and decompress when needed.

Clearly they hadn't been on the same page back then. They'd both had dreams, but they'd branched off in different directions. Looking back, maybe that had been the best thing that could have happened to them.

Luke cleared his throat and reached for his door handle. "Let's go have some fun."

She was out of the truck before he could come around and get her door. The late-summer breeze surrounded them, sending her hair dancing around her shoulders. Cassandra lifted her face into the wind and closed her eyes. An instant punch of lust to the gut had him catching his breath. He hadn't thought of the impact bringing her here would have on his mental state. Luke had just wanted to apologize and have a relaxing day.

He hadn't taken into consideration all they'd discussed so long ago. At one time, this was exactly what Cass had dreamed of and what she'd wanted them to share together. He'd always planned on having a place where they could escape from their work and just be alone.

And that's exactly what they were doing now, but definitely not under the circumstances he'd originally envisioned.

Without thinking, Luke reached for her hand and Cassandra's gaze snapped to his. Now that he was holding her, he didn't want to let go and it had nothing to do with faking this relationship. He couldn't help how he felt. Turning off his desire for her wasn't an option—it never had been.

He curled his fingers around hers and couldn't help but feel an extra lick of lust when she returned the gesture. There was something building here that had absolutely nothing to do with the outside world and nothing to do with their business arrangement.

"I don't remember the last time I went riding," she told him. "This definitely gets you brownie points."

"So I'm forgiven for the other night?" he asked as he led her toward the stable.

"There's nothing to forgive. Things got heated, Luke. It's bound to happen given our history."

Maybe so, but their history had nothing to do with why he felt a pull toward her now. He was intrigued by the woman she'd become and he wanted to learn more. He wanted to know what she'd been doing since she'd left. Maybe he was a masochist for wanting to spend more time with her, for wanting to uncover everything about their time apart. She was only back in town for a short time and Luke wanted to make the most of it.

But he had to remain guarded. She'd been such an intricate part of his world at one time and yet she'd walked away. Getting too emotionally involved now would be such a foolish, naive mistake. He knew better, and quite honestly, he still wasn't looking for anything more than something physical.

"And given the attraction that's still there," she murmured.

Luke's stomach tightened as she tacked on that bold statement. Considering she'd put the brakes on things the other night, he respected her enough to let her take the lead. If she wanted more, then he'd sure as hell give her everything she wanted. But if she only wanted to be friends while she was in town, then that's what he would do, no matter his own desires.

Nobody had ever affected him like Cassandra and now that she was back in town, she had him mesmerized all over again.

He was doomed. That would be the end result of all of

this. He might not be in love with her anymore, but that didn't mean he didn't want her. He wanted the hell out of her and the more time he spent with her, the deeper that desire took hold. It threatened to consume him.

As they stepped into the stables, Luke spotted the stallions at the end of the path. Their reins were looped around the hooks and the horses were all set to go. Luke had told his stable hand to make sure everything was set and then make himself scarce. Luke wanted privacy and he wanted Cassandra to enjoy her day without any interruptions.

"They are gorgeous," Cassandra exclaimed as she headed toward the animals. "What are their names?"

"Carl and Stan."

Cassandra laughed. "Those aren't quite the horse names I was imagining. I figured like Thunderbolt, or something strong and powerful."

Luke laughed and reached out to stroke one of the stallions.

"Carl and Stan were two of my regular customers when I first opened The Cheshire. They were best friends who'd been widowed. They came to drink every Thursday night and stayed until I closed. We ended up getting close, as one does with regular customers. They both passed within six months of each other."

"They clearly left an impact on you." Cassandra reached up and slid her hand along Carl's nose. "You're more sentimental than I remember."

Only because he'd become that way after she'd gone. He'd realized what was important in life. When he was left with only his businesses and his dreams, he'd thrown himself into every bit of them to make everything a success. He'd been so close to commitment when he'd lost her—he'd vowed never to lose anything or anyone else again.

"Which one am I riding?" she asked, turning to face him.

"Either one. They're both gentle giants and love to be ridden."

Cassandra unhooked one of the reins and easily slid up into the saddle. "I'll take this guy. I can't wait to see the land. It's so gorgeous from out here. Does it go back far?"

Luke took his own horse and mounted him before easing the reins to turn the stallion. "I own about five hundred acres."

"Five hundred?" she exclaimed. "What are you going to do with all of that property?"

"One day I'll build a house, but I just haven't gotten around to it. I built the stable about five years ago, but I've been too busy to design the house."

Not to mention he couldn't bring himself to zero in on the plans he wanted. It seemed rather silly to build a large house for a party of one. His place now was too big for him. He wasn't looking to marry or start a family, but maybe it would happen for him one day. Hell, he had no idea what his future would look like. He was living in the now and enjoying every minute of the life he'd created.

His mother would love nothing more than for him to catch that marriage bug like Will and Cash, but that just wasn't happening.

When Luke had told his parents about the fake engagement, his mother had scolded him for multiple reasons, but mainly for not bringing Cassandra around so they could see her.

"Show me around," she told him with a smile.

Luke followed her out into the pasture, wondering if this day would bring more for both of them than just a time to relax.

Hell, what was he thinking?

This day and this fake engagement weren't going to end in some damn fairy tale. Clearly, his brothers' engagements were messing with his head. Luke would do good to remember that Cassandra had walked away once and there wasn't a doubt in his mind she would do it again.

The diamonds on her engagement ring glinted in the sunlight and the pearl seemed to glisten even whiter than before. Cassandra tried to ignore the shimmer and shine as she took in the beauty of Luke's property. All of this seemed so surreal. There were too many elements that were thrusting her back into the past.

At one time this property, and this engagement, would have been real, would have been hers. It would have been her actual life and she would have been living her dream with the perfect man. Would they have children by now? That was one area she hadn't allowed her mind to wander to before, but now that she was seeing all that she had lost, she couldn't help but let her imagination go into that hidden corner she'd kept locked.

But none of that mattered.

No matter how wayward her thoughts were, she

couldn't go back in time. And now she was only pretending to have that life she'd once dreamed about. The
ring would go back, the fairy-tale romance of riding in
open fields would be gone, Luke would go back to his
bars and she would go back to her life in Lexington.
She'd come to Beaumont Bay only to get the wedding
of her career and boost Be My Guest into high-society territory. She'd done that. So why was she wanting more?

"Back here is where I plan on building."

Luke's statement cut into her thoughts and she focused on where he was pointing. There was a slight
knoll and just in the distance was a large pond. She
could practically picture a stone-and-log home standing tall. Wraparound porches were a must and maybe a
second-story balcony off the master. Something masculine and demanding of attention with thick wood beams
and dark stone chimneys.

"So you're going to give up living in the Bay?" she
asked.

"Eventually. There's a little too much drama in town
and I like the peace and quiet this place has to offer."

"Drama? You mean that's still a problem?"

When she'd lived here years ago, there was always
something major going on. The place was almost like
living in a soap opera. Typically, the emotional chaos re-
volved around Mags Dumond—self-dubbed First Lady
of Beaumont Bay. Even though her husband, the mayor,
had passed away long ago, the woman still believed she
ran the town. Maybe it was the outlandish parties she
threw or maybe it was the money she flaunted in ex-

cessive ways, but Mags had always made it a point to be in everybody's business.

"Cash was arrested for a DUI a few months ago," Luke revealed then shook his head. "All bogus charges that were ultimately dropped."

"DUI," Cassandra gasped. "That doesn't seem like Cash at all, not the way I remember him. I mean, he might be country music's bad boy—"

"Reformed bad boy," Luke amended. "Presley changed him."

"Yes, well. Drunk driving isn't something he would do, is it? How in the hell did he get arrested?"

"Because he was set up by Mags."

Yep. There it was. The woman who stirred up trouble. Some things never changed in this town. Surprisingly, Cassandra hadn't had a run-in with the eccentric woman since she'd been back.

"Why would she do that?" Cassandra asked.

"I'm sure she had her reasons. She's jealous of the success of Elite Records—she wants to always come out on top no matter the cost." Luke shrugged. "Hell, who knows what she'll come up with next, but we're always on our guard with her."

Cassandra knew Mags was powerful, but for the woman to take on all of the Sutherland brothers…well, that was ridiculous. That would be a battle Mags would definitely lose.

"None of that is important now," Luke added. "I really don't want to ruin the day with talk of Mags."

"Fine by me," Cassandra agreed. "So how long are we riding?"

Luke glanced her way and winked. "We're almost there."

Confused, Cassandra glanced around and saw nothing other than the pond. She turned her attention back to Luke.

"Where?"

He gestured up ahead. "Right over there."

He took the lead with his stallion and circled the pond. That's when she saw a display that made her gasp.

"Lunch is served."

Luke dismounted his horse and looped the reins to the post next to the pond. When he came over to her, he reached up and gripped her waist to assist her down. Cassandra was so stunned by the blanket, the basket and the wine chilling in a pewter bucket, she didn't notice the way her body slid right against his until she found herself gripping his shoulders.

Luke's eyes met hers and he smiled. "I figured that even though you're a big city wedding planner now, that country girl is still inside and you'd find a picnic by the pond romantic."

Cassandra's breath caught in her throat. "Is that why we're here? Romance?"

His dark eyes locked with hers and that bond they'd formed long ago was still there. It couldn't be denied. Whatever was happening had started the second she'd stepped into his office a few weeks ago. As much as Cassandra thought she'd been in control of this entire situation, she realized right then that she hadn't grasped an ounce of control.

"I know you don't want a fling," he told her. "I didn't

bring you here to seduce you or anything else, but I do know you're a romantic at heart and I thought since you were wrapped up in the wedding and—"

Cassandra kissed him.

She'd cut off whatever he was saying with her lips because she couldn't stand another second of not touching him. Luke churned something deep inside her that had been dormant for eight years. Only this man could convince her to ignore the alarm bells going off in her head and finally take what she'd been craving.

Cassandra intended to do just that.

Ten

The last thing Luke expected was for Cassandra to suddenly kiss him like she'd been just as achy as he had been. Had he known a horse ride and a picnic would have her practically climbing up his body, he would have done this weeks ago.

Luke wrapped his arms around her and splayed his hands over her back, pulling her flush against him.

Finally.

This wasn't a quick kiss or something for a social-media post. This was Cassandra taking charge, taking what they both wanted.

And if nothing else came from this kiss, then Luke would still be okay. All he'd wanted to know was if they still had those embers between them... he hadn't expected the flames.

Cassandra framed his face and shifted, taking the kiss deeper as she sighed. Arousal and anticipation slammed into him and Luke gripped her backside and positioned their hips just right.

She pulled away from the kiss, panting and looking at him as if waiting for him to do something. But this was the one time he had to relinquish control. She'd made it apparent that a fling or anything else was off the table. He respected her enough to let her take the lead...though he would be more than willing to follow anywhere she wanted to take him.

"Are you sure you didn't bring me here to seduce me?" she asked.

"That wasn't my intention, and if we're making accusations, you've been seducing me since you came back into town."

Cassandra's eyes widened as her tongue darted out and licked her bottom lip. "I didn't come back for that... or any of this."

He waited because those murmured words that had fallen from her damp, swollen lips led him to believe she wasn't done with her thoughts.

She closed her eyes and shook her head. "But I want you. It's a ridiculous fight that I've been losing for weeks."

Some sense of calm eased into his chest. He hadn't realized he'd been waiting on her to admit that, but he had. While he'd wanted Cassandra since she'd come back, he also still cared about her. He would never push her out of her comfort zone or make her feel like she wasn't fully respected.

At the same time, he also had to be true to himself and honest with her about how he was feeling. Not that he was one to dig deep and get in touch with his emotions, but damn it, she pulled out things he thought he'd buried long ago.

"You do something to me, Luke." Cassandra opened her eyes and refocused on him. "No matter what has happened in the time I was gone, that doesn't change what we shared and what I want now."

She'd summed up his thoughts exactly. Luke reached up and slid his fingertip along her forehead, smoothing her hair back behind her ears. She shivered beneath his touch as he trailed along her jawline and down the column of her neck.

Cassandra kept her eyes locked on his and his heart pounded even faster. Was she ready to cross that line? Because he'd mentally crossed it every single day since her return. He'd give anything to know the thoughts running through her head.

"There's nothing wrong with taking what we want and there's no reason to feel guilt or worry."

Luke listened as she seemed to be talking to herself. She reached up and traced the V of his T-shirt and he instantly held his breath.

Then he got a smile that he'd only seen back when they used to be together. It was a sexy grin that held a hint of naughtiness and a whole hell of a lot of promise.

"Tie up my horse," she commanded as her eyes remained on his. "And take a seat on the blanket."

Hell yes. She didn't have to ask him twice. Luke secured the stallion with the other horse before sinking down onto the large, soft quilt that had been left out here with their picnic.

Cassandra came to stand above him and kicked off her boots, then she went for the waist of her riding pants and slowly, so agonizingly slowly, eased them down her thighs and ultimately kicked them aside. She stood there in a plaid button-up shirt that hit just below her panties and he'd never seen a sexier sight than this woman with her hair disheveled from the ride and those long, dark legs that were just begging for his touch.

"Are you sure?"

He couldn't believe he was pausing to ask, considering she was half-naked, but he wanted zero regrets after this.

Cassandra quirked an eyebrow and started at the top button, easing each button through its hole as she continued to stare at him in silence. Of all the scenarios he'd envisioned since Cassandra had returned, this was definitely not one of them.

As if he hadn't found her sexy enough before, now she was taking charge, taking what she wanted on her terms. Looks only went so far and confidence was absolutely everything. Cassandra had never faltered in that category.

She eased off the shirt and let it fall to the blanket. Wearing only her white lacy bra and panties, she dropped to her knees and started tugging off his boots. He jerked his shirt up and over his head and they both reached for the button on his jeans at the same time.

Their eyes met and she gave him that saucy smile

once again and it had him laughing. Damn, she was something and he was not about to waste this moment.

In a flurry of hands and a few chuckles, they had his jeans and boxer briefs stripped off and tossed aside without a care. Now she remained on her knees staring down at him and Luke wanted nothing more than to reach for her and pull her on top of him. Instead, he used every ounce of willpower to keep his hands to himself.

But that didn't mean he couldn't get his point across.

Luke leaned back and laced his hands behind his head as he kept his attention on her. He smiled, waiting on her to make her next move.

Without moving her gaze, she reached around and unfastened her bra, then eased it down her arms and off to the side. Then she wiggled out of those flimsy excuse for panties.

Luke didn't even try to hide the fact he was raking his gaze over her bare body. It had been too damn long since he'd seen her like this. She was still breathtaking, still stunning, still the sexiest woman he'd ever seen.

Her curves had filled out more than he recalled. The flare of her hips and the dip in her waist were more accentuated than before, and that young woman he'd fallen in love with had turned into a strong, confident, damn fine woman. And for now, for right now, she was his.

Cassandra rested her knees on either side of his hips and straddled his lap, flattening her hands against his chest. The wind kicked up and sent her hair dancing around her shoulders. He'd never seen a more beautiful sight. His heart tightened and he refused to dwell on the feeling. His heart was just getting confused with the past, but his mind knew full well what this was… and what this wasn't.

"Tell me you don't have workers who are going to come out here anytime soon," she laughed.

"They're paid well to set up and then leave."

He couldn't wait another moment to touch her. Luke gripped her hips and eased her right where he wanted her.

"I don't have protection with me," he told her. "I honestly wasn't planning on this."

She slowly rocked against him, very nearly sinking into him, but was clearly relying on her willpower, as well.

"I don't have anything, either, but you are the only person I've ever not had it with."

He shouldn't have let his ego swell at that statement, but he did. She trusted him, in the past and now.

"I've always been careful, too," he told her.

He said nothing else as she joined their bodies, then immediately closed her eyes and tossed back her head. The way she remained still and tightened her entire body around him had Luke groaning and unable to restrain himself anymore.

Jerking his hips, he set the pace and continued to hold on to her. Cassandra shifted and leaned forward, placing her hands on either side of his head. Luke tipped up his head just enough, silently seeking her mouth. She didn't hesitate to cover his lips with hers as she started moving even faster.

This was the passionate Cassandra he'd missed. No

matter the distance between them over time, this was so familiar…almost like coming home.

But that couldn't be, and it sure as hell wasn't something he wanted to be thinking about while entering this moment. He didn't want to think of the future or wish for more from Cassandra. All he wanted was this, right now. He couldn't mentally or emotionally afford anything else.

Luke flattened his hand on the small of her back and fisted her hair with the other hand. He nipped at her lips as her body jerked even harder. She released his mouth and cried out, then bit down on her bottom lip as if she'd just realized she was losing control.

"Let go," he demanded.

Her back arched and she came undone. Strands of wayward hair clung to her neck, her bottom lip, and she cried out as her knees squeezed against his sides.

Luke couldn't take his eyes off her. Damn, he'd missed her. How the hell could this be happening? He only wanted a temporary fling, one last bit of time with her before she vanished again for good.

Before he let his mind travel too far down a dangerous path, Luke's body climbed and he pumped his hips faster, harder, until he followed Cassandra over the edge.

Eleven

"No regrets?"

Cassandra reached for a piece of cheese and met Luke's gaze over the picnic lunch he'd set up while she'd gotten dressed.

"Regrets? No." She chose a cracker and took a bite before finishing her thoughts. "I was fighting the inevitable. I guess my only concern is what now? I like plans, you know, and I like to know what's going to happen. This is out of my comfort zone."

Luke chuckled. "You seemed pretty damn comfortable a few minutes ago."

Cassandra couldn't help but smile. Oh, she'd been quite comfortable, but that was all physical. Mentally she was a hot mess. For someone who made a career out of planning every single detail down to the minute, not knowing what was going to happen between her and Luke was rather unsettling.

But there was no way she could regret the sex. Intimacy with Luke had always been the best, and the eight years between them had only made it even better.

Her heart fisted. Maybe part of her wished she hadn't let down her guard, but common sense prevailed... barely. They'd had sex. Amazing, outdoor sex, complete with a picturesque background and a romantic picnic.

Luke claimed he hadn't planned for this to happen, and she believed him, but the day couldn't have been any more romantic. Even if she hadn't been in the business of love and happily-ever-afters, she would still have found this moment to be one of the sweetest, most tender, most passionate in all her life.

So how was she just going to leave when the time came? Luke had reopened that spot in her heart she'd thought she'd sealed off. Cassandra hadn't expected her heart to open up, or those deeper emotions to rise to the surface, but they were. And now there was no way to protect herself. He would still never give her the marriage and commitment she wanted. There was no reason for her to allow herself to think otherwise.

So while her heart would be aching when she left town, at least she'd had this physical connection with him one last time. That was something, right?

"I'm not sorry we did this," she told him. "Given our past and the close bond we've always shared, I am comfortable with you. It's strange, even after all this time, that I still trust you with my body."

Luke shifted to lie on his side and propped himself

up on his elbow. He'd still not put on his shirt, which was certainly not helping Cassandra's mental state. He'd left his jeans unbuttoned and now he was just lying there with all of that excellent muscle tone on display. Between the naked chest and the scruffy beard and her still tingling body, Cassandra's clothes nearly melted right back off.

"There was a time you trusted me with more than your body," he reminded her.

Cassandra stilled, then set down her food on a napkin. She wasn't sure what to say to that statement, but she needed to defend herself. Bringing up the past again wasn't something she wanted to do, but considering what had just happened, she supposed there was no other choice. Their past was what had brought them here today.

"I trusted you with everything." Cassandra swallowed the lump in her throat and shifted to cross her legs in front of her. "I would've done anything for you."

"Except stay."

"You know why I didn't."

Now he rose up and rested on his hand, his eyes holding hers in place. "Yeah, I do. I wasn't ready to marry, Cass. I had too many things going on, too much I wanted to do with my career, and I wasn't in the same place you were. I thought we were both chasing our own dreams first."

"We were," she agreed. "Until your dream became all you could see. I became invisible and what I wanted wasn't on your agenda."

That muscle ticked in his jaw as he continued to stare

at her. Maybe her comment sounded selfish, but she couldn't just negate how she'd felt at that time.

"Never once did I think you were invisible," he insisted.

Hearing him say that now didn't help. She'd wanted those words then, she'd wanted him to fight for them, for what they'd planned together. But he'd been stubborn or preoccupied or something, because when she'd walked out, he'd let her go.

"You were so worried about your bars and everything going along with that, I was getting pushed farther and farther away from your priorities. And when I asked you what was more important, you said nothing. That's all the answer I needed to know. I didn't compare."

He leaned in closer as his lips thinned. "Did you ever think that I was trying to build a solid foundation for our lives? So that way when I was emotionally ready, I could give you everything you ever wanted?"

Cassandra listened and couldn't deny the passion, the frustration in his tone. Why hadn't he told her that back then? Why did he have to be so damn stubborn?

With a sigh, Cassandra reached for her stemless glass of wine and swirled the contents.

"Rehashing everything now won't change the people we were or are," she told him. "And if that's really what you were thinking back then, you should have said as much instead of letting me walk out."

"I didn't say anything because if you were hell-bent on leaving, then nothing I did or said would have stopped you," he countered. "I shouldn't have had to beg you to stay."

"No, but I deserved more than silence."

Cassandra's heart tightened again at the flashback of that moment as she recalled the ache. She wanted out of this conversation and off this topic. Because no matter what was said now, it wouldn't erase the years of pain they'd endured, or the outcome of their relationship.

"My mom says everything happens for a reason."

The reminder that she'd left his family as well as him just layered on more pain.

Cassandra smiled despite her inner turmoil. "How are your parents? I can't believe I haven't seen them yet."

"Oh, they're dying to see you," he laughed. "And, just a heads-up, they aren't convinced that our engagement is fake."

Cassandra glanced to her ring, then back to Luke. "Why is that?"

"Probably because my parents have always loved you, but I told them this isn't going anywhere."

Before she could comment, his cell chimed. Part of her hoped he would ignore it, but he shifted to pull the phone from the pocket of his jeans.

Luke stared at the screen and sighed before setting his phone to the side. Cassandra couldn't help but look at the screen, and she saw the name *Emma*.

"Friend of yours?" she asked.

He shrugged and didn't say a word. Irritation now had Cassandra sitting up a little straighter.

"Are you still getting many calls since we started this charade?" she asked.

"Not as many, but still more than I'd like," he replied.

Luke searched through the basket of food, then pulled out a small plate of brownies and placed them on the blanket between them. Cassandra had suddenly lost her appetite.

"How about at the bar when I'm not around?"

Cassandra couldn't help but ask. She really had no right to probe and no claim to him because all of this was only a farce. But moments ago, when they'd been as close as ever, that had felt too damn real.

"The attention at the bar has definitely not slacked off," he chuckled.

That low, sultry laugh of his pissed her off even more.

Again, though, she knew she had no right. They were doing each other favors, and apparently, he rather enjoyed having the extra attention. Maybe, in spite of what he'd said when he'd asked her to become his fake fiancée, he liked living with his new title of Most Eligible Bachelor.

If that's what he wanted, then Cassandra had no place to say a word.

"Does this bother you?" he finally asked, looking back to her.

"What?"

He cocked his head, looked toward the phone and raised his eyebrows.

"Fine," she conceded. "It bothers me."

There, she'd said it. But she didn't want him to get the wrong idea. She wasn't about to admit any more of her feelings. She was done being vulnerable for the day.

"If we're supposed to be engaged, then you should respect me enough to play the part."

"You think I don't respect you or is that jealousy talking?"

Cassandra tipped her chin. "I'm not jealous," she insisted.

"No? Then why do you care who wants to be with me or who I talk to?"

Why indeed?

"I rarely date because I spend all my time with my family or with my businesses," he went on. "I sure as hell am not advocating for the attention of these women. I run successful bars and restaurants, I make music careers, so chatting and being overly friendly are part of my job."

Cassandra listened to him and let out a sigh as she shook her head. "Maybe I am jealous, but I know I have no right or reason to be."

Luke met her gaze and she saw that hunger she'd seen countless other times. Every time he looked at her beneath those heavy lids, she wondered how they hadn't worked out the first time. How they couldn't have just lived on their attraction. She thought about how damn well they got along when they only let their bodies do all of the communicating.

He reached across and swiped his thumb along her bottom lip.

"What would you say if I told you I love the idea that you're jealous?"

Instinctively, the tip of her tongue flicked at the pad of his thumb. That fire in his eyes burned even brighter and arousal nearly consumed her.

"Luke," she murmured.

He blinked and eased his hand away, pulling them both from the moment.

"We both know this can't go anywhere." His words seemed to ground out through gritted teeth. "No matter how much I want more of you, no matter if you're jealous or not. We're still in different places in our lives."

He was right and they both knew what was at stake here.

"So what do you suggest?" she asked.

He gestured toward the brownies. "Chocolate."

Cassandra eyed the plate and couldn't help but chuckle at the switch from desire to dessert. "Are these your mother's?"

Luke let out a bark of laughter. "They're her recipe, but I made them."

"You made them?" Her focus snapped back to Luke. "When we were together before you didn't know how to do much in the kitchen."

His face sobered. "A great deal has changed since you left."

On the contrary. Cassandra feared not much had changed at all because she was starting to feel too much while Luke was still not ready for anything real.

Nothing had changed after all.

Twelve

With the wedding now only days away, Cassandra had officially hit panic mode. Every wedding she worked on had her nervous, but those nerves were always the giddy kind, filled with anticipation.

This was the first time she'd been a bundle of unidentifiable energy. Maybe that was because she was doing the wedding of someone with Hannah Banks's stature, or maybe it was because she was back in Beaumont Bay once again.

Or perhaps it was because she still couldn't get that romantic, sexy man out of her head.

Cassandra hadn't seen Luke in person for a couple of days, since he'd surprised her with the picnic. He'd texted a few times, but she kept telling him she was too busy to come up to the bar.

In truth, she was not only too busy, but she was also forcing herself to put some distance between them.

With the wedding happening in less than a week, that also meant Cassandra would be going back to Lexington soon. And once she was back home, working on building Be My Guest, she would have to put Beaumont Bay and Luke Sutherland out of her life for good.

Cassandra glanced to the piano and vowed that she would play later with a glass of wine once she could unwind and relax. For now, though, she had to get to the lake to meet with the florist and finalize plans. Then after that she had to follow up with the security detail because this wedding could not be crashed by unwanted paparazzi.

As she closed her computer, Cassandra checked her cell and calculated how much time she had before she had to get down to the gazebo by the north end of the lake. Not for another hour, which would be just enough time for—

The penthouse alarm echoed and had Cassandra jerking her attention toward the door. The only visitor she ever had was Luke. Her heart pounded and she pulled in a shaky breath. She couldn't dodge him forever, she just had to remember to keep her clothes on this time.

Cassandra crossed the spacious room and flicked the two locks before opening the door.

"Dana," she exclaimed.

"Oh, my darling."

Dana Sutherland barely got the words out before she threw her arms wide and pulled Cassandra in for an embrace. Thrilled to see Luke's mother after all this time, Cassandra returned the hug.

After a moment, Dana eased back and smiled.

"You are even more beautiful than the last time I saw you," she declared. "I hope this isn't a bad time, but I kept asking Luke to bring you to the house and he clearly has ignored me."

Cassandra stepped back and gestured. "Come on in. I have an hour to spare."

"Working on the big wedding, I assume."

Cassandra led Dana into the sitting area and took a seat on the sofa. "Are you ready for this?"

"I can't wait to finally gain a daughter," Dana replied. "Hannah is so perfect for Will. Then again, I thought you were perfect for Luke at one time."

Is that why Dana had stopped by? To prod at the current status of Cassandra and Luke's relationship?

"That wasn't meant to be," Cassandra told her. "But Hannah is so lovely. You're all very lucky to have her join your family."

"Presley is an amazing woman, too. I can't believe I'm gaining two daughters in such a short time." Dana crossed her legs and rested her arm on the edge of the sofa. "So tell me all about your life in Lexington. Luke tells me you've branched out on your own and started a wedding business."

"I did, which is why Hannah and Will's wedding is so important. This will not only be my first high-society event, this will be the first for Be My Guest."

Dana smiled. "What an adorable name. I love it. Now, tell me if I'm overstepping, but do you plan on sticking around the Bay or are you set on going back to Lexington?"

Cassandra couldn't help but laugh. "I built a life for myself in Kentucky. I have friends, and when I get back I have interviews set up so I can start adding employees because I'm hoping this wedding blows up my new business."

"I'm quite confident it will," Dana assured her. "Hannah has told me what a dream you have been to work with. She will most certainly give you a glowing recommendation to anyone who seeks your assistance."

That's what Cassandra was counting on. The possibilities were endless. This was everything she had ever wanted. A reputable wedding company of her own and a solid foundation that would lead to growth. When she'd left Beaumont Bay years ago, she'd struggled both emotionally and financially. But over time, she had gotten stronger in both areas and now she had every intention of pushing forward. Looking back on any aspect would only put a dark cloud of doubt over her dreams.

Dana gasped and pulled Cassandra from her thoughts.

"That ring…"

Cassandra glanced to her hand and back to Dana, who was still staring with the oddest look on her face.

"Are you all right?" Cassandra asked.

Dana blinked and shifted her focus. "What? Oh, um, yes. I just… That ring is beautiful."

That vise squeezed tighter around Cassandra's heart. She'd worn this ring for a couple of weeks, and as foreign as it had felt before, now she was getting more and more used to the band. Luke had really outdone himself on a ring that wasn't supposed to mean anything.

"It's quite something," Cassandra agreed. "I've seen so many different rings in my line of work, but there's something so simple and elegant about this one that really makes a statement."

Dana still seemed stunned, as if the ring in question had shifted something within her. Cassandra had no clue what was going on in her mind.

"It's really great to see you again," Cassandra stated. "Do you want something to drink or anything?"

Dana shook her head. "Oh, no, no. I just stopped in to see you. I don't want to take up too much of your time. But I would kick myself if I didn't speak my mind while I had the chance."

Cassandra braced herself. She knew what was coming, but she loved and respected Dana enough to listen.

"I don't think you coming back to the Bay is a coincidence," she began. "I know you wanted this job, I know my son propositioned you into some ridiculous fake engagement, but I've always believed everything happens for a reason."

"I would agree with that to some extent," Cassandra replied.

Dana eased forward on the sofa and turned to face Cassandra even more. She reached over and patted her knee, while offering that motherly smile that was a precursor to advice.

"I can't help but think you two have been given a second chance," Dana said with utter conviction. Cassandra almost wanted to believe the words. "What if this is where you are supposed to be? What if Luke never got over you?"

She couldn't help but let out a soft laugh. "Luke is getting along just fine without me. All he ever wanted was those bars and to make a name for himself. He's done all of that."

"But at what cost?" Dana countered. "He's still got a void in his life, and as his mother, I can tell you that he was a disaster when you left."

"That would make two of us," Cassandra said, defending her actions. "But I couldn't stay."

Dana nodded. "I understand and nobody blamed you. In fact, we all pretty much told him to go after you and get his priorities straight."

Clearly that hadn't happened and Cassandra had actually waited for exactly that. Not to mention he'd pretty much refused to marry her.

Though she'd wanted him to fight for her, she hadn't been playing a game or leaving to get him to chase her. She hadn't issued an ultimatum because she was being a difficult girlfriend. She truly needed to remove herself from the place where she felt she was no longer appreciated. But she had honestly thought he *would* have fought for her…for them.

"Have you two discussed what happened?" Dana asked, then sighed. "I'm sorry. I don't like to be a meddling mother, but I just can't help it when I know you and Luke were so right together."

"We were," Cassandra agreed. "And then we weren't. It happens. People grow apart and move on."

Dana tipped her head and smiled, but the gesture

didn't quite reach her eyes. Cassandra loved this woman like her own family and would have loved to be considered one of her daughters, but there were some things that just weren't possible.

"Would you like to join me this afternoon?" Cassandra offered. "I'm meeting with the florist and finalizing security down by the gazebo."

"Oh, I don't want to get in the way."

Cassandra came to her feet. "Nonsense. You're the mother of the groom. Maybe after we can grab a late lunch at the new little café on the water."

Dana nodded and rose. "I would actually love that. Travis is out at an open house all day, so I could use some girl time."

Cassandra was excited to spend more time with Dana. They'd once been so close, and when Cassandra had left Luke, she'd been heartbroken over leaving all of the Sutherlands. Now if only she could remember that this, too, would be coming to an end in less than a week.

"Luke, darling."

He turned at the familiar, grating tone and found himself face-to-face with Mags Dumond. Her hot pink smile widened when he met her gaze.

"Mags," he greeted.

She glanced around the rooftop bar, seemingly scanning for something, before she focused back on him.

"Do you have a private area where I can meet with a potential new client?" she asked. "We don't want to be disturbed."

Luke resisted the urge to laugh. Maybe coming to a

rooftop bar where there was nightly music wasn't the best place to have a business meeting. Then again, nobody understood Mags or her way of thinking.

He was actually surprised she'd shown up here considering it wasn't long ago she had set up Cash with a bogus DUI charge. Luke wasn't quick to forgive and forget. But he was in the business of making money and he sure as hell would take hers as a patron.

"I have a VIP room," he offered. "There's a two-hundred-dollar fee up front, but you will have a special menu and your own private bartender."

She pursed her lips and ultimately nodded. "Sounds perfect. Show me the way and then you can send my guest back. Her name is Sandra Collins."

Sandra Collins. Luke had heard of her. Her agent had actually contacted Luke about Sandra playing at The Cheshire, but he hadn't heard her music yet so he hadn't made any final decision. Luke figured Mags was here just to be her usual, busybody self and show off the fact that she was adding new artists to her label.

Since Hannah had left to sign with Will's label, Elite, Mags had been out for blood.

Luke motioned for one of his employees to come over.

"Marcus will take care of you," Luke assured Mags. "Let him know if you need anything at all."

"Wonderful." She started to turn and follow Marcus, but glanced back to Luke. "Oh, will you be open on Saturday?"

"Saturday? Of course. Why?"

"Well, with the wedding and all, I wasn't sure. I plan on having another meeting."

"My staff will take care of you, but I, of course, will not be here."

Her smile thinned. "Of course. Give my blessing to the happy couple."

As she walked away, Luke nearly groaned.

Her blessing? What the hell? Hannah and Will could care less what Mags thought or said about their nuptials... hence the reason she wasn't invited to the wedding. It was likely she just wanted to raise his awareness of that fact because her ego had taken a hit at being snubbed.

"Mr. Sutherland?"

He turned to see a fortysomething lady with a drink in hand and smile on her face...and in an extremely low-cut dress.

"Yes?"

"My name is Tracy." She held up her cell phone. "Could I get a quick picture with you? My best friend couldn't make it tonight and I promised I'd send her a selfie."

Before he could politely deny the photo, Tracy leaned in, held up the phone, and snapped a picture. Luke stepped away and offered her a smile, trying not to be rude, but also trying to respect his "fiancée's" wishes about playing the part that he had created for himself.

"My fiancée might not like you posting a picture of us on social media," he half joked.

Tracy immediately glanced down to her phone, obviously not worried about what Luke was saying. She was already sending out the photo.

Luke slipped away and headed to his back office,

needing to escape for a bit before he introduced the band in an hour. They should be arriving anytime to set up, but they were return guests, so Luke had put one of his staff out to greet them.

Right now, he needed a reprieve.

Earlier he'd met his brothers for their final suit fittings and Luke had been warned that his mother had spent the day with Cassandra. Nothing good could come from that. Luke was well aware of how his mother loved Cass. Will had given Luke a heads-up, since Hannah had met the other ladies at the gazebo this afternoon.

Luke took a seat at his desk and leaned back in the chair. Rubbing a hand over his beard, he let out a sigh. Part of him didn't want Cass to leave after the wedding, but the other part knew the sooner she was gone, the sooner he could get back to his normal life. Maybe he'd start making time for dating again. Maybe he'd do more socializing outside of work.

Those ideas were all well and good, but none of them seemed to settle right within his mind.

His cell vibrated in his pocket and he pulled it out to see Cash's name with a photo attached. Luke opened the text and groaned. There was a photo of Cassandra, Hannah, and his mother all laughing and enjoying lunch. Obviously, this had come from earlier today and the caption read:

All in the Family

Of course. How lovely this image was, as it relayed assumption that everyone was one big happy family. Appearances could be convincing, but the more Luke studied that photo, the more his heart flipped in his chest.

He couldn't quite describe what he was feeling while looking at this, but he did know he had a sense of... Hell, he couldn't put a label on it. All he knew was that this was a scene that could have been his life—*his real life*—had he been ready.

At one time, his mother and Cassandra had been extremely close and they would have planned an amazing wedding. Dana had loved Cass like her own daughter, but Luke just couldn't quite commit at the speed they seemed to want him to. He couldn't be sorry about how it had ended, because he'd been true to himself. Had he given in to what everyone else wanted, he would have lost himself along the way and resented Cassandra and their relationship.

No doubt his mother had enjoyed their day out together today. He hoped she didn't get too heartbroken when Cassandra left town again.

The fact that she wouldn't look back once she was gone kept playing over and over in his head. This was it. Their last time to be together.

Luke stared at his phone another minute before he got to his feet and went out to talk to a few members of his trusted staff. He had plans and nothing was going to keep him from what he should have done long before now.

Luke had more of a solid foundation than he'd ever thought possible. He was much more advanced in his career and in a better position to have a life he could be proud of.

He wanted Cass back in his life.

Thirteen

Finally.

Cassandra dried off from her relaxing bubble bath and slid on her pink silk robe. She picked up her glass of wine from the edge of the bathtub and headed down the hall and into the living room.

The one-way windows provided a breathtaking view of the lake and all the lights of the homes and businesses while giving her the privacy she needed. Taking a seat at the piano, she set her glass on the top and lifted the cover to expose the keys.

This was what she'd been waiting to get to all day. A perfect relaxing ending to a fun, productive day.

Not only was everything going smoothly for the wedding, but Cassandra was also thrilled she'd gotten to reconnect with Dana. The woman was just as amazing as ever and Cassandra had promised that even when she went back to Lexington, she would stay in touch.

Which only meant she'd have that loose lifeline to Luke. As much as she wanted marriage and a family of her own, she was also realizing that she would have an extended family if she and Luke reconnected. His family had been hers at one time. Who said she couldn't let that kind of family fill the part of her that wanted kids and marriage, and then accept Luke as he was, in whatever kind of relationship he was ready for? Would he want to take that next step eventually? With seeing his brothers fall in love and marry, would that make him see that he could have it all?

Just as she started to play a familiar song, the bell chimed through her penthouse. Her hands stilled on the keys. She knew who was out there. At this time of the night, there wasn't a doubt in her mind.

Cassandra got to her feet and glanced down. No need in changing. She hadn't planned on visitors and Luke probably just wanted her to come up and hear the music. Tonight, though, she planned on staying in and decompressing before the mad rush that would start rolling into the weekend.

She crossed the penthouse and went to the door, where she flicked the dead bolts. As soon as she opened the door, Cassandra smiled as Luke stood before her, but her smile faltered at the look on his face.

His eyebrows had drawn in and muscles clenched in that strong jawline, but those were nothing compared to his intense, dark stare.

"Is everything okay?" she asked.

"No, it's not."

He took a step in and Cassandra moved out of his way, then shut and locked the door behind him. When she turned to face him, he was close, so close.

And she knew that look. Aside from the fact that they'd been together for years, she knew the look of a man who was hungry for passion. Her body instantly stirred with arousal. The realization that she was only wearing an extremely thin robe that could be discarded with one expert jerk of the knot only made her desire grow.

"I can't get you out of my mind," he murmured, keeping that penetrating gaze locked on her. "I can't concentrate on work and I can't escape through social media because you're all over it. My family thinks you're amazing and you're driving me out of my mind."

Cassandra opened her mouth, but the words vanished as Luke took a step forward, then another, until her back was pressed against the door. She tipped up her head and swallowed at the vulnerability looking back at her. For the first time in her life, she finally saw the unimaginable—Luke Sutherland conflicted and vulnerably exposed.

She reached up and cupped the side of his face with her hand. His nostrils flared as he leaned in to her touch.

"I need you," he whispered. "Now."

Cassandra nodded and eased up onto her tiptoes as she wrapped her arms around his neck and pressed her lips to his.

Then Luke seemed to snap as he picked her up and carried her away from the door. Her world seemed to

tip as she released his mouth and buried her face in the
crook of his neck. She inhaled that familiar, woodsy
cologne of his. All masculine and rugged, just like the
man.

He laid her down on the oversize sofa and stood
over her, raking his heavy-lidded stare down her body.
Cassandra couldn't stand the wait, the torture, any longer. When her hands went to the tie on her robe, Luke
reached for her and shook his head.

"Let me," he commanded.

Slowly, he pulled the silk belt until the garment
came untied, then he peeled away the material from
her heated skin. Cassandra arched her back, seeking
more of his touch, needing him to fulfill that promise
she saw staring back at her.

"You're so damn perfect," he muttered.

And she felt perfect. The way he looked at her, with
more passion than she'd ever seen, made Cassandra
feel beautiful, cherished and, dare she think it…loved?

Luke reached behind his back and grabbed a handful
of his T-shirt, then yanked it over his head and discarded
it off to the side. Cassandra watched as he continued to
undress until he was completely bare before her.

She reached up for him, silently inviting him to join
her. As he placed his hands on either side of her head,
Cassandra shifted her legs to allow him space to settle
between.

The moment he aligned their bodies, she closed her
eyes and relished the feel of his weight pressing her
into the cushy sofa. Cassandra brought up her knees

on either side of his body and tipped up her face to nip at his chin.

"You make me want too much," he murmured as he slid his lips back and forth across hers. "I can't stop this need."

Cassandra wasn't sure if he was just talking sex or if he meant something else, but now was certainly not the time to start discussing such things. She only wanted to feel. He'd come here because he'd needed her and something clicked with Cassandra…something she thought had been forgotten long ago.

When Luke joined their bodies, Cassandra wrapped her legs around his back and locked her ankles. He rested on his elbows and covered her mouth with his as he started setting the pace. Clutching his firm, broad shoulders, Cassandra opened for him and let Luke take control. He clearly needed more from this than she knew. Never before had he shown a vulnerable side. Her Luke had always been in control, always in charge, and ready for anything life threw at him.

Something had gotten into his head, and whatever it was, he needed to exorcise it out. Cassandra had told herself not to get intimate with him again while she was here, but there was no way she could turn him away. All it took was one look, one touch, especially when he showed up looking like she was the only one who could save him.

Cassandra tightened her legs and her arms, wanting him to know that she had him. As he increased the pace, she felt her body climbing. He murmured something against her lips, but she couldn't make out the words.

At this point, no words were necessary. She wanted to feel, she wanted him to take all he needed.

Luke reached down and gripped the back of her thigh, pulling her leg up even higher. That's all it took for her to come undone and cry out. Moments later, Luke followed her and his entire body tightened. Cassandra continued to hold on to him as the tremors ceased.

When Luke's body relaxed and settled heavier against hers, Cassandra stroked her hands up and down his back, silently offering comfort.

When he started to shift, Cassandra flattened her palms against him.

"Stay."

"I have to be hurting you," he murmured.

Cassandra straightened her legs a little, loving the feel of his rough hair against her silky skin. This certainly wasn't the way she had planned on spending her evening, but she wasn't about to complain. Having Luke here might just have been what they'd both needed.

"You're not hurting me," she assured him.

"I know I shouldn't have come here," he told her, easing up to look down at her. "I just—"

"This is where you belong."

She hadn't meant that the way it sounded, but she wasn't sorry she'd said the words. Cassandra wanted Luke here. Part of her needed him here. Coming back to Beaumont Bay had been terrifying, personally and professionally. She'd known coming back would open up all of those old wounds and it had. But, somehow, Luke had filled those newly exposed cracks.

She didn't know what would happen after tonight. She wasn't about to ask. All she knew was that Luke needed her and she wasn't going anywhere yet. For the next few days, she would offer him whatever he needed...and hope she could walk away when the time came.

Luke stared at Cassandra sleeping with the sheet wrapped all around her. Her dark shoulders and one shapely leg were exposed. Her black hair was in disarray on the stark white pillowcase.

His gut tightened. This was the only woman who could make him second-guess everything in his life. She made him wonder why he'd let her walk away so long ago. She made him question how the hell he hadn't been on the same page back then, when all she'd wanted was to be his wife.

Why hadn't he gone after her when she left? Why hadn't he just told her to give him time? Maybe it was pride, maybe it was that he had been afraid that making a commitment meant he'd lose a part of himself.

So here they were. His mother was convinced this was the second chance he and Cassandra deserved. Luke wasn't so sure about that. He wasn't sure this was much more than a fling, but he had feelings...and these feelings had nothing whatsoever to do with the past and everything to do with the woman who was lying so peacefully and beautifully before him.

Maybe his pride was still standing in the way, even today. Luke wasn't ready to risk asking her to stay, to see if they could maybe try again. Putting his heart on the line like that wasn't smart when he was likely just getting too caught up in all the wedding nonsense.

Between Will and Hannah's wedding and Cash and Presley's engagement, was it any wonder he was getting confused while playing pretend with his ex?

But the intimacy he'd shared with Cassandra wasn't pretend. The posts on social media, the affection in public—those were all for show. There was so much that wasn't for anyone else, though. All of this behind the scenes was strictly for them.

Luke's eyes drifted to the ring on her hand and that did nothing to calm his nerves or ease his mind.

He'd known that ring would look stunning on her hand. He'd known she would love it because Cassandra had always been more of a romantic than someone who went for bling and flash. The pearl was absolutely the perfect choice for her.

Yet she'd already told him she'd be giving it back. He wanted her to keep it. He'd wanted her to have it since the moment he bought it eight years ago. Maybe it had been naive and pathetic of him to hold on to it.

Oh, he hadn't kept the ring because he thought she'd come back. No. He'd kept that piece locked in his safe so that every time he opened it, he would have that reminder of all he'd lost and all he'd sacrificed to have what he did today.

Luke pulled in a shaky breath and turned from the room. It was early and he knew she had a full schedule ahead. The wedding was only a few days away and Cassandra would be up to her ears in flowers, seating charts, catering questions, and rehearsals.

He went to the kitchen and started up the coffee maker. After searching through the cabinets, he found two mugs. He pulled his cell from his jeans, then sent a text and ordered breakfast to be sent up ASAP.

While waiting for the coffee, he glanced around the penthouse and spotted the piano. A glass of unfinished wine sat on top and he figured he'd interrupted her last night. He wanted to hear her play again. She had a knack for music, just like Cash and Will. Luke and Gavin hadn't gotten that talent, but they did love music, so they'd entered the industry in a different manner.

Luke went to retrieve the glass and got it washed and put away just as the coffee finished brewing. He poured a mug for himself and took a sip. That first taste of hot caffeine in the morning always did wonders for his soul.

Spending the night in Cassandra's bed also did his soul wonders. He wanted to stay here again tonight and every other night until she left.

No, he wanted her in his bed. On his turf. He wanted to see how well she fit in…

Wait. That would be a mistake.

Taking her home, seeing her in his house, would not be smart because when she ultimately left, as he knew she would, he would have those reminders in each and every room.

Maybe he could convince her to let him stay here until she left. He wouldn't mind being closer to The Cheshire. He had to pop in to his other establishments today and do some inventory and payroll, but he mainly could be found at his favorite rooftop bar.

He had no idea what the hell he truly wanted when

it came to Cass. Every scenario scared him to death, but he knew he wasn't ready to let her go.

Luke grabbed his mug and went back to the piano. He slid onto the bench, took another sip, and stared down at the keys.

"He makes coffee and plays the piano."

Luke glanced over his shoulder to Cassandra, who was leaning against the doorway coming off the hall. She'd put that silky robe back on and he knew damn well she had nothing on beneath.

"I'll take credit for the coffee, but I'm terrible with any instrument."

She padded barefoot across the marble floor and slid onto the bench next to him. He wanted to scoop her up and take her right back to bed, but they weren't at that point in this relationship.

Hell, they weren't even in a relationship. They had great sex between them and a fake engagement. They hadn't made things work the first time they were together because he hadn't been ready for more. Was he ready now? Could he give her everything he wanted and not lose part of who he was?

Luke had to just keep pressing on with this physical relationship, enjoy her while she was here, and remember that once she was gone, he would go back to the life he had created, the life he loved. He wasn't sure what else to do and he wasn't ready to take the risk to find out. Doing so, and failing, could ruin both of their lives and he sure as hell wasn't about to do that.

"Play for me," he told her.

Cassandra turned to face him, her bed head of curls

falling over her shoulder as she smiled. "What do you want me to play? I usually only play for myself and to relax."

"You look pretty relaxed." He reached up and smoothed her hair away from her face, tucking the strands behind her ear. "Play anything. I had no idea until I heard you that you were so good."

Cassandra's eyes darted to her lap, then back up. "This was my outlet when I left. I had to do something or I would have gone insane."

He understood. He'd poured himself into his work even more than when she'd been here. Had he not, he would've gone out of his mind. Besides the fact that she had left, Luke had been berated by his entire family for letting Cass go.

She said nothing else as she adjusted her position on the bench and delicately placed her fingers on the keys. Instantly, the room filled with a soft, slow song. Cassandra closed her eyes and lost herself in the music. Luke couldn't take his eyes off her.

The longer she played, the more Luke found himself getting lost right along with her. The juxtaposition of feelings continued to confuse him. He wanted her, and not just in bed, but how was that even possible? She hadn't been in town long enough for them to even discuss their past or what had happened.

Oh, they'd touched on it, but never fully resolved anything. Should he try? Should he defend his actions? Maybe let her tell her side and really listen?

But what would that solve? Going over something that happened eight years ago wouldn't change a thing and he wasn't sure he was ready to jump back in with her. Damn it, he wanted to, but he refused to get hurt again.

Keeping part of his guard up was the only way because Cassandra had never given any indication she wanted more, or that she would even consider staying here, with him, after the wedding.

When she finished playing, she glanced back to him, but all Luke could think about was that the bed was probably still warm.

"How soon do you need to be out of here?" he asked her.

A smile spread across her face and she turned to meet his eyes. "I have a little time before I need to shower, if there's something you had in mind."

Luke got to his feet and lifted her into his arms.

"I haven't had my coffee yet," she said, resting her head against his chest.

He maneuvered down the hallway toward her room. "Oh, this is much better than morning coffee."

Fourteen

Cassandra smoothed down her dark green pencil dress. She wanted to wear something appropriate for the autumn season, but still perfect for the wedding of the year. She definitely didn't want to be flashy, as she was supposed to fade into the background.

Granted, nobody would be looking at her and that's the way things should be. As a wedding planner, her only duty was to make the entire day flawless and stay behind the scenes…almost like a magical fairy had taken over and everything just appeared as it should be.

But she would be remiss if she didn't try to sneak in a selfie or a public kiss with Luke. They were still playing the part, after all.

But she was fooling herself.

Because they'd both fallen into this "role" a little harder

than they should have. Now they were coming to the end
of this tête-à-tête and she'd pack up her feelings, along
with her suitcases, and be done with Beaumont Bay and
Luke. That was the only way to prevent heartache again.

Cassandra glanced to the aisle and the flowers on
the back of each chair cover. The flowers Hannah had
chosen were absolutely perfect and the weather couldn't
be more beautiful. The lighting was exactly right and
their pictures were going to be stunning.

As Cassandra bustled around making sure everything was in place, she was also texting Miles at The
Cheshire to make sure everything was going smoothly
for the reception setup.

There were so many working parts to making a wedding go off without a hitch. Everything happened at
once. But this was what Cassandra lived for. And every
time she reached this moment in her job, she always
thought about what her own day might be like.

Maybe that's why she excelled at her job. She treated
each wedding like her own to make sure the bride and
her party didn't worry about a single thing.

But would she ever have her own wedding? That ring
on her finger continued to mock her. It was like Luke
knew exactly the type of engagement ring she would
want, but couldn't see how much marriage meant to her.

She'd actually put on her pearl earrings today to
match the ring. How silly was that? She would be giving it back tomorrow and packing up to head back to
Lexington. The only other reason she'd have to return to
Beaumont Bay would be for another celebrity wedding.

By the time Cassandra finished making her rounds

and handling final touches so everything was perfect, the five-piece orchestra started playing while the guests arrived. Hannah and Will had decided to keep the guest list small at only one hundred people.

Cassandra smiled at an usher as she walked by and made her way to the lakeside community building, where the wedding party was all getting ready. It was go time and Cassandra had to make sure each person went out on cue.

The men were on the second floor and the ladies were on the first. As Cassandra approached the side entrance that the men would be using to bypass seeing any of the ladies, she was glad to see them lined up and heading in her direction.

"Ready to go," she greeted. "You all look devastatingly handsome."

And that was quite the understatement as Will led his brothers down the walkway. Cassandra's eyes naturally gravitated toward Luke. Seeing him in a tux was quite different from seeing him in jeans and T-shirts. If she'd thought he was sexy before, that was nothing in comparison to his hair perfectly parted and fixed, that scruff along the jawline, and the broad shoulders filling out that dark jacket.

Was this how he would've looked on their wedding day had they gotten to that point? Would he ever get there?

Cassandra forced away the thoughts because this wasn't the time for a self-pity party. Hannah and Will were counting on her. Any emotions or dreams or other feelings she had regarding Luke would have to be put on hold.

But the way his eyes raked over her would certainly make concentrating difficult. He might as well have been stripping her down because she felt just as exposed. Then his gaze traveled back up her body to her face and he smiled.

Oh, what that smile did to her. There was a promise there. He'd spent the past few nights in her penthouse and he'd only left her bed just this morning. Would he be back tonight? Even though they said they would be finished after the wedding, would he want one more night?

She hoped so.

"The music has started," she told them, circling back to her job. "Do everything just like last night at rehearsal."

Will looked like he was either going to pass out or run in the other direction. She'd had an amazing track record of no runaway brides or grooms and she fully intended to keep it that way.

"Look at me," she demanded, getting right in front of his face. "Your bride looks stunning and this is the best day of your life. You ready?"

He pulled in a breath and nodded. "I didn't think I'd be this nervous."

Cassandra smiled. "You're nervous because this matters. That's a good sign. And, if it helps, Hannah is a wreck. Hallie is calming her down as we speak."

Hannah had been nearly in tears questioning everything from her cake flavors to why she wore a fascinator instead of a veil. Hallie had been the only one to talk Hannah off the proverbial ledge.

Wedding jitters were a real thing and this couple sure as hell had them. But Cassandra had been serious when she said nerves were a good thing. Will and Hannah were too in love to let anything stand in their way and nothing would stop this dynamic duo from taking on the world together.

A ping in her heart had Cassandra nearly faltering, but she pasted on a smile, pushed through and gestured toward the venue.

"Let's get this beautiful moment underway."

She stepped aside as the guys walked by. As Luke passed her, he leaned down to her ear and whispered, "I can't wait to peel that dress off you tonight."

And then he kept on walking in a line with his brothers. Mercy, those men were a force when they were all banded together like this. All sexy in their own way, wearing perfectly fitted suits with wide shoulders and devilishly handsome looks.

None of the men got to her like Luke.

And it wasn't just the other Sutherland men who didn't do it for her. Nobody since she'd left Beaumont Bay had affected her or given her those thrilling vibes like the man she'd fallen in love with when she'd lived here.

The promise for tonight that he'd left her with had her shivering despite the warm autumn breeze. Cassandra made her way to the front of the community center building and walked through the atrium and toward the rooms where the ladies had been getting ready.

When she stopped in the doorway, she couldn't help

but gasp at the beauty. She'd seen Hannah before, but there was something about her radiant smile today that had Cassandra jealous of such love and happiness.

"We are ready for the grandmother and the bridesmaids."

Eleanor Banks, Hannah's grandmother and mega country-music star, grabbed the hand of the flower girl and headed out the door. The entire wedding party looked like something from a magazine...which worked out well since Cash's fiancée, Presley Cole, was getting the exclusive.

Presley was the only one Will and Hannah trusted with their special day. Cassandra knew the photographers Presley had on the premises were trusted or they wouldn't be here.

So far, so good.

"If we could have the bridesmaids line up in order," Cassandra announced.

Once they were all lined up and out the door, Cassandra walked to Hannah and took her hands.

"Your groom is waiting and the sun is shining," she told the bride. "You ordered up the perfect day."

"This wouldn't have happened without you," Hannah stated.

"Oh, you still would have gotten married, but I agree. I was your best bet for a wedding planner."

Hannah laughed, just like Cassandra had hoped she would. She'd said it to take off a little of the nervous edge.

"Ready?" she asked.

Hannah nodded and glanced back to the full-length mirror one last time.

"Travis will be waiting on you at the beginning of the aisle just like you rehearsed."

Will's father was going to give Hannah away since her father was no longer living. The entire ceremony was so sweet and perfect, Cassandra couldn't recall a wedding she'd loved working on more.

She truly only thought her own would surpass everything she'd ever done for this one. Granted, that day would actually have to happen for it to surpass anything, but for now, she was thrilled with the direction of her business.

"Thank you," Hannah told her. "I truly would have gone mad without you during all of this."

"You would have been just fine," Cassandra assured her. "Now go get married."

Hannah lifted her dress and slipped through the doorway. Cassandra double-checked again with Miles about the reception and he confirmed that all was set and ready to go. The bridesmaids should be going down the aisle now, and soon Hannah would be, too.

All was right and Cassandra made her way toward the gazebo area. She remained in the background as the ceremony took place. She couldn't help but watch Luke at the end of the aisle as he stood next to his brother. At one time in her life, she had pictured him waiting on her as she glided to his side in a designer dress. She envisioned him tearing up or smiling and telling her how beautiful she looked.

None of that was real, though. As Cassandra glanced at the ring on her finger, she couldn't help but wish second chances weren't just for fairy tales.

Fifteen

"What is she doing here?" Cash asked. "This reception is family and close friends only."

Luke turned toward the elevator and spotted Mags as she stepped off. She waved to someone and instantly lifted a champagne flute off the tray of a passing waiter.

"Hell if I know, but I'll take care of it."

He maneuvered through the small crowd and approached the unwanted guest. She caught his eye and had the nerve to smile like everything was perfectly normal with her crashing a wedding reception.

"What a beautiful wedding," Mags declared as he came closer.

"You weren't invited. How would you know?"

Mags laughed and took a sip of her champagne. "Luke, darling, Hannah is a stunning bride. I can see her from here. And that woman of yours outdid herself. Who knows, maybe if I marry again, Cassandra can plan my wedding. I hear she might be busy planning yours, though."

Luke wasn't taking the bait.

"You have no reason to be here, Mags."

She jerked back, her eyebrows drawn in as if she was literally hurt.

"And I thought you had a meeting with someone today," he reminded her.

"Oh, I rescheduled. Wishing my former star all the best in this new chapter of her life was much more important."

There weren't many people who grated on his nerves, but Mags Dumond was sure as hell one of them. Will and Hannah purposely hadn't invited her and she damn well knew it. But he wasn't going to cause a scene on his brother's wedding day. He would, however, keep his eye on the busybody.

"Don't ruin their day," he warned. "You're not the only one with power."

Her eyes widened slightly and she held her free hand to her chest. "I would never," she gasped. "I just want to give the happy couple my best wishes."

Luke snorted and moved away. The woman didn't have an innocent bone in her body. She lived to stir up trouble. She was like a walking soap opera and Luke would never forgive her for setting up Cash to get arrested for that DUI.

She'd been jealous that Hannah had left her studio to team up with Cash at Will's label. The DUI falsehood had been a petty move that no one could actually prove was Mags because she was too slick, but the Sutherland brothers knew exactly who had tried to destroy Cash's reputation.

"You're frowning."

Luke blinked and realized Cass had come to stand in front of him. He'd been preoccupied with his own thoughts, but now he shoved Mags to the back of his mind.

"Something wrong?" she asked.

Luke shook his head. "What could be wrong on this day? My brother married the love of his life in a beautiful ceremony that people will be talking about for years."

A wide smile spread across her face. "That's what I'm counting on," she told him. "I only had one minor hiccup, but I don't think anyone noticed but me."

He hadn't noticed that anything had gone wrong. All he'd seen was Cass in that body-hugging green dress that was supposed to look polished and professional, but made him think about how damn amazing her curves looked. And he couldn't wait to fulfill the promise he'd made to peel her out of it.

"You've got that look in your eyes," she murmured.

Luke eased closer and snaked an arm around her waist. "What look is that? The one that says I want to kiss you or the one that says I want to tear this dress off you?"

Cassandra's eyes darted to his mouth. "Both."

"Soon," he assured her.

"We probably shouldn't be so affectionate here," she

whispered. "This is your brother's reception and I'm the wedding planner."

"And we're still engaged," he reminded her.

"This is our last day for that."

Her statement might be true, and one he'd agreed to, but that didn't mean he liked the situation. That didn't mean he was ready to give her up, take that ring back, and have it again as only a reminder of all he'd lost.

But was he ready to be vulnerable again? Was he ready to ask her to stay? Was that even fair of him? To ask her to uproot the life she'd made and move back here?

"This is a nice-looking couple."

Luke turned to see his parents both beaming at him and Cass. Of course, they would love to see Luke and Cassandra back together, but Luke had made things perfectly clear…or at least he thought he had.

"The wedding was absolutely gorgeous," Dana said, beaming. "You really have a special talent."

Cassandra smiled and took a step away from Luke. "I love what I do, so I always hope that comes through."

"I imagine you are going to be one very busy lady after today," his mom added.

"I hope so."

Travis slapped Luke on the back and gave him a half hug. "Has my son convinced you to stay in Beaumont Bay yet?"

Luke glanced to his dad and willed the man to be quiet.

Cassandra's eyes darted from Luke to Travis and back again. "Are you going to ask me to stay?"

Luke shook his head. "Ignore them. They're still living in the past."

A flash of something moved over Cassandra's face, but he couldn't identify it and it was gone before he could truly put a label on it.

"Second chances don't always come around," his dad said. "Maybe you two should think before just parting ways."

Think? That's all Luke had been doing since Cassandra had stepped into his office. He thought of the past, he thought of the present and now he was forced to think of the future. Did he want to allow himself to be vulnerable enough to admit he wanted to try again? Would she even want to? Would she trust him with her heart again? She'd never said as much and she'd insisted she wouldn't keep the ring. Hell, she probably already had her bags packed.

"We both have such different lives now," Cassandra said. "Sometimes two people can get along perfectly, but are just not meant to be."

Luke watched as his parents exchanged a glance and he knew Cassandra was wasting her breath. Clearly, she meant what she was saying. She did not think they were meant to be anything more than what they were.

At least Luke had his answer. He would keep his feelings to himself. Disappointment and loss settled deep. He was the one who hadn't been able to commit before, so all of this pain and heartache and frustration rested on his shoulders.

But they weren't twenty-five anymore. They had set

down roots and were growing each day in their journeys that took them away from each other.

"Well, a mother can hope," Dana added.

"It looks like your brother has his sights set on someone, as well," Travis added with a nod toward the corner of the rooftop.

Luke glanced up and spotted Gavin and Hallie deep in what appeared to be a serious conversation. Then Hallie shook her head and Gavin laughed. Good grief, was his brother seriously hitting on Hannah's twin? The woman looked like she'd rather be anywhere else than where she was.

"I just want to see all my boys happy," Dana said with a sigh. "And then I can start having grandbabies."

Travis chuckled. "Let's give the boys some time to adjust to being in love before you throw babies into the mix."

"The only ones in love are Will and Cash," Luke demanded. "Everyone needs to calm down."

Cassandra laughed. "Relax," she told him with a pat on his arm. "Your mother is happy and who can blame her. Today was a wonderful day."

"Just as long as she doesn't expect a wonderful day coming from me anytime soon," Luke murmured.

Damn it, he wanted out of this situation, but he couldn't exactly be rude. Thankfully, the DJ announced it was time for the first dance for the bride and groom. Everyone's attention turned to the center of the rooftop, where Will and Hannah stepped up and embraced each other with the happiest smiles Luke had ever seen.

That pang of jealousy he hadn't expected took him

completely off guard. What were all of these emotions attacking him? He didn't want to be jealous or confused. He didn't want to second-guess every decision, past or present, where Cassandra was concerned.

When he glanced to her, all of her focus was on the happy couple. Cass had the softest smile on her face with tears brimming in her eyes. There was that hopeless romantic he'd fallen in love with so long ago and she paid him absolutely no mind. She had moved on and, as soon as he got that ring back, he should, too.

Cassandra had never felt more conflicted in her entire life. This wedding couldn't have gone any better. She had already received an email yesterday from a record producer in Nashville who wanted his daughter to meet with Cassandra and discuss her upcoming wedding in the spring.

Once Presley went public with this exclusive story and the first photos were sent to the rest of the media, Cassandra hoped her inbox would be flooded with so many potential weddings that she had to hire even more staff than she first intended.

Wouldn't that be something? To have to hire several staff to keep moving forward with Be My Guest.

On the other hand, as much as Cassandra was riding high now that the day was drawing to a close, she knew her time in Beaumont Bay was done. It had taken all her willpower to keep her true feelings to herself when Dana and Travis came over and were blatantly and boldly telling her to stay.

Luke hadn't mentioned her staying and he'd never

acted like he wanted marriage any more now than he did before. He certainly hadn't even pretended to be jealous of his brothers and their nuptials.

As Cassandra helped work on cleaning up after the reception, she ran over every detail of the day and knew the events couldn't have gone any better. She was damn proud of herself, though she was so ready to get back to her penthouse and relax.

"Cassandra."

She turned to see Presley and smiled. "Hey. I thought you and Cash left by now."

"We wanted to help clean up," she stated. "And I stuck around for a more selfish reason."

Cassandra motioned toward one of the sofas and led Presley around Luke's employees, who were working hard on transforming the reception back into a bar.

Once they were seated, Cassandra let out a sigh and leaned back against the cushions.

"I bet you haven't sat all day." Presley laughed. "You outdid yourself with this wedding. It was beyond anything I had imagined."

"Thank you. And, yes, this is the first time I've sat, but that's my job and I love it."

Presley's bright smile widened. "That's what I want to talk to you about. I was hoping I could get on your schedule before you get too busy."

Cassandra couldn't help but return the smile. "I would never get too busy for you and Cash. Working on your wedding would be amazing. What date are you all thinking?"

"Honestly, I'm just so thrilled to be getting married,

we're open. I don't want cold weather and I'd love something outdoors if possible."

Cassandra's mind started racing with the possibilities. No matter how tired she was now, she was always in the mood to get creative and plan a couple's perfect day.

"I'm sure we can come up with something amazing for the two of you," she promised. "Why don't you email me any ideas you have so far, whether it be colors or venue or even a dress style you like, just so I can get an idea of what you're thinking. Also, feel free to tell me things you absolutely do not want."

Presley clapped her hands together. "I will. Oh, my gosh, I can't believe this is really going to happen."

"Believe it. Cash is completely in love with you and he had one of the most romantic proposals I've ever seen."

Pulling Presley up on stage during one of his concerts and producing a ring from his guitar had blown up the internet and there wasn't a woman in the world who hadn't watched that clip over and over.

"You might just be the next one to make a Sutherland brother give up his bachelor status," Presley joked.

Cassandra shook her head. "I doubt it. We were just pretending, you know."

"Oh, Cash filled me in on the arrangement you and Luke made," Presley claimed. "But I've seen the way Luke looks at you and the way you look at him. I'm assuming you're both stubborn."

Cassandra laughed.

"Sorry," Presley quickly added. "I just can't help but

say what I feel and it would be such a shame for the two of you to walk away from each other again when it's so obvious to everyone around you that you're meant to be together."

Why did everyone keep saying that? Of course, she and Luke were looking at each other in a certain way... likely because they were both still sexually attracted to each other and there was no hiding that. But there was no way to build a future, a lifetime, on sex or lustful glances. It didn't work the first time and it simply wouldn't work now...no matter how much she longed for Luke and that life they'd talked about. Dreams didn't always come true and there always came a moment when one had to put aside a fantasy and focus on a new dream.

"I think this whole family is so swept up in wedded bliss that they just want everyone to walk down the aisle," Cassandra joked, hoping to deflect the attention off things that could never be.

"Maybe so, but I still stand by my statement that you and Luke are too adorable together."

"Well, thanks, but we're just friends."

Friends? They hadn't actually decided to stay in that zone once she was gone. Right now, they were lovers, but after tonight... Well, she really didn't know what they would be. Likely a distant memory and the thought of never seeing him again hit her hard.

The pang of intense loss had her throat burning and her eyes stinging. Cassandra got to her feet and forced a smile.

"If you will excuse me, I have a few things to finish up here, but get me that email and we will get this wedding ball rolling."

Presley rose and looked like she wanted to say more as her eyebrows drew in. Cassandra was terrible at hiding her feelings, but she really didn't want to go further into the topic of Luke.

Ultimately, Presley nodded and Cassandra excused herself. After checking with the staff of the bar to make sure everything was under control, she made her way to the private elevator.

Once she was in her penthouse she could fall apart. Now that everything was over and there was no more reason for her to stay, every emotion came crashing down around her.

Cassandra stepped into her suite and stilled. Across the way, standing with his back to her as he glanced out at the starry night, was Luke. When he tossed a glance over his shoulder, Cassandra knew this was it. He was going to make good on that promise to peel her out of her dress and they were going to share their last night together before she left Beaumont Bay.

Sixteen

Too many emotions stirred within Luke, but he couldn't concentrate on them. They all felt too damn vulnerable, as if he was losing control. He never lost control and he sure as hell couldn't afford to now.

Raw physical need was all he could manage because at least he could remain strong and dominate that familiar territory.

The day had been long and he imagined Cassandra was exhausted. As he turned fully to face her, the weariness in her expression was apparent, but there was something else—something he couldn't quite pinpoint.

"I wasn't sure you'd wait for me," she told him as she slipped out of her heels and padded barefoot toward him. "You must be tired."

"I was just thinking the same about you." Luke met

her halfway and reached for her. His hands rested on her shoulders and he gave a gentle squeeze. "Why don't you let me take care of you now? You've done so much for everyone else."

She let out a groan as he continued to massage her. Her lids slowly lowered as her head tipped to the side. Luke touched his lips to her forehead before releasing her shoulders. Then he scooped her into his arms and headed toward the bedroom.

"I can walk," she laughed. "I'm not that tired."

"You can do many things, but right now I'm taking over."

She rested her head against his shoulder and sighed. "I like the sound of that."

So did he…more than he thought. As Luke set her on her feet and moved to her back to unzip her dress, he realized he wanted to take care of her for more than just tonight. He wanted to be the one she leaned on after her stressful days. He wanted to be the one that she turned to for every aspect of her life.

He'd been juggling her needs, this fake relationship, and his businesses just fine since she'd come into town. She knew exactly what he did and how much he put into his work, just as he knew how much she loved her own career. Why couldn't they both have it all and enjoy each other? They could support each other and work through this life together, right?

Right now, he just wanted to feel her. He wanted to show her, without words, that he had come to care for her again.

Did that mean he loved her? He'd loved her when

she'd been here before, but his feelings were quite different now and he had no clue what to do with them or how to label them. One thing was certain—these feelings were much more intense, much more overpowering.

As promised, he peeled the fabric down her curvy body and left her in her black lacy bra and panties.

"And I thought you looked sexy with the dress on," he murmured, taking in the beautiful sight of her.

Cass smiled and stared up at him. "I wore this set for you," she confessed. "I was hoping you'd spend one last night with me."

One last night. That's what she had in her head… that's what he should have in *his* head. But, damn it, he didn't know if he could let her go.

That was a conversation for another time. Right now, he didn't care about words, he only cared about making her feel and clearing her mind of anything else but him.

Luke encircled her waist with his hands and lifted her. She let out a little gasp as he carefully settled her back onto the bed. She was lying there looking up at him with all of that dark hair around her. Those heavy lids had nothing to do with her being tired and everything to do with her arousal and passion.

No woman had ever looked at him the way Cassandra did. No woman had the power to make him want to relinquish every bit of control the way she did, either.

And that was new, different from when they were younger.

That was also how he knew he was in a whole hell of a lot of trouble if she ended up leaving again.

"How long are you going to stare?" she murmured.

Luke pulled from his unwanted thoughts. They had no room here, not when he wanted to solely concentrate on Cassandra.

He wasted no more time as he stripped out of the rest of his tuxedo. When she reached for him, he shook his head.

"Not yet," he told her. "Just lie back and relax."

Her hands fell to her sides as her eyes remained locked on him. Damn, he never tired of that look she gave him. This was the moment he wanted to keep locked in his mind forever…and maybe in his heart.

Luke eased back just enough to take her delicate foot between his hands. The second his thumb raked up her arch, she let out another moan. Clearly, she liked this and he'd barely gotten started.

Luke couldn't take his eyes off her as he continued to massage first one foot and then the other. He worked his way up her calves, her thighs, and that's when she began to get impatient. Her hips jerked and she whimpered.

"You're not relaxing," he chuckled, reaching for the lace scraps across her hipbones. "You seem to be a little too on edge."

"On edge?" she asked. "I'm aching, Luke. Please."

A begging Cassandra was something he'd never been able to turn down and now was no different. Selfishly, he didn't want to wait, either. He'd had to watch her all day long rushing from one area to the next, all while wearing that body-hugging dress and a sweet smile on her face.

He didn't realize how much he'd wanted her in his life until she'd come back into it.

Luke clenched his jaw to keep from saying something in the moment he might not want her to know afterward. His vulnerability was teetering on the line and he was about ready to expose himself.

Sliding her panties down her legs, Luke focused on her dark eyes. Cassandra rose up onto her elbows as he moved up her body. He reached around her back and flicked the clasp on her bra as she wiggled it off and tossed it behind her.

Luke gathered her and flipped until she was straddling his lap. Her hair went wild around her shoulders as she smiled down at him. Damn it. His heart flipped in his chest and that's exactly what he didn't want to happen.

Too late.

Flattening his hands on her thighs, Luke slid up to that crease at her hips. He gripped and jerked his hips beneath her. She instantly took his silent gesture and joined their bodies.

When she braced herself against his chest and started moving, Luke absolutely got lost in the sight. The passion from this woman, the bond they shared, wasn't something he'd felt since she'd been gone. Luke couldn't help but wonder if she was it for him. Was he just getting caught up in nostalgia and his brothers' happiness, or was Cassandra the one for him?

Luke shifted and rose, taking her legs and wrapping them around his back. She continued to move with him as he wrapped himself around her. He couldn't get close enough. He wanted her, in bed and out. He wanted some magical moment where she knew how he felt and he didn't have to bare himself completely by telling her.

Just as she started to come undone, Luke leaned in and captured her lips. He wanted to experience every single aspect of her passion as he was closing in on his own climax.

Cass trembled against him and Luke couldn't hold back any longer. He joined her as he held on, never wanting this moment to end...never wanting to say goodbye.

He was lying sleeping in her bed and she didn't have the heart to wake him. Cassandra leaned against the doorframe of the en suite and took in the man who had made love to her all night with such passion and care.

And today she would be leaving. They hadn't talked, even though that's exactly what she'd vowed to herself to do. She didn't want any heartache or ill feelings before she left. They'd found some common ground and she'd come to care for him once again. Or maybe she'd never stopped.

Regardless of her feelings, they'd created such successful lives in completely different cities. Being in Beaumont Bay for just over a month wasn't near enough for her to drop everything and stay. She'd had eight years of rebuilding and couldn't give all that up...not that he'd asked her to.

A fierce, invisible grip on her heart had her nearly tearing up. She had to remain in control of her emotions, though. She'd known this day was coming and she'd known Luke wouldn't need her anymore after the wedding.

That had been the entire plan, right? They'd both gotten what they'd wanted, had an intense fling on the side, and now they were both ready to go about their lives just like before.

Only she wasn't sure she'd ever be like before because all she'd done here was reopen all her old wounds and reach into that pocket where she'd kept her emotions regarding Luke. They'd all come spilling out and now she had to figure out how the hell to pack them all back in.

But she didn't want to pack them back in.

She wanted to leave them out, and she wanted Luke to admit he wanted her, to admit that maybe they could try for something they hadn't been ready for before. Was any of that even possible? Was all of this worth the risk?

Cassandra padded quietly into the kitchen and ordered room service. What was the protocol for saying goodbye to an old lover and fake fiancé? Surely a nice breakfast was a good start. But what was there to talk about?

The nerves seemed to pile higher and higher. Cassandra closed her eyes and took a deep breath. She needed coffee and she needed to just calm down. Luke wasn't expecting anything from her…and that was the crux of her issue right now.

Last night, she could have sworn he was going to say he loved her. Just the way he held her, the way he touched her, the man was in love. Maybe he didn't know it. Maybe he didn't want to be. Or maybe he refused to face reality.

So if he wasn't going to say anything, despite their passionate night, then she wasn't going to say anything, either.

Damn it.

Presley was right. They were two stubborn people and maybe that had been the problem all those years ago. Maybe if she'd told him what she needed from him, things would have been different. But, in her defense, she hadn't wanted to beg for attention or fall second to his work.

Several minutes later the elevator chimed, indicating a visitor, and Cassandra tightened the belt on her robe and went to the door to meet the waiter. Once she'd tipped him, she wheeled the cart inside and laughed. Maybe she'd been a little out of it when she'd called. Luke had her so confused, it looked like she'd ordered for the entire wedding party from yesterday.

"Damn, woman. How long are we staying in and eating?"

She glanced up to see Luke rubbing a hand over his bare chest as he shuffled from the bedroom. His eyes were on the silver domed trays.

"I wasn't sure what you'd want and I really didn't know what I was in the mood for."

His eyes moved to her and there it was…that hunger. She couldn't get sidetracked, though. They'd had their last night and there were still some loose ends to tie up before she left.

"Do you want to eat first or talk?"

Luke stilled and his eyes locked onto hers. "What is there to talk about?"

Everything, but nothing she wanted to get into. She twisted the ring on her finger and ultimately slid it off.

"For starters, this is yours."

Cassandra extended her arm, but Luke just continued to stare at her. She wanted him to take it, to make their break as simple and painless as possible. After all, this had all started as a business arrangement, so shouldn't they end things that way, as well?

"I want you to keep it."

Cassandra dropped her arm and sighed. "I can't do that, Luke."

"Why not?"

Because it would remind her of what she didn't have. Because she would look at it every day and think of him, which was something she could not afford to do.

"We aren't engaged," she told him.

"Maybe not, but that ring is yours."

He took a step forward, and then another, until he stood toe-to-toe with her. Those dark eyes seemed to penetrate her, as if he could read her thoughts. That was the last thing she needed. Because no matter the gap of time that had separated them, Luke still knew her better than anyone. She'd never let anyone get as close as he had. That bond they'd shared still hadn't been severed. Despite everything, there was a piece of her heart that would always belong to Luke Sutherland.

"I suppose you're leaving today," he said, still studying her face.

Cassandra nodded, fisting her hand around the ring.

"Will you come back?" he asked.

"Come back?"

"To visit," he added. "I know my family loved seeing you and my parents said you told them you'd stay in touch."

She swallowed the emotional lump forming in her throat.

"Are you asking on their behalf or yours?"

The muscle in his jaw clenched and he took a step back, raking a hand over his jaw. The morning stubble bristled against his palm, breaking the silence surrounding them. Her heart beat so fast... She wanted him to answer. She wanted him to tell her what he was thinking and what he wanted.

"Maybe I'm asking for both of us," he finally replied.

Cassandra truly didn't think their morning talk would get so emotional. She'd hoped he'd take the ring, they'd share breakfast, maybe a few kisses, and he'd be gone.

That wasn't going to be the case, so she had to shore up all her courage, all her willpower, to get through this. She couldn't leave town with heartache again. She didn't know if she'd survive it.

"Are you asking me to come back?"

"What if I am?" He rested his hands on his narrow hips and waited a beat. "Would you come back if I asked just for myself?"

Confused, Cassandra needed something to focus on besides these unwanted feelings. She moved to the cart and poured a mimosa. Once she had the tall, slender glass in hand, she turned back around and wrapped her arm around her waist.

"I don't want to play games," she told him. "If there's

something you want from me, you need to say it. Otherwise, I should start packing."

His eyebrows rose and he let out a low, humorless laugh. "I don't want you to pack."

"Then what do you want?" she asked as her heart kicked up.

"I don't know, Cass, but I'm not ready for you to just pack and go."

Cassandra nodded and took a sip.

"The last time you broke things off and just left. There wasn't much discussion."

Unable to stand still under his penetrating gaze, Cassandra moved around the penthouse and made her way to the wall of windows overlooking the lake. She didn't like the unsettling nerves that came with her relationship to Luke. They'd been there since she walked into his office a month ago and had only grown with each passing day.

"I had to leave, Luke. I realized we were obviously wanting two different things at that time and staying would have only shattered both of us even more."

Maybe she was a coward for not facing him, but she just couldn't. They were entering into a conversation that was long overdue and even after eight years, she still wasn't ready for it.

"I had to put myself first," she added, forcing herself to turn and take this head-on. "I'm not placing the blame on you. I know it takes two people to make a relationship work. Maybe I should have told you long before that I wasn't going to be second to anything, including your work."

Luke jerked. "Is that what you thought? That you were second to my businesses?"

"That's not what I thought, that's what I know."

Luke crossed the room with purpose and stood right before her. He took her drink and set it over on the table by the sofa. Then he came back, took her fisted hand and opened her fingers.

"See that ring?" he demanded. "I chose that for you eight years ago. I intended to propose to you, so we could officially start our lives together. But I wasn't ready, not when you were. I needed time and I wasn't sure when I'd be ready for what you wanted."

"Then why didn't you fight for me?" she demanded. "Why didn't you tell me you were needing more time?"

"Because you said you were leaving and I knew if you felt that way, then there was nothing I could say. If you wanted to go, then maybe we weren't right for each other and you *should* go."

She stared at him another minute and truly didn't know what to say or what had gotten them to this heart-wrenching point.

"Damn it," he muttered as he spun around and gave her his back.

"Luke."

"Forget it."

But she couldn't forget it because now they were entering a whole new territory, one she hadn't even known they needed to explore…and she had a feeling more emotions than she ever wanted to admit were about to be exposed.

Seventeen

He'd never wanted to tell her that. He'd never wanted to admit he'd been a damn fool and had gotten her a ring and then, like the pathetic heartbroken man he'd been, he'd kept the damn thing for all of this time.

"Talk to me."

Cassandra's soft, questioning tone had Luke turning back around. He hadn't been strong enough the first time she was in his life, but he damn well would be now. Maybe this was risky, maybe this was all a mistake and he was going to end up looking like a fool again, but he had to know. He had to.

"I never put you second in my life." He held her gaze, wanting her to see he was absolutely telling the truth. "You know I invested everything I owned and took out loans to get those bars up and running. I wanted a solid foundation and a firm income before proposing to you. I didn't want to come to you before I knew I could provide the life you deserved. But then I was afraid. I feared if I took that step that I would lose myself and all I had created. I didn't know how to have it all and the risk scared the hell out of me."

Her eyes widened and instantly started brimming with tears. Luke clenched his jaw and waited for her to say something…and he also cursed the man he used to be for not standing up for what he wanted and for being too damn stubborn.

"Everything I did was because I was putting you first," he added. "But then… I just wasn't ready."

"I didn't know," she whispered.

"I was so busy trying to pave the way to an easy life for us, and then all I could think of was how I could juggle it all…and I let you go."

Cassandra blinked and a lone tear slid down her dark skin. Luke reached out, cupped her cheek, and swiped away the moisture. She leaned in to his touch.

"I never knew you were that afraid. I should've asked. I should have made you talk to me." She closed her eyes as another tear escaped. "What have we done?"

"We were guarding our hearts. That's why we didn't communicate properly."

Her lids fluttered open as she focused on him. Luke hated seeing her cry, hated knowing he'd had any part of her unhappiness and heartache.

"So what happens now?" she asked.

This was the tricky part, the hardest part…but maybe the most rewarding.

"You can decide to go as you had planned or you can decide to stay a bit longer and see how this plays out."

When she remained silent, he reached up with his other hand and framed her face.

"I would never make you decide between your life in Lexington and Beaumont Bay," he told her. "That's not fair for either of us. But if you want to make this work, we will find a way. I can go to Lexington if that's what you want. I can still own my bars, I have managers I trust to run them, and I can come down every few weeks to check on things."

"Luke."

The emotional whisper had his heart clenching. He'd gone this far, he might as well finish the rest.

"Did you look at the planner I bought you?" he asked.

Her eyebrows drew in as she shook her head. "I mean, I looked at it, but I haven't gone through it or anything. Why?"

"Go get it."

She eased back, still looking at him like he was crazy. Hell, maybe he was crazy for putting himself on the line like this. But he hadn't gotten this far, been this successful in his life, without taking risks and putting himself out there.

Cassandra went to her bedroom and then came back out with the planner. She started to hand it to him, but he pointed to it.

"Open it to today's date," he told her.

She flipped through the pages until she came to the date. When her eyes landed on the square and the red writing he'd added, she gasped.

"'Tell Cass how much she is loved,'" she whispered.

Then her eyes darted up to his. The shock on her face made him realize he'd never seen her this shocked and that meant he'd done a terrible job of letting her know just how much he'd fallen for her all over again. He'd hoped she'd pick up on that on her own, but clearly she hadn't.

"You love me?" she asked.

Luke nodded. "I do."

"But you gave this to me weeks ago. You already knew then?"

"I'm not sure I ever stopped loving you, Cass," he told her. "When you came back, all of those old feelings came back, too, but then I started with new feelings as I got to know the new Cassandra."

"You think you know me well enough now to say those words?" she asked.

Damn it, he wanted her to say them back. But he wanted her to mean them. His heart had been exposed and he wished like hell she'd take it again.

"I know when you set your mind to something, you make it happen," he began. "I know you're a successful wedding coordinator, which was a dream you made come true. You're strong, resilient, loyal, loving to my family like they are your own, sexy as hell, and I don't want to be without you anymore."

Her eyes filled once again as she glanced back to the planner.

"Luke, I…"

She closed the planner, but kept her head down. Luke's breath caught in his throat and he had no idea what she was thinking, but he wished she'd clue him in. He'd never been so nervous or on edge in his entire life.

Finally, she glanced up to him as tears streamed down her cheeks...but she was smiling.

"I love you," she told him. "I never thought I'd get the opportunity to tell you that again, but your mom was so right. Second chances happen for a reason and this encounter happened to force us back together... where we belong."

A wave of relief washed over Luke. He hadn't been sure she felt the same—he'd hoped, he'd suspected, but he hadn't been certain.

Now he knew. And there was no way in hell he would ever let her go again.

Luke took the planner from her and tossed it over to the sofa, then banded his arms around her and lifted her. She squealed as he spun her in a circle and kissed her firmly on the mouth.

"How soon can you plan our wedding?" he asked.

She laughed. "Well, I hadn't thought of that considering we just decided to go from fake to actually engaged."

Luke sat her down, took the ring and slid it back onto her finger. "This is where my ring belongs. I'm ready now and I know with your support and love, I can have it all. We both can. Our careers and a successful relationship are what we both deserve."

"Where will we live?" she asked.

"I don't care about that, either." He honestly didn't. So long as he had her by his side. "We can discuss details later. Right now, I'm taking you back to bed."

"Shouldn't we call your family and tell them the good news?" she asked.

Luke scooped her up into his arms and headed back toward the bedroom. "I have more important things to do, like make love to my fiancée."

Her smile widened as she looped her arms around his neck. "Presley was right. She said I'd make you fall for me. Now there's only one Sutherland left."

Luke laughed. "No way in hell will Gavin settle down. My mom better be happy with the three new daughters she has."

Cass started to open her mouth again, but Luke tossed her onto the bed, then climbed in after her.

"No more talk." He came to settle over her, his heart completely full of more than he'd ever thought possible. "Let me show you just how much I love you."

She smiled. "Kiss me again."

* * * * *

A NINE-MONTH TEMPTATION

JOANNE ROCK

In loving memory of my favorite NYC roommate,
Rebecca Schaeffer.

One

B̲est. Job. Ever.

Sable Cordero sipped the fine champagne and toasted herself in the full-length mirror at the Zayn Designs studio in Manhattan, where she'd been working as a stylist for three months. What other line of work would give a backwoods Louisiana divorcée with more ambition than savings the opportunity to drape herself in haute couture from the most lauded new brand of the year? She didn't own the sample-sized dress, of course. It was far beyond her financial means. But tonight she got to wear the silk work of art for the sake of a social media video she was creating after hours. The designer, Marcel Zayn, had been fully supportive of her wish to help develop content for the brand, not even blinking at the idea of her remaining late in the studio unsupervised.

And damn, but she appreciated his faith in her. At twenty-nine years old, Sable was older than anyone else employed by the fashion house, except for the designer himself. She couldn't be more thankful for the opportunity to chase her dream of being a stylist after the brief detour of an unhappy marriage.

She'd been given a second chance at life. One she would not take for granted.

Once upon a time, she'd nabbed a fashion degree from Louisiana State, but she'd gotten sidetracked by a smooth-talking political science major who convinced her she wanted to share his dream instead of her own. In hindsight, she could hardly be surprised that he moved on when she stopped fulfilling his vision of what he wanted in a wife. She'd learned the hard way that some men just marry women as placeholders, human mirrors to reflect back what they want to see.

Sable was mostly cured of the bitterness surrounding her ex. Nevertheless, she cranked up the stereo volume as Beyoncé sang about putting middle fingers up and saying, "boy, bye."

She couldn't be bitter after scoring this dream job. She might be living hand-to-mouth for a while in the Brooklyn apartment she shared with three other women, but at least she had a great place to call home.

Sable danced around the hardwood floor in bare feet. Tonight, she was filming after hours, incorporating the champagne brand that had approached Zayn about some sponsored ads—a budget-friendly way to extend the fledgling design house's marketing reach. She didn't need to be model-gorgeous since she was filming herself from the back, where the dramatic ribbon ties of the neckline fell over mostly bare skin until they grazed the sexy-as-hell silk that wrapped her hips.

Careful not to spill her drink, Sable went around the Tribeca loft space making sure all her props were positioned for the series of short videos. She'd culled the designer's most visually interesting furnishings, dragging them all into the open section of the loft where she'd walk among them in her dress. She'd flipped on a few spotlights and filled in the dark areas with a couple of borrowed floor lamps. It wasn't high tech, but it would get the job done. Her video concept wasn't super fancy, either. She planned to film the same basic movements twice—once tonight while wearing the black version of the silk dress, and again during daylight hours clad in the same dramatic dress in white. Then she'd interpose the segments in editing.

She was almost ready. She just needed a little more mojo to fuel her attempt at a catwalk swagger.

"Cheers to me." Sable lifted the flute to her lips again, savoring the way the bubbles tickled her nose before she downed another sip.

She wanted the champagne bottle to be half-empty in her video, and she *obviously* couldn't dump the contents of a ridiculously expensive vintage down the drain. The only appropriate action was drinking it herself. Besides, she needed the confidence boost those bubbles provided since the silk fit like a second skin and she was about to film her ass in unforgiving high definition. Alcohol and Queen B on the stereo were both re-

quired, considering the Zayn videos were getting over
a hundred thousand views.

And yeah, maybe she'd opted to put herself out there
tonight in the latest video as her final middle finger to
her ex. She'd gotten a call from her mother today that
he was expecting a baby with his new wife, the woman
who'd taken her place even before Sable had realized
she wasn't wanted anymore.

While she no longer resented him moving on, she
resented the hell out of him leaving her because of her
inability to give him a baby. She'd tried. Yes, it had hurt
her that she hadn't been successful in keeping their marriage afloat. But what hurt more was the memory of her
miscarriage, which had filled her with a deep sense of
loss. So it was galling that her ex had replaced her with
someone more fertile.

That warranted the badass babe music and all the
boss-woman attitude she could bring to this dress. Sable
slid on the sky-high stilettos guaranteed to make any
woman's legs look delicious. She hadn't felt sexy in a
long, long time.

Unbidden, an image of Roman Zayn came into her
mind. Roman was the design house's owner, Marcel's
older brother, and the power behind the throne. Or
maybe Sable just saw him that way because Roman's
brand of tall, dark and brooding had slid past her professional reserve and done something wicked to her insides the lone time they'd met. They'd only exchanged
a few words during her first week on the job before he
returned to LA, where he ran Zayn Equity, a global
wealth management company. Yet the man's probing

stare had stripped her bare and sent her sensual imagination off and running.

It had been silly, really. Just a fanciful turn of her
thoughts that would never come to anything since
Roman had little to do with the day-to-day workings
of the fashion house. But that moment alone with him
when he'd asked about her experience—in fashion, of
course—had been the last time she'd felt a hint of feminine power.

So she let that memory wash over her as she took
a deep breath, finger hovering over the record button
on her phone where it rested in a cradle on the tripod.

Hell yes, she was moving on. Chasing her dream.

In three, two, one…

Roman Zayn heard the music as soon as his black
Town Car pulled up outside the Vestry Street building
where his brother worked. Considering the Zayn Designs loft was on the seventh floor, that struck Roman
as…excessive. But definitely not out of character for
Marcel, the family black sheep to everyone but Roman.
Marcel lived by his own lights and Roman admired the
hell out of him for it, which was why he'd agreed to be
his business partner. Marcel might not have Roman's
financial know-how, but the man knew clothing.

Besides, Marcel had been there for Roman during
the darkest year of his life. He'd been the only family
member to show up for him with more than just plati-
tudes during the hell he'd gone through when his wife
died. Roman owed him for that.

But as much as he loved Marcel, he also understood

his brother's tendencies to overspend in order to bring his art to life. Roman had committed to putting in an appearance at the atelier as often as possible to keep the design house within budget while they found an audience that could sustain the kind of business Marcel envisioned. Roman hoped the pop anthem blaring out the seventh-floor window at 10:00 p.m. meant his brother was working overtime toward that goal. He hadn't planned to meet with him personally tonight, thinking he'd duck into the small suite attached to the workshop and catch a few hours of sleep before intercepting his brother first thing in the morning. He'd been trying to avoid seeing anyone else at the studio.

Namely the newly hired stylist Roman had met on his last trip to New York. The Southern siren who'd ignited a flashfire of lust with just a few words spoken in her molasses-thick drawl.

He'd stayed away from Zayn Designs longer than usual to avoid her. Roman didn't deny himself feminine companionship since his wife's death. But he preferred to slake that thirst with women who didn't stir quite so…much. Curvaceous, delectable Sable had "too much" stamped across her perpetually bee-stung lips.

If Roman could speak with Marcel tonight, he could leave early for his other meetings tomorrow morning before anyone else arrived at the studio.

"Have a good night," Roman called to the driver through the open window after he got out.

Stepping into the building's brick archway, he swiped his keycard and opened a wrought iron door to access the elevator behind it. He noticed the sound of the music was fainter here as he unearthed a second security key for the elevator.

Once inside the industrial-sized lift, Roman loosened his tie. He'd kept it on for video conferencing during the flight from LA, but his brother would only harangue him about his too-conservative clothes. No doubt, the customer base for a wealth management firm was a world away from high fashion. His shirt, at least, had been made by his brother. Sure, Marcel designed more women's garments than men's, but his clothes for men were fantastic, from the mother-of-pearl buttons to the French seams and custom tailoring.

Roman stuffed his tie into his briefcase as the elevator door opened onto the loft. R&B music made the floor vibrate, the horns blaring and drums thumping as loud as in any dance club. The lights shone brightly in the center of the work area, while the edges of the room remained in shadow.

But it wasn't the light or the music that hit his senses like an assault.

That honor went to the woman strutting away from him in a black silk dress that molded to her curves like it had been poured over her. Her lustrous, dark hair was piled haphazardly on her head, a braid coiled around the mass like an afterthought to keep it in place. The dress had no back. Zero. The fabric only covered the soft swell of her ass, the silk cupping the bared dimples at the base of her spine as if to highlight that undeniably sexy feature.

Two thick ribbons cascaded from a knot at her neck to sway between her shoulder blades. As she moved, her hips rolled in a come-hither rhythm so seductive he found himself following in her wake even from ten yards away. A champagne flute dangled carelessly from her fingertips as she wove her way between stylized dress forms and the kitschy busts of composers that Marcel collected. She moved among them like they were adoring lovers, caressing a cheek here, bumping hips with a mannequin there.

She was so sexy she took his breath away, his pulse pounding in time with each step of her stilettos.

Tap. Tap. Tap.

How had the beat synced up? He wanted to catch her. Pull those teasing hips against him.

Right up until she paused to cast a sultry glance over one shoulder. And promptly screamed at seeing him.

The champagne glass shattered on the hardwood.

Damn.

It was *her*. Recognizing the very woman he'd been hoping to avoid, Roman regained his faculties at once.

"It's just me," he assured her, moving toward the stereo system on the shelf between two of the huge arched windows overlooking the street. Dialing down the volume, he turned toward Sable, the woman who'd populated far too many fantasies since his one and only meeting with her. "Roman," he reminded her.

He couldn't help feeling the flash of annoyance that she was staring at him like she'd seen a ghost. The thought of her forgetting him when she'd made an indelible impression on him was a definite kick to the ego. Not that it mattered.

"Of course I remember you." She hastened to speak,

possibly hearing the irritation in his voice. "I'm sorry." She started to take a halting step, her movements jerky. Was she embarrassed? "I wasn't expecting anyone," she rushed to explain, color flooding her cheeks.

Seeing that she was about to step on glass, he crossed the floor to help her. Somehow, that meant lifting her off her feet to remove her from the danger. Roman realized how unwise that decision had been the moment his fingers encircled her almost-naked waist. His fingers caressed bare skin while his thumbs pressed into the black silk just above her hips. For a scant second, her breasts grazed his chest as he picked her up.

He didn't want to let go. Not when he could feel the tight points of her nipples brush against him. Not when he heard the swift intake of her breath, felt the rush of air along the heated skin at his neck, saw the flash of awareness in her hazel eyes. Hell no, he didn't want to release her.

Which was why he forced himself to put her down, prying his fingers free from the magnetic force that was her gorgeous body, then jamming them into his pants pockets where he balled them into fists.

She looked up at him, confusion in her gaze as if she had no idea why he'd picked her up. Or maybe she was unsure why he let her go. And didn't that thought mess with his head? He ground his teeth together and brusquely said, "I need a broom."

Stalking away from her, he went to find one to clean up the glass, knowing he sounded rude but needing to keep his hands busy. Definitely needing his hands off her.

"I can get it," she called, following him into the tiny galley kitchen someone had added to the loft in a long-ago renovation. "I made the mess. I can certainly clean it up."

From the softness of her footfall, he guessed she'd taken off her shoes. And it disturbed him how acutely attuned his senses were to her movement.

He could only brace himself and hold his breath when she leaned past him to reach for the broom and dustpan in the recess between the cabinets. The scent of her hair tickled his nose, something lemony and sweet.

Her hip bumped his and she murmured, "Excuse me." She lifted her face to his again. "I'm just so mortified to have screamed like some ninny in a horror movie. I'm Sable, by the way, in case you don't remember. Marcel never mentioned you were arriving tonight, so I thought I was alone."

Roman's pulse ticked in his temple as he stared down at her, willing himself not to touch her again. Seeing her now reawakened every hot fantasy he'd had about her since they'd met three months ago. She was still too *much*, the feelings she awakened stirring something that felt more ominous than simple lust. And yet…what if acting on the lust deflated things back down to a manageable level? He was so keyed up he was tempted to try, except that she worked for Marcel.

Hell, technically, she worked for *him*. So taking a taste of her was out of the question. He needed to shake off this spell she had him under and take control of the situation.

"I remember you." He let that sink in for a moment

before he took the broom out of her hands and charged toward the broken glass. He'd help her clean up and then he'd get a hotel. "And Marcel didn't expect me. The fault is mine for not warning him. Tonight, it never occurred to me that anyone but him would be here at this hour. When I heard the music outside, I assumed he was working late."

He tackled the glass shards with a vengeance, drawing the bristles over the hardwood, the bright lights making it easier to find all the pieces. She was quiet for a long moment, but she'd followed him into the work area with a towel in hand, careful to remain outside the ring of glittering shards.

"You remember me," she repeated in a barely audible voice, almost like she was turning the thought over in her head.

Her tone was so...wistful, almost, that it made him look up from sweeping. She leaned a bare shoulder against one of the columns scattered throughout the room, her sinfully sexy dress clinging to a body any 1940s pinup would have envied. Something twisted in his gut.

He wanted to call it lust, but it sure as hell felt like something more.

"Definitely. You aren't exactly the kind of woman a man forgets." He wasn't happy about it, either. He couldn't help it if some of that frustration bled into his words.

She straightened from where she'd been slouching, her chin tipping higher as something defensive lit up her gaze. She folded her arms. "I am, actually. So excuse me if I found it momentarily flattering that someone like you would recall the meeting. But I can see I've disrupted your evening, Mr. Zayn." Her Southern accent slid over his name, dragging out the vowel. "I'll get out of your hair now."

Spinning on her bare heel, she presented him with her back again. The same view that had tied him in knots the moment he entered the loft. Only this time, he was close enough to catch her. Without giving himself time to think about it, he slid an arm around her to halt her.

Immediately, he recognized the error. Knew he was crossing a professional line. He hung his head in defeat.

"I'm sorry." He sounded like he'd swallowed the broken glass. Once more, he took his hands off her with an effort, cursing his impulsiveness. Cursing himself for landing in a situation where he was alone with a woman he'd thought about too often. "You didn't ruin my evening. I should have called Marcel before barging in here tonight."

He tried to keep his eyes off the long ribbons that trailed down her back, but even when he wasn't looking at them, he was thinking about trailing them over her skin. Would it make her shiver? The mere thought of it made his body react.

She glanced back at him over her shoulder.

"You own the building, Mr. Zayn. I'm sure you don't need to call when you want to visit your own company." She scooped up a pair of jeans and a T-shirt lying over the back of an armchair. "I'll just slip out of this dress and be on my way."

He wasn't sure what bothered him more: that he was responsible for her leaving, or that he wouldn't be the one to untie those ribbons for her tonight.

Hell.

"Don't. Go." He articulated the words carefully, keeping his tone neutral-ish. "I've interrupted you, and you're obviously doing a lot to help Marcel if you're here at this hour. If it's just the same to you, I'd much prefer you stay. Tell me what you're working on."

Slowly, she turned to face him. The anger had left her features, but she arched a skeptical brow. "You really want to know?"

She had no idea.

But now that he was here, the idea of Sable walking away from him tonight was almost painful. He knew this woman was the most talented stylist Marcel had on the payroll, so Roman couldn't afford to scare her off. But he also couldn't ignore the way she made him feel alive again after years of going through the motions of his day-to-day world. Now that he'd admitted as much, maybe he could figure out what to do about it.

"I really do." His pulse spiked at the possibilities. "And please, call me Roman."

Two

She shouldn't let the owner of the fashion label sweep the floor. But when she'd stood close to the broken glass earlier, Sable had ended up wrapped in Roman's arms as he transported her away from the mess.

Awareness of the fact that she wore nothing, nada, *zilch*, beneath the silk dress had made the contact even more intense. She was still feeling light-headed from his touch.

So she forced herself to wait patiently while Roman carried the dustpan of glass to the bin and stowed the broom. He washed his hands at the sink in the galley kitchen, the pendant lamp above the counter illuminating his high, sculpted cheekbones and the thick scruff along his square jaw. With dark eyes and dark hair that curled just above his shirt collar, he had the same Lebanese heritage that informed his brother's good looks. And yet Marcel had never lit a fire inside her. No, that special explosion to her senses was reserved for Roman.

After he dried his hands, Roman set aside the towel and flicked open the buttons on his shirt cuffs, folding the sleeves up as he spoke.

"You're very quiet for a woman who was about to tell me what you're working on." He lifted an eyebrow as he glanced her way.

Right.

No sense explaining she'd been distracted by his raw sex appeal. She'd already made enough of a fool of herself tonight. Setting aside the jeans and T-shirt she'd been ready to put back on, she crossed to the center of the room to turn off one of the spotlights.

"I'm working on some video content for the Zayn Designs social media accounts." She headed to the tripod and released her cell phone from the clamp. "The back of this dress is so unique that I thought it would be fun for viewers to see it in motion. The video just follows me as I walk away from the camera."

"May I see?" he asked, closing the distance between them to reach for her phone.

His fingers brushed hers.

She passed it to him, her body twitching with the memory of his arms around her. "Just keep in mind it's not edited."

"Of course." Gaze fixed on the screen, he tapped the play button.

Music blared from the speaker. She resisted the urge to arch up on her toes and look with him. Even though she hadn't seen the playback yet and was curious, venturing that close again seemed dangerous to her sanity.

Besides, with his attention fixed on the device, she had the chance to study him. To try to work out what it was that drew her so completely. She'd been attracted to him the first time they'd met. Tonight—once she'd recovered from being startled at his arrival—she'd been even more fascinated, experiencing a shivery awareness that wouldn't go away. And that was *before* he'd made that cryptic comment about not being able to forget a woman like her.

The remark had raised her hackles at first when she wasn't sure it had been sincere. After all, her ex had made her feel entirely forgettable. Replaceable. But after Roman's insistence she stay, she couldn't dismiss his remark. If he found her so very memorable, had he felt the same pull as she had from the very first time they'd met three months ago?

Unobserved, she allowed her gaze to rake over him from his muscled thighs up to his narrow waist. From the flare of his back to his broad, powerful shoulders. By the time she reached his face, his dark gaze had shifted from the phone to *her*.

He was alert. Intense. And very, very aware of her attention.

"Like anything you see?" The sexy rasp of his voice skated over her skin like fingernails.

Heat bloomed in her cheeks. Pooled between her thighs.

"Whether I do or not is hardly the point," she managed, her voice a thin husk of its normal sound. Or maybe it was just difficult to hear it over the racket her heart was making, ricocheting around her rib cage like it needed a way out. "My job is too important to me to risk it with poor decisions."

"Ditto." He nodded amiably as he set her phone down on the back of a low-slung sofa. "I feel the same way about my job. Which is why I waited three months to return to New York after we met the first time."

Her breath stuck in her throat. Had she moved closer to him? They were near enough to touch. Near enough for her to wonder at the texture of the stubble along his jaw. Would it leave a mark if he rubbed his cheek over her bare skin?

Along the more sensitive flesh between her legs?

"I don't understand." She needed him to clarify. Her senses were too high on him to make sense of words right now. "You stayed away from the studio on purpose?"

"I did." A muscle twitched in his jaw, a ripple of movement even the facial hair couldn't hide. "I told myself to respect Marcel's workspace by keeping clear of his tempting new stylist."

Would a more confident woman take that comment at face value? Sable couldn't be certain. But when *she* heard it, she had the urge to look around the room for a hidden camera and someone to reveal she'd just been punked.

Maybe some of her thoughts showed on her face because he lifted an eyebrow. "You don't believe me?"

"You run a billion-dollar company in a city famous for its beautiful people. I have no doubt there are scads of *tempting* women who throw themselves at you on a regular basis."

"Funny thing about attraction, it has to work both ways," he countered, not backing off an inch. If anything, she felt like they'd gotten closer during this exchange. "Like it is right now."

His gaze lowered to her mouth. It took a superhuman effort not to lick her lips. Her throat was as dry as dust, and she couldn't have spoken if she tried.

A small sound did escape her lips, though. A telltale, hungry whimper. His dark eyes narrowed. A growl vibrated in his chest.

His mouth hovered over hers, a breath away from kissing her. Yet not kissing her. They stood close together but not touching. And it took all her willpower not to grip his shirtfront and drag him the rest of the way to her.

"This is a bad idea." Even saying the words put her lips closer to his. Had her breathing his air.

She didn't dare look up to meet his eyes. She had the feeling she'd fall right into their dark depths.

"Probably." He didn't move away, his rough exhale fanning a loose tendril of hair that had fallen near her cheek. "That is. Unless—"

He broke off.

"Unless what?" She knew better than to grasp at straws. Didn't she? Yet her body very much craved any scenario that would end with his mouth on hers.

Was it wrong to crave his healing touch after the blow to her ego and heart she'd received today? Memories of the call from her mother still lingered. Memories that made her feel inadequate. Unwanted.

"I could leave again tomorrow," he finally continued. He clasped her chin between his thumb and forefinger, lifting it to study her face and forcing her to meet his gaze. "Stay on the West Coast for a couple of months. Try again to let things cool off."

"You're going to leave already?" She felt bereft at the thought. Rejected even.

An old pain had split open inside her. But she was sure Roman Zayn's touch could ease it. Unless he left her again.

"Tomorrow," he reiterated with new emphasis. "That way we have tonight. A window of time together where we don't have to think about work or Marcel or the consequences."

The magnitude of what he was suggesting should have daunted her. But she was too hungry for his touch. Too desperate for forgetting. More than ready for any answer that would allow her what she wanted.

"We'd be walking a fine line." The ethics were questionable. But they weren't the first people to ignore professional boundaries to indulge in hot sex.

And she knew without question it would be hot. Even now his thumb stroked the underside of her chin, stirring a deluge of longing.

"Tricky, but not impossible," he acknowledged. "It's up to you, Sable. What do you want to do?"

She knew without question he could have convinced her with a kiss long ago. He hadn't pressed that advantage, though. That he wanted her to make the call, to take ownership of what she wanted, spoke well of his intentions.

"It might be a fine line, but I have excellent balance." She lifted her hands to his chest, letting her fingers curl into the fabric of his shirt. She needed whatever he could give her tonight. "And I might die if you don't touch me soon."

Roman fused his lips to hers. Kissing. Claiming. The need to taste her had been a fire in his blood from the moment he'd stepped into the studio, so her acquiescence came not a minute too soon. She tasted like strawberries and champagne, her flavor going to his head faster than any drink.

He wrapped his arms around her and held her close, only to be reminded her dress had no back. A groan went through him at the feel of her smooth skin through the long, silky ribbons. He fought the urge to untie them and send the thin fabric to the floor in a heap. He didn't want to rush things.

"You're not wearing one damned thing under this dress." He spoke the words against her damp lips, then nipped the lower one between his teeth. "Are you?"

She sucked in a startled breath before arching her hips into his. Robbing his brain of thought. Torching any restraint he might have salvaged.

"There was no room for anything but me." She smoothed her hands down his sides and then hauled his shirttails free so she could tunnel beneath the fabric.

He ground his teeth at the feel of her nails gliding lightly over his abs, tracing the muscles, until the last of his blood rushed south.

"Don't move," he warned her, backing away to find

the condom he needed. "And don't even dream about taking that dress off without me."

He spotted his bag and speared a hand into a side pocket, withdrawing what he needed before returning to her. She made one hell of a vision with her dress rumpled from his touch, her dark pile of hair slipping to one side of her head as if it would spring free of its confines at any moment. She caught her lower lip with her teeth, nibbling as she watched him.

He could swear he felt those teeth on him.

Tugging her by the hand, he led her to the suite in back, a tiny afterthought of a space with just enough square footage for a queen-size bed and nightstand. But he didn't need much room considering he wanted her all over him. Or under him. All night long.

She started to reach behind her to shut the door, but he caught her in time.

"Leave it. I need to see you." Though the lamp was off in the bedroom, the open door allowed the light from the studio to filter in.

Reaching into her hair, he found the clip that held the silky mass and undid it, watching the dark strands tumble to her shoulders.

"Good idea. I want to see you, too." She was already at work on the buttons down his shirtfront, flicking them open one after the other. Her hazel gaze followed her progress, absorbed in the sight of him. Almost as if she found him every bit as fascinating as he found her.

Impossible. Yet it felt incredibly good.

He waited until she finished, then helped her by shrugging the garment off his shoulders. There was no sound in the room save their harsh breathing and the fall of clothes to the floor, noises that only amped him up when he wanted to take his time. Savor her. Especially if he was only going to get one night.

Her gaze fell to his pants and his need surged, throbbing an urgent beat in response to the growing want in her eyes. But he wouldn't let himself get distracted from getting her out of that dress first.

"Turn around." Hands on her hips, he spun her away from him until she presented him with her back, where her hair now tangled with the long ribbons that dangled from her neck. Carefully, he gathered it to one side before pushing it forward over her shoulder.

He traced one swath of black silk with his finger, watching goose bumps rise on her skin until a shiver undulated up her spine. Satisfaction pumped through him that he could elicit a reaction from her so easily. He couldn't wait to catalog every single thing she liked. Every movement that made her breath catch and her body quiver. If he only had one night, he needed to make certain it was one she'd never forget.

Too bad he was so wound up to have her that it already took monumental effort to keep himself in check and make this about her.

Bracing himself for the feel of her against him, he slid a hand around her waist, palming the space between her hips to draw her to him. With the sweet curve of her ass pressed tight to his erection, the need to grind away the ache was fierce. Especially when she moaned at the contact, her hips doing a shimmy that had him gritting his teeth and seeing stars.

From somewhere, he gathered up enough restraint to refocus on her, the length of her lithe body visible to him over her shoulder. One ribbon still in his hand, he tugged the fabric until the front of her dress dipped low, clinging precariously to the swell of her breasts for a moment before falling to her waist. The perfect mouthfuls tipped with dusky nipples were begging for his touch. His tongue.

He licked a path down her neck while he molded the soft flesh in his hands, running his thumbs over the sensitive tips in a way that made her push back against him until they both groaned.

"I need my mouth on you." He turned her back around, the dress falling the rest of the way down her body.

He stepped over the silk and laid her on the bed, her dark hair fanning out around her. Her breath came faster as he reached for his belt, and their eyes fastened on each other. With impatient hands he stripped off the rest of his clothes before he fell on her, keeping his weight off her with one arm while he feasted on her breasts. First one, then the other, sucking and kissing, tracing circles around the tight, pebbled peaks.

But she thwarted his plan to take his time by reaching between them to stroke him, her fingertips slowly exploring him in a way guaranteed to make him lose control if he didn't stop her. Yet the sweet tentativeness of her touch forced him to endure the sexy torment. He remembered too well the way she'd bristled when he'd talked about not being able to forget her—as if someone in her life had made her feel forgettable. Unwanted.

No way would she leave his bed without feeling thoroughly appreciated.

He kissed his way down her body, veering toward her hip before returning to her navel. Circling. Dipping. She shifted beneath him, her movements restless. Needy. He skimmed a touch down her leg before tracking back up the inside of her thigh. When she made a soft, hungry sound, he guided one leg over his shoulder and tasted her.

Her back arched, hips lifting off the bed as she offered herself to him. Roman lost himself in her, eager to feel her pleasure against his lips for the first time. He didn't have to wait long before her muscles were spasming, hips twisting. He held her steady, stroking every ounce of pleasure from her until she eased against the bed again.

By the time he lifted himself higher on the bed, he was already plotting how many ways he could take her to that brink again before the sun rose. But first, he needed to be inside her. Had to be.

She must have thought the same thing because she already had the condom packet in her hands, shaking fingers ripping open the foil. Even in the half-light from the outer room, he could see the flush in her cheeks. Color he had put there.

Possessiveness clawed at him, a feeling he hadn't experienced since—*hell*. He shut that thought down as fast as possible, then took the condom from her, a flare of anger at himself making him all the more desperate to lose himself inside her.

"Roman?"

His name on her lips gentled the self-recriminations in his head. He took a moment to roll on the protection.

"I'm right here with you," he assured her, stroking her cheek. "So ready for you."

"Can I be on top?" She sounded breathless. Excited. A little nervous?

He quieted the turmoil in his mind to tune into her. "You can have anything you want, beautiful Sable." To prove it, he rolled to his back and hauled her on top of him; she looked like a goddess straddling his thighs. "I want to see you from every angle anyway."

Her bee-stung lips curved in a satisfied smile. He searched her eyes, making sure she was totally on board with this. But her attention was already on his body, her focus glazing with desire as she lined up her hips with his, then dragged her sex over his.

Heat blasted through him. He couldn't have held back the thrust of his hips if he tried. He gripped her waist to steady her and buried himself deep. The feel of her around him was incredible. So much better than the mindless release he'd occasionally allowed himself in the past five years.

So much better that he couldn't even dwell on the hows or whys of that. He just let the sensation build until he had to move. Had to take more.

"Sable." His grip tightened on her, fingers flexing into her softness. "I need—"

"Me, too," she gasped, wriggling on him.

Rewiring his brain so she was the center of it.

With a curse that was both pleasure and pain, he answered her movement with his own, a rhythm syncing between them that drove all thought out of his head, leaving him with nothing but burning need.

They moved as one, feasting on each other, finding out what one another liked. Which was everything. There wasn't a thing she did that didn't make him feel amazing. When he'd held off as long as he could, he reached between them to stroke her, taking her higher. He could feel when she got close, when her legs started to quake on either side of him. Only when he was sure she was there, when her body started to clamp hard around him, did he let himself go.

The release went on and on, his shout coming from the depths of his gut. When he became aware of himself again, he lowered her to her side on the bed, needing her next to him while he checked to be sure he remembered his own name.

Because, damn.

Once his breathing was somewhat back in the range of normal again, he opened an eye he hadn't realized had fallen closed. In time to see Sable bending to kiss his chest. That possessiveness he'd felt before simmered again, so he was grateful when she looked up at him through her long lashes.

"Don't go to sleep yet, Roman." She repositioned herself to tuck an elbow under her head.

He had no intention of sleeping while she was in his bed, but he didn't share that with her.

"No?" He twined a dark strand of hair around his finger, and was amazed to feel his body stir again. "What did you have in mind instead?"

"If I only have one night with you, there are other…

things… I want to try," she confided, her tone a sweet mixture of bold and shy that socked him in the gut.

And definitely had his body stirring now.

"Anything you want, beautiful girl." He hauled her closer to kiss her neck, savoring the brush of her breasts against his chest. "But you're going to have to be more specific."

He couldn't wait to hear what she wanted. And to deliver. But he was seriously regretting the deal he'd made with her about this lasting just one night. Already he was plotting to find a way around it without complicating things for her.

Because he would honor the pledge to leave town tomorrow. And he'd give her some time to miss him while he worked out a way to ensure that seeing her again didn't compromise her job. But once those two months were up, he had every intention of returning for more.

Three

In the eight weeks that followed her toe-curling, mind-blowing, breath-stealing night with Roman Zayn, Sable sometimes thought she must have dreamed the next-level sex with the man who owned the company she worked for.

Now, seated on the edge of the tub in the fourth-floor bathroom of her shared Brooklyn apartment, watching a second pink line appear on her pregnancy test indicator, was not one of those times.

This can't be happening.

But according to the third pregnancy test she'd taken that week, it absolutely was happening, whether she wanted to believe it or not. She just couldn't understand it. They'd used protection. Except for one time, just before dawn when they'd been half asleep and she'd straddled him before remembering the condom. Even then, it had only been a momentary error. And Sable hadn't thought twice about it because when she was with her ex-husband getting pregnant had been such a struggle.

She let her head fall against the white sink basin, wondering how and when she was going to tell Roman. He'd followed their bargain to the letter, leaving her life two months ago without a word since. While she appreciated the way he was respecting boundaries, a tiny part of her couldn't help wondering if he'd thought of her. Or if he sometimes wanted a redo of that night.

A knock sounded at the door.

"Sable?" It was Tana Blackstone, the aspiring actress who'd moved into the apartment the month before her. She was pacing in the hall outside, the volume of rock music on her phone rising and falling depending on how close she was to the door. "I'll never get this job if I go to my audition with unwashed hair."

"Coming," Sable muttered. Shoving the pregnancy test in the trash, then covering it up with a tissue for good measure since she wasn't ready to share the news, Sable stepped out into the hall.

Still wearing a sleep shirt that said Coffee, Nap, Sparkle, Repeat, Tana darted past, a guitar solo blaring from the phone in her hand. "The landlady is waiting downstairs to see you, I think," she said before shutting the door between them.

"Cybil Deschamps is here? In the house?" Sable's feet stalled on the hardwood outside her bedroom, wondering what the philanthropist cosmetics heiress could want with her.

Cybil not only owned the gorgeous brownstone that

Sable now called home, but also handpicked the occupants as part of a well-publicized social experiment. The seventy-something society maven had long ago resided in the storied Barbizon Hotel, a women's residence that she credited for helping her find her footing in New York while she got her career as a model underway. Last year, Cybil had decided that pricey Big Apple real estate was making it impossible for young women to chase their dreams, and started a women's apartment of her own. As one of the city's wealthiest women, she just happened to have a Brooklyn brownstone available, and she'd offered reasonably priced rooms to talented people she deemed worthy—after a lengthy and rigorous application process, of course. Sable was grateful to her since it had been the only way she could have afforded to take the internship at Zayn Designs.

"I think so," Tana called back through the door. "Three floors up is a long way to eavesdrop so I'm not a hundred percent sure."

Sable grabbed her bag from her bed and began the trek down to the main floor. Logically, she knew Cybil couldn't already be here to kick Sable out of the apartment, even though she suspected that having a baby while in residence would be frowned upon. Was it perhaps even in the lease's fine print? She couldn't remember but wouldn't be surprised. This gorgeous refuge overlooking Fort Greene Park was intended for single women working to get ahead in artistic careers, not accidental baby mamas faced with giving up their career ambitions to raise a child.

Her belly knotted at the thought of walking away

from her career. But she wanted a baby. She'd had so much trouble getting pregnant when she'd been trying, and then there'd been the miscarriage that devastated her. While her circumstances weren't ideal for parenting right now, she would never risk this opportunity to be a mother that—for all she knew—could be her one and only chance. But she hadn't really thought about what that would mean for the dream job she'd been working so hard to get off the ground. She was on track to be a celebrity stylist, putting in extra hours to build the Zayn Designs social media accounts along with her own so that she would have a following and some contacts by the time her internship ended.

Now? She needed to rethink everything.

What would Roman say when he found out about the baby? Should she call him? Wait for him to show up again in New York? She'd been rejected by her ex for not being an effective baby-maker, so she had a lot of unresolved feelings about a partner's role in parenting. Not that Roman was anywhere close to a partner. For that matter, she wondered what Marcel would think once he learned she was pregnant with his brother's child. Would he even want her to finish the internship?

She'd almost reached the main floor—the *parlor* floor, as Cybil Deschamps called it—when she heard voices coming from the great room.

"Here she is now." Cybil's voice rang with authority across the foyer, bouncing off the twelve-foot ceilings.

Tall and blonde with perfect skin, Cybil thrived on her reputation as a charity gala queen, never missing an opportunity to network. She wore a pink-and-white vintage Chanel suit with nude pumps and a T-shirt from a recent breast cancer benefit. Beside Cybil stood a man she recognized as her son, Lucas, and a younger woman Sable had never seen before but who shared Cybil's height and Nordic good looks.

Lucas and the newcomer seemed to be studiously avoiding looking at one another, yet studying each other at the same time. Like they wanted to check each other out but didn't want to be caught.

"Hello, Cybil." Sable attempted a cheery welcome but suspected her smile was flat because her mind was still on her baby news. "I was just on my way to work. Did you need me?"

"I want to introduce you to your new housemate." She put her arm around the younger woman next to her. "This is Blair Westcott. She's not only a talented makeup artist, she's going to be working for our family business, too."

Sable thought she saw Lucas Deschamps tense at this remark, but she focused on the newcomer and extended her hand. "Sable Cordero, fourth floor. Welcome."

"Nice to meet you," Blair murmured as she shook her hand, a heavy silver charm bracelet sliding down her thin wrist. Meanwhile, Cybil went on about how much Blair and Sable could help one another with their "complementary skill sets."

"Absolutely," Sable agreed, guilt settling on her shoulders at the reminder that soon she wasn't going to be using her stylist skills anymore. Cybil would be filling her spot in the apartment in no time, and then Sable wouldn't even be around to offer the new tenant any help. "We can talk more when I get home from work, but I'm already running late."

It was true. She'd somehow lost half an hour to her pregnancy test freak-out. Still, she felt a little twinge of guilt at the idea of leaving Blair to her own devices with Cybil, who would take up the rest of her morning with name-dropping and mapping out the younger woman's future.

Not that a map always mattered. Sable pushed open the front door to the street as she considered how far off course her own life was veering from the direction she'd envisioned.

"Good morning, Sable." It was the sexy voice from her dreams.

Roman Zayn stood at the bottom of her stoop, dressed in gray pants and a custom-fitted white shirt that she recognized as one of his brother's designs. He tugged off the aviator sunglasses.

He looked...hot, with his *GQ*-worthy style, plus a whole lot of lean muscle beneath the clothes.

"Um." She realized she was staring.

The street was quiet around them, although the park on the opposite side of DeKalb was already busy with joggers, cyclists and women pushing babies in strollers.

Babies.

The reminder made her even more tongue-tied.

"So. I picked up some coffee on my way over here." Roman nodded toward the black SUV with deeply tinted windows parked behind him. A driver sat behind the wheel. "Why don't you join me for a cup, and I can take you to work?"

She blinked and nodded, telling herself to pull it together.

Why did he have to show up now of all times? If only she could have had a couple of days to absorb the changes in her life before he came striding through her door and tilting her world all over again.

Well, she didn't have the luxury of time now.

"Sure. Thank you." She needed to figure out a way to explain to her boss she was expecting his baby despite their one-night deal.

She didn't think there was enough coffee in the city to fuel that confession.

As receptions went, Roman could have wished for better.

The woman now seated next to him in the SUV had filled his waking thoughts and starred nightly in his dreams ever since his last trip to New York. He'd royally pissed off his brother by staying away from the fashion house for so long, and Marcel was even angrier when he learned that Roman had made a brief trip to Manhattan without even staying long enough to speak with him.

Roman regretted that. But he'd taken his promise to Sable seriously. He refused to put her in a compromising professional situation, and he had been hell-bent on establishing that being with him wouldn't be a conflict of interest with her work. Because he wanted to be with her again.

No woman had gotten under his skin since his wife's death the way Sable had. And while he would never remarry or replace the only woman who would ever hold his heart, he could at least take pleasure with someone who fascinated him. Someone who seemed to enjoy their connection as thoroughly as he had.

Or so he'd thought.

But seeing Sable's reaction to him today made him second-guess what he'd remembered from their one night together. Sure, there'd been the flash of heat and awareness when their eyes met. He didn't doubt the attraction was still strong on her side, too. He'd felt it in those tense moments when they'd faced off in front of her building.

Then, she'd seemed to slip away from him. Her thoughts had gone somewhere else and he didn't have a clue how to get them back.

He watched her sip from one of the coffees he'd bought, her gaze focused on the river as they crossed the Brooklyn Bridge. Dressed in denim capris and a pink sweater that drooped off one shoulder to reveal the white lace strap of an undershirt, she looked entirely edible.

He'd been dying to taste her again for months.

"You seemed surprised to see me," he remarked finally. "Did you think I wouldn't return?"

She hit him with the full force of her hazel gaze as she put the foam cup in the molded console holder. The morning sun brought out the gold and green flecks in her eyes, subtleties he hadn't been able to appreciate in the darkened studio bedroom.

"I never doubted you'd visit the studio again, but I wasn't expecting you at my apartment." She adjusted the leather strap of her bracelet, making him wonder if he made her nervous. "I guess it makes sense that, as my employer, you'd know where I live."

"I never looked at your personnel file," he clarified. "You're easy to find in an internet search since you're living in Cybil Deschamps's apartments and they get a lot of publicity."

He hadn't realized that Sable had captured the eccentric heiress's attention through a highly competitive vetting process to award the housing situations to talented applicants.

"I couldn't have afforded to accept the internship otherwise." Her shoulder brushed against his as the vehicle turned north, and she edged back quickly. "But you probably know that, too. My hometown paper gave the story a lot of coverage."

Along with coverage of her divorce from a local would-be politician, a media angle he would have found intrusive and in poor taste even if he hadn't felt protective of her. But seeing her in an old photo with another man had been…uncomfortable, to say the least. He shouldn't feel jealous of another man in her life, but the feeling had been stark. Obvious.

His phone vibrated on the seat beside him, but he barely glanced at it, wanting to savor this time with Sable.

"They should have focused more on your accomplishments and less on your personal life." He was grateful for the gridlocked traffic; it gave them a private moment together, especially with the partition between them and the driver raised. Roman hadn't had nearly enough time to talk to her. He still needed to convince her to see him again. "Your professional track record is commendable. It was obvious why Marcel wanted you."

"Thank you. I've always wanted to be a celebrity stylist, and Marcel has given me so many opportunities to make that happen once I finish my commitment to him. I'm not even halfway through my internship, and I've already had some interest—"

She broke off suddenly, turning from him so he couldn't read her expression. Was she upset? She sounded uneasy.

"That's a good thing, isn't it?" He didn't know enough about the fashion world. The only reason he was the head of Zayn Designs was his knowledge of business and his personal capital.

He reached over the console to touch her shoulder. Encourage her gaze. When she turned back toward him, he couldn't identify the emotions in her eyes. But they swirled there.

Intensely.

"It *would* be a good thing," she started again, her voice low. "If I could take advantage of those opportunities."

She lifted her coffee for another sip while he tried to make sense of that.

"Why can't you? Are you afraid they won't still be there when you finish your year with Marcel?" He wanted to help her. To pave the way for her to use her talents. But he also didn't want to overstep.

He had to handle this relationship carefully, but being respectful of her as a professional didn't mean he shouldn't acknowledge her contributions to his business. Far from it. And if she was having problems related to the fashion house, he wanted to know about them.

The muscle beneath her right eye twitched and he

wondered again if she was nervous. And it occurred to him that this conversation would be easier if she was on his lap. In his arms. Under him.

Hell. He shifted uncomfortably, beginning to think he'd underestimated her effect on him. How could he concentrate on what she was saying when he wanted her this badly?

"I can't take advantage of those opportunities, Roman." She drew in a deep breath as she met his gaze. "Because I just found out I'm pregnant."

The words he'd never expected to hear left a phantom echo in the silence.

They circled in his head. Blanked his brain of everything else. He had questions but didn't trust himself to ask them in a way that would be appropriate. Hell, he didn't have the brainpower to determine what *was* appropriate. Knowing that, he waited. Watching her. Hoping if she spoke again maybe he could make sense of the pronouncement.

Licking her lips, she continued. "I only just found out for certain, so I'm still trying to wrap my brain around what it means. But you're the only man I've been with in the last year, so even though we took the right precautions. Well, mostly…"

Her words trailed off.

She didn't need to finish the sentence, though, because he recalled that last time they'd been together when they hadn't been careful enough.

"I remember," he acknowledged, knowing he wasn't doing enough to take responsibility. To support her. "It never occurred to me to follow up with you about that—"

With a hand on his arm, she halted his words. It was the first contact she'd initiated.

"That wasn't on you," she said, shaking her head as her hand fell away again, retreating toward her coffee cup. When she spoke again, her voice was quieter. "I didn't think twice about it at the time because I had trouble getting pregnant when I was trying."

The unexpected admission—and the hint of old hurt it revealed—felt like the most intimate thing he'd learned about her so far. Oddly, that small glimpse of vulnerability finally nudged his brain into gear.

Later, he'd think about the repercussions of this. Figure out what it meant for him and for his future. Right now, it was imperative to solidify some trust with Sable. Ensure she wouldn't cut ties with him or Zayn Designs to return to Louisiana and her family. If she was carrying his child, he needed her here.

"I'm sorry the timing isn't ideal for you, Sable." He shifted toward her in his seat to look her full in the face. Then, wanting to emphasize what he said next, he took both her hands in his and squeezed. "But I'm here now, and I can help. I'll support you in whatever comes next."

He meant it, too. But he also knew, underneath that offer of support, there lurked a sharp ache that he had missed out on this with his wife. He scrubbed a hand over his face to give himself time to school his expression.

Annette had wanted so badly to be a mother. And while Roman planned to keep his most personal vow to her, grief knotted in his chest that he would be sharing this with another woman. He felt disloyal.

"I'm keeping this baby," Sable told him emphatically

as the SUV rolled to a stop outside the Zayn Designs building. A defensive note lurked in her voice. "That's my next step, Roman. I'm going to make a doctor's appointment and do everything in my power to have a healthy pregnancy. I won't ask you to be a part of the baby's life if you would rather not, but I *will* see this through."

"Good." Relieved, he felt some of the knot in his chest ease. He couldn't afford for Sable to misread his tension. He squeezed her hands again to indicate to her they wanted the same thing. "I'm glad. And rest assured, I will also see this through. I'd never abandon my child. I hope you'll allow me to attend the doctor's appointment with you."

Her lips parted in an O of surprise; clearly, she hadn't been expecting that. But something softened in her expression, and the wariness faded in her hazel eyes, giving him hope that his declaration wasn't unwelcome.

"Of course." She tugged her hands free to retrieve the leather handbag on the seat beside her. "I'll text you once I set it up." She moved to get out of the vehicle, then turned to look at him over her shoulder. "Aren't you coming upstairs?"

"Not yet." Mostly because the baby news had thrown him for a loop. He wasn't ready to conduct business as usual with his brother right now. He also had a lot of planning to do, beginning with securing a place to stay in New York now that he'd be spending more time here. "I've got a couple of other appointments this morning, but I'll connect with Marcel later today."

He passed her the coffee cup after she stepped onto the sidewalk.

"Oh. Well, thanks for the ride, then." She nibbled her lip for a moment, drawing his attention to her delectable mouth. "And can we keep this news to ourselves for a little while? Just until we've had some time to get more comfortable with it?" She drew her jacket tighter around herself, the movement drawing his attention to her narrow waist. The curve of her hips.

And damn, but he wanted the right to touch her again. Taste her. But he couldn't risk pressing her right now. She was too jittery.

"That's fine," he agreed, even though he hadn't thought that far ahead. "We'll talk more soon, and I hope to hear from you later about that appointment."

She gave him a nod before turning to enter the building. Roman watched her leave, then used the call button to let the driver know their next destination. He had a lot to accomplish today, but one good thing about the baby news was that he wouldn't have to talk Sable into spending time with him again.

With the doctor's appointment coming up, he didn't have to. One way or the other, he'd be seeing her soon. He just hoped by then she would be open to his next proposition. Because if she was already pregnant, he couldn't imagine a single reason they couldn't indulge in many more heated nights together.

Four

Sable battled her dread of doctors' offices and showed up at the obstetrician's early the next week. She'd texted Roman the details of the visit the same day she'd dropped the baby bombshell on him, and he'd replied that he'd be there. Outside of that communication, she'd only seen him briefly one other time at the studio and they hadn't spoken. He'd texted her a few times, however, checking in to see how she felt. Asking if she needed anything.

That had been…nice. In fact, she appreciated the space to get her head together as much as the reminders that he was willing to be a presence in her life. Well, the baby's life. She had no illusions about where his loyalties lay given that they barely knew one another.

"Sable Cordero?" A nurse dressed in pink scrubs

and carrying a clipboard waved her into an exam room for the ultrasound.

Still no Roman.

She blinked away the hurt she shouldn't be feeling. So what if he'd only been paying lip service to wanting to be a part of this pregnancy? She planned to move forward with or without him, so not having him beside her today shouldn't upset her so much.

It was just that she had hoped Roman would distract her from how nervous she was about being here, and how it reminded her of all the other times she'd wound up at her physician's office in Baton Rouge. Or later when she'd visited the fertility clinic. The memories brought a thorny sense of failure and shame she'd scarcely admitted to herself, let alone shared with anyone. Those emotions were too personal, too negative. What was worse was that she didn't even feel *entitled* to them after having met women who'd struggled with infertility far longer than she had.

When the nurse left, Sable dove for her handbag to find her phone in an effort to distract herself. She'd find a social media feed full of puppies, maybe. Or cats in costume. That was always good for a smile. She had just unlocked the screen to see two missed messages when she heard a commotion outside in the lobby.

And was that Roman's voice?

A knock sounded at the exam room door and the nurse poked her head in.

"Ms. Cordero? There's a gentleman here for you—" She didn't finish speaking before Roman appeared behind her.

Sable felt a spark of awareness at the sight of him. His hair was messy, like he'd tugged on it a few times. His cheeks were flushed, his expression agitated.

"He can come in." Sable cursed her sudden breathlessness at the sight of him, her voice sounding all wrong.

Still clutching her phone, she wrapped her arms around herself, feeling suddenly self-conscious in the thin exam gown.

"Sorry I'm late." Roman strode in, his dark eyes sweeping over her as the nurse let the door fall closed behind them. His presence seemed to fill the room, making it feel smaller than it had just a moment ago. "There was an accident on the West Side Highway. I tried to call."

"I've had my phone off," she explained. Remembering that she was still holding it, she slipped the device back into her handbag. "I'm one of those overly compliant types that actually follow through on shutting it down at a doctor's office." She should have thought to check for messages instead of assuming the worst. But then, she'd grown used to doing baby-related doctor visits on her own, so maybe she'd been expecting Roman to bail on her.

The tension in Roman's shoulders eased a fraction at her admission, and the corners of his lips lifted in a smile. "So the temptress of my fantasies is a rule follower at heart?"

"If you mean me, um…yes. Too much so," she admitted, trying to ignore the warmth in her cheeks. She'd been so consumed with worries about making responsible decisions for a baby's future that she hadn't thought as much about that night with Roman. Let alone if he might want a repeat. "And the ultrasound technician should arrive soon to listen for the heartbeat. All you missed were paperwork and blood work."

He jammed his fists in the pockets of his tailored black pants. "I missed being here with you. My goal was to support what you're going through, not to waltz in for the fun part."

Sable was saved from picking through all the ways that statement appealed to her by another knock at the exam room door. The ultrasound technician entered and introduced herself as Melissa. The tall, stately woman was shadowed by Pink Scrubs, who helped Sable get comfortable on the exam table before disappearing again.

The flurry of movement around her made what was happening become more real. More exciting and scary at the same time. Sable took deep breaths and hoped for the best. Her blood work had confirmed a pregnancy, so at ten weeks, they ought to hear a heartbeat. She'd confided her concerns about her miscarriage earlier, prompting the doctor's decision to go ahead with an ultrasound even though the practice usually waited until after the eleventh week.

Strictly a precaution, the doctor had said, adding that it would give Sable peace of mind. The woman hadn't recommended she curtail any activities, insisting she'd done a thorough review of Sable's health history and saw no indication that her previous miscarriage would be a cause for concern. Still, some of her worry must have shown on Sable's face because Roman laid a hand on her shoulder.

"Are you ready?" His focus remained trained on her face while the tech prepared the wand.

Unable to restrain herself, she gripped Roman's wrist and held tight, grateful he was here. That he cared what happened. Blinking through the onslaught of emotions, she nodded up at him.

"Ready."

Two things stood out to Roman as the tech wielded the wand on Sable's flat belly like she was conducting an orchestra.

First, the gorgeous woman on the exam table in front of him was carrying his child, and the start to this pregnancy was healthy and perfect in every way. He heard it for himself in the strong heartbeat. He understood it in the reassuring way the tech kept pointing out all the normal markers of a ten-week pregnancy.

That part was nothing short of awe-inspiring.

But the other thing that Roman couldn't help noticing during the ultrasound was that Sable was scared.

His first clue had been her death grip on his hand, making him all the more pissed at himself for not being there on time to get a better read on her. What had her so worried? Granted, there were a million possible answers to that question since she hadn't been expecting to get pregnant while trying to establish herself in a competitive industry. No doubt she had a lot on her mind with all the changes ahead. But since his one and only role in this baby business prior to the birth was to make sure Sable was safe and happy, he couldn't help feeling he was already failing.

Which was simply unacceptable.

Ten minutes later, with Sable dressed in a leopard-print trench coat she wore open over a white shirtdress and ankle boots, they took the elevator down to street level in silence while Roman strategized his best approach. He needed to spend more time with her, figure out what was bothering her, and fix it. The sooner she started trusting him, the better for the sake of shared childcare. And if they ended up working out some of this attraction that had him on edge whenever he was around her, so much the better.

But first things first. He'd already texted their driver to meet them out front.

"You look great," Roman told her as their shoulders brushed inside the elevator cabin. He hoped to transition from the easy compliment into touchier subjects. He skimmed his fingers over her sleeve strap, feeling an answering shiver through her. "Is that one of Marcel's designs?"

She laughed; it was the first smile he'd seen from her since he'd returned to New York. "I can't afford your brother's clothes. But thank you. I have fun putting outfits together. The coat was a good vintage find."

The elevator settled on ground level with an unsteady jerk that had his arm wrapping around her. The possessiveness he'd felt that first night with her had only intensified since learning she carried their baby.

"It's not just the clothes." He released her as they headed toward the exit so he could hold the door for her. "You have the pregnancy glow working for you today. Have you been feeling well?"

He resented missing the first half of her appointment since he'd lost the chance to hear her talk about her health. He wanted to know how she was sleeping, if she was eating enough.

"A little more tired than usual, but I've heard that's normal." Her words mingled with the screech of a fire engine's siren as it careened past.

"Should you ask Marcel about modifying your schedule?" He'd agreed to keep the news between them for now, but he needed for his brother to be understanding about her condition.

"Not yet." Eyes wary, she hesitated outside the SUV when he opened the rear door of the vehicle. "I worked so hard to land this job, Roman. As long as the doctor says I'm okay to continue, I will. And I was going to hit some consignment shops in this area while I was up this way."

Meaning he wasn't going to have a chance to find out why she'd been scared in the doctor's office, let alone fix it.

"You need lunch," he urged, thinking of her health. "I thought we could share a bite and talk more about what's ahead."

"I have a whole list of items I need to find for a photo shoot." She withdrew a scrap of paper from her pocket, still making no move to enter the vehicle. "One of the stores is just around the corner."

"Dinner then," he suggested, but was unwilling to push her. He didn't want to add to her worries, but the thought of not seeing her for another week was like a vise constricting his chest. "We deserve to celebrate, Sable. Hearing that heartbeat was pretty incredible."

"Yeah, it was." A gravity in her hazel eyes told him how much that moment had meant to her, too. She dropped her list back into her pocket.

It still blew him away that he was going to share this monumental thing with her when they'd spent so little time together. He couldn't afford to screw it up.

"It's not like I can celebrate with anyone else," he reminded her. "Since we're keeping it just between us."

Finally, she nodded. "I should be done with the photo shoot by seven if you want to meet afterward."

The stranglehold on his chest eased. "Should I pick you up at the studio?"

"That would be great." Her lips curved slightly. Not a real smile like he'd glimpsed before, but at least he was grateful that he'd have more time with her tonight.

They could get on the same page about the future and what this baby meant for them. As long as he could keep the feelings he had about the pregnancy separate from the red-hot attraction he still felt toward Sable, he'd be fine. He could indulge the latter without threatening the vow he'd made to stay true to his wife's memory.

One day at a time. It was the only way he knew how to move forward after life had stolen everything precious to him.

"Great work today, Sable." Marcel Zayn stood in front of an antique mirror near the loft's elevator, putting on a dinner jacket. "I hope you snapped some images for your look book. I already posted a few candids on the Instagram page. The clothes and concept really worked well together."

Sable hugged the praise close to her chest as she put the last few sample garments back on the rolling rack. A new digital magazine had done a focus piece on Zayn Designs, and Marcel had okayed a photo shoot of their own to overlap the time the reporter was on site so they had some control over the images that would run with the story. They worked hard to leverage as much content as possible out of opportunities like today's, and Sable appreciated the designer's generosity in giving her credit.

"Thank you. We lucked out with the models. They really got on board with it." Sable had suggested a few poses, and the models had been so comfortable with each another. Their chemistry had resulted in a great shot of the male model untying the ribbons on the back of the woman's dress.

No mystery where she'd gotten *the* idea for *that* sexy sequence of shots. She probably owed Roman a creative credit.

Marcel laughed as he tugged his shirtsleeves to the perfect length underneath the jacket. "You think? There were sparks flying all over the place. It was so damned steamy to watch I ended up calling Parker for a second date." His phone chimed in his pocket while he was refastening a French cuff. "That's probably him now."

He stepped onto the elevator when it arrived. Sable watched him, noticing the resemblance between the designer and Roman in the way they moved with athleticism and grace.

"Night, Marcel." She was relieved Roman hadn't crossed paths with his brother since it was almost seven now. She'd asked Roman to keep the baby news quiet, but she wasn't sure where they stood in regard to letting other people know they occasionally…dated?

Hooked up?

Hell, *she* didn't know where they stood with one another, so no wonder she wasn't sure how to explain it to anyone else. Add to that the taboo factor of an intern dating the CEO, and she really wasn't ready to draw attention to it.

That was one of many reasons she'd been wary about spending more time with him. It was not like the attraction had dimmed since they'd torn off their clothes and feasted on each other all night long. Even today during her appointment, when she'd been stressed and anxious, she'd felt the tug of awareness for him. What would it be like tonight when they were alone over dinner?

Especially now, with the memories of that sexy photo shoot that had her reliving every second she'd spent in this studio with Roman ten weeks ago? She'd basically memorialized it by having the models reenact the encounter—up until the clothes came off, of course—in the photoshoot today. She allowed her fingers to walk from one hanger to the next on the rolling rack in the quiet studio, lingering on the dress she'd worn that night with Roman.

How would she put those thoughts out of her mind once she met Roman tonight? Her focus needed to be on the practical matter of sharing parenting duties, not remembering all the ways he could take her to extraordinary sensual heights. She couldn't afford to lose focus on what was most important.

Not with a baby at stake.

The thought had her returning to her bag and taking out the printed ultrasound image from the doctor's office. Studying the profile of her baby's face had her spine straightening, her shoulders braced for the weight of the world. Because she'd take it all on for the sake of that heartbeat she'd heard today. So strong and fierce.

The memory was precious, the moment unforgettable. And it was made all the more so by the fact that the man beside her had seemed as blown away by it as she'd been. Roman had gripped her hand tightly when the sound of the heartbeat had filled the exam room. She'd glimpsed his face, and there'd been a moment of raw emotion there. Deep. Complex. Hope and awe, but perhaps tinged with a hint of regret?

She'd looked away fast, feeling like she'd seen something overly private. Personal. He'd made it clear afterward he'd viewed the strong heartbeat as a reason to celebrate, but she couldn't shake the sense that there was more to it than that for Roman.

Still, whatever he felt about her pregnancy, at least he'd been there with her. That was more than she could say about her ex-husband, whose work had always trumped the doctor appointments he viewed as Sable's responsibility. She respected Roman's desire to be there. Admired it. And yes, she'd been glad to share something momentous with the only other person who had as much connection to this tiny life as she did.

A moment later, the elevator doors reopened with a soft swish and she slid the ultrasound photo back into her bag.

Even before she saw Roman, her body hummed with

the sensation of being watched, her skin tingling and the hair at the back of her neck lifting.

"Sable." His voice rubbed over her like a touch, the low tone giving her goose bumps.

She wished she could write off the reaction as pregnancy hormones, but it had been the same exact way as that night they'd spent together. Right here, in this same spot.

Memories crowded her as he drew closer. He'd changed clothes since the appointment. His hair was still damp around the collar of a black button-down as if he'd just showered. The gray pants he wore had a subtle weave, and his loafers were casual. He looked good enough to eat. She wanted to drift closer, guessing he smelled even better.

But she had her priorities straight now, and she wasn't going to waver on them.

"Hi." She reached for her coat, which was hanging on one of the rolling racks of the clothes she'd used for the photo shoot. "You didn't have to come up. I could have met you downstairs."

He was instantly at her side, taking over the task of settling her coat on her shoulders, sliding her hair out from under the collar so that it fanned out over her back.

"From now on, whatever I can do to make your life easier, Sable, I will." He turned her around, and she was suddenly facing him while he wrapped one side of her coat over the other before tying the belt at her waist. "Get used to it."

The gesture was both intimate and sweet, accelerating her pulse and making her feel cared for at the same time. And, just as she'd suspected, the scent of him—like woodsmoke and pine—only made her want to lean into him.

"Where are we going?" She retrieved her bag, moving away from him to collect herself.

"It's a surprise." He returned to the elevator and pressed the button, then lingered by the rolling rack where the clothes from the shoot were lined up on hangers.

With an unerring eye, he zeroed in on the dress she'd worn the night they'd been together. While he waited for her to shut down the lights, he slid his thumb and forefinger over one long ribbon. The hanger swayed gently in the wake of the movement.

Sable was pretty sure she did, too.

The elevator doors slid open.

"Ready?" he asked, turning dark eyes on her when she hesitated.

Was she ready for more time with this charismatic man who turned her inside out? She should be resisting him. But for practical purposes, she had to plan a way forward with Roman so they could raise a child together. She could ignore her hormones for a couple of hours to engage in what amounted to a business dinner, couldn't she?

It wouldn't be easy. But she owned her choices, and she would be the mother her baby deserved.

"I am." Reaching his side, she stepped into the elevator. "Let's go."

Five

"How are you feeling?" Roman asked Sable on the short drive from his brother's studio to their dinner destination.

He'd told himself that it was just as well that she'd declined his lunch invitation since it had given him more time to work on his game plan with the woman seated next to him. After her ultrasound, he'd been both elated and gutted at the reality of becoming a father, and he ran the risk of letting too much slip in front of Sable. He wasn't going to begin their co-parenting relationship while she thought he wasn't fully on board with raising a child.

Now he'd had time to lock down that unruly knot of reactions so he could make this evening 100 percent about her.

"I'm not as tired today as I have been the last couple of weeks, so that's a win." She gave him a small smile, her dark hair trailing over one shoulder. She'd tied it with what looked like a fabric swatch, the ends of the red velvet unfinished and fraying.

"No morning sickness?" He still resented that he'd been late for her appointment and hadn't heard the full dialogue with the physician.

"None so far." She sounded relieved about that as the vehicle rolled to a stop in front of the Madison Square Park Tower. She glanced up and down the street around the granite base of the soaring sculptural glass building. "We're eating here?"

"I ordered in for us in case you wanted to put your feet up," he explained. "I know you had a busy day preparing for the photo shoot, so I had the concierge coordinate a restaurant delivery. Although it's not too late to do something else if you prefer."

"No. That sounds great, actually." She picked up her purse while he exited the vehicle.

After helping her down, he released his hold on her hand, wanting her to be at ease. If he had his way, he would have been touching her every second since he'd set foot in the design studio, but this wasn't about him. He needed her to feel comfortable with him.

"Did you find everything you needed for the shoot?" he asked as he led her past the door attendant and into the elevator that would take them to the fiftieth floor.

"I found all I wanted and then some." Her soft drawl lingered over the words like a caress, a smile teasing around her lips. "Marcel was really pleased with how it all came together and we got a lot of great images."

"Are they posted on the social media accounts yet?" He pulled his phone from his pocket. "I checked about an hour ago, but I didn't see an update."

"You did?" She sounded surprised. "I mean, it makes sense you'd follow the account. I just didn't know how much of your professional time was devoted to the design house since you've only been in the studio a couple of times."

He paused in the middle of scrolling to meet her gaze. "That was in deference to you, Sable. I was trying not to make you uncomfortable with how much I wanted—how much I still want—you."

She swallowed, her legs shifting beneath her dress in a way that sent a growl up the back of his throat. He only just barely managed to suppress it, but he did because that was not what this night was about.

Even if pregnancy had made her all the more irresistible, with deeper color in her cheeks and added curve to her breasts. He'd noticed the changes earlier at the doctor's office. He wondered what other subtle things he would notice about her body if he had the chance to explore it more thoroughly.

The elevator door opened on his floor, providing a much-needed distraction from the temperature spike between them. Still clutching his phone, he gestured the way to his door and let her in.

"And, to your point," he added, hoping to pick up the thread of their conversation before he mentally undressed her anymore. "I spend about one quarter of my time on Zayn Designs, running the business side so Marcel can concentrate on what he does best."

He took her coat from her, careful not to linger over the body he wanted to touch so badly. Sable seemed to be on the same page since she quickly darted away to check out the view through the floor-to-ceiling windows in the living room while he turned his attention to the catering bags on the marble kitchen counter.

"Your place is really nice," she observed softly, her white shirtdress reflecting a blue glow from lights near the clock tower visible at 1 Madison Avenue. "Did you just move in? I remember you were staying at the studio last time you were in town."

He ground his teeth at the reminder of the only time they'd shared a bed. "Our father owns this apartment. He was in Manhattan at the same time as me two months ago, so I chose not to stay here. But he doesn't use this space often. He and my mother are in London for the next six weeks, so there's no chance we'll run into them here." He withdrew a platter from the warming drawer beneath the oven and carried it to the dining table that bridged the kitchen and living room in the open-concept layout. "But I've already looked at a few other places around town since I'll need something of my own."

"You're moving to New York?" she asked quickly, clearing away a pewter bowl that was a centerpiece on the table, making room for the food he carried.

Was it his imagination or was there a hint of panic in her voice?

"Not full-time." He kept his answer casual, returning

to the kitchen to bring in the catering bags, plates and silverware. "Zayn Equity is based on the West Coast, so I'll maintain a presence in Los Angeles. But you're in New York, and so is my firstborn, so it makes sense to maintain a home base here."

She turned away to retrieve the two glasses he'd left on the kitchen counter, and her face was momentarily hidden. When she returned, her gaze was trained on the table, prompting him to check in with her.

"I hope that's not a problem," he said, taking the glasses from her and setting them on the table. It was killing him not to just wrap her in his arms and offer her the undeniable physical connection they shared. But since he knew they couldn't solve their deeper problems that way, he withdrew her chair for her instead.

"No. Of course not." She took the seat he offered. "I'm just not sure that I can afford to stay in New York once the baby arrives. Even if I can find work here, I'll need to move out of my current apartment since it's intended for women launching careers in creative fields, not working mothers."

He took that in—along with the obvious tension she felt about the situation—and hoped to distract her with the meal before resuming the topic. These were issues he knew damn well he could solve if she'd allow him. For now, he pulled out the containers from the catering bags and poured two glasses of water from a chilled bottle.

"Dig in," he urged as he took the seat across from her. "I didn't know what you'd be in the mood for, and I wanted to be sure there was something you'd like, so I ordered a little of everything."

"Oh, wow," she murmured as she raised the silver lid on one of the dishes, revealing an assortment of pastas. "This looks delicious."

"And I've got some chicken options over here." He lifted the lid on the dish closer to him to show her. "The bread is in there." He unwrapped a tea towel from a basket, then began to fill his own plate. "Do you mind telling me what you had planned for work after the internship if you hadn't gotten pregnant?"

"I counted on Marcel's connections to keep me working as a stylist in New York for at least another year or two so I could build my network and my reputation." She slid some fettuccine, chicken and tomato slices onto her plate as she spoke, and it pleased him inordinately to see her eat. To know he'd fulfilled a need for her when she was carrying his child. It made him all the more certain he wanted to do more. "After that, I would have tried to make the leap to working in Hollywood, dressing celebrities."

"So don't leave New York for the baby's sake if you'll want to resume working here eventually. Take a sabbatical to give birth and see how you feel. Come back in a year when you're ready, and you'll be able to pick up where you left off."

She laughed. "Spoken like a man. A wealthy man, at that."

"Is that so?" He wasn't accustomed to his input being dismissed.

Perhaps his frustration came through in his voice because she straightened in her chair and met his gaze.

"Yes. Because I'm not asking you to solve my problems for me. And even if I had solicited your advice, there are subtleties you're not taking into account."

"So let's talk through them." He pushed the bread-basket closer to her, wondering how he could convince her to let him help. "Figure out a plan."

"Okay. First of all, it would be difficult enough to finance a year off even if I return to Baton Rouge. But I'd never be able to afford it in New York." She paused to take a sip of her water, and he noticed how the sky-line behind her had turned fully dark through the wall of windows. "Furthermore, my life will change radically once a baby arrives. I'm not sure I'll even continue chasing my professional dream once my priorities shift to accommodate a child."

Her words tugged at a memory, an old conversation with Annette about having a family and what it would mean to her. How she wanted to stay at home to finger-paint and run the sprinkler in the backyard so their kids could play in it on hot afternoons. She'd been so certain of what kind of mom she wanted to be that she'd made Roman able to envision it, too.

That sting of disloyalty jabbed him again, but he forced himself to ignore it to focus on Sable.

"You're right." His jaw felt stiff when he spoke, making him realize he'd been grinding his teeth, gnawing on the past. "You deserve more time to figure out what works best for you. Why don't I look for a bigger space so you can move in with me for a year?"

This was all moving too fast.

Sable didn't want to appear ungrateful for Roman's

generosity, but she absolutely couldn't allow him to step into a role where she could grow dependent on him. Jack had been her husband and she couldn't count on him. She sure as hell couldn't trust that Roman Zayn, her too-sexy boss with no legal tie to her at all, would follow through on what he proposed.

Better to remain independent.

"I can't do that." She twirled her fork through the fettucine noodles. "And I need more time before I make any big decisions about what's next."

"But you don't want to be in the middle of the move when you're eight months pregnant. Wouldn't it be best to relocate somewhere else soon, so you have time to get settled without exhausting yourself?"

It was a valid point. And yet…

"Could we revisit that in a couple of weeks?" She was stressed enough about the pregnancy without heaping more decisions on top of it. "After I get through the first trimester?"

He frowned. "Do you have any reason to…be concerned?"

She let out a sigh, knowing he deserved the truth, but still hating to dredge up the hurt.

"I told you that I had trouble getting pregnant," she began softly, taking a roll from the basket and buttering it. "But I didn't tell you that I also had a miscarriage."

His fork clattered onto his plate, and the next thing she knew his arm was around her, his chair drawn close to hers so he could give her the comfort of…him.

"I'm sorry, Sable." He spoke into her hair, his lips pressing close to her temple.

Touched at his kindness and understanding, she set aside her bread and allowed herself a moment to turn to him, her forehead tucking into the crook of his neck to absorb his strength. His empathy.

Had Jack ever held her like this when she'd needed desperately to be comforted? Her eyes burned as she realized how much she'd needed that, and how Roman offered it so completely.

"Thank you." With an effort, she picked her head up and tried to resume their conversation.

Except then they were just a breath apart, with his arm still a warm weight around her shoulders. His jaw was close enough for her to kiss. Taste. Bite.

She closed her eyes to dial down the temptation.

His hand shifted slightly to palm the middle of her back.

"How far along were you?" He cupped her face in his other hand, tipping her chin up.

She opened her eyes and met his dark scrutiny. In that moment, she was grateful for the physical attraction. The raw tug of it kept her from falling into unhappy memories.

"Twelve weeks." How long had it been since she'd shared the story? "I started bleeding the day before my first ultrasound appointment. I felt so relieved when I hit that twelve-week mark, too. But then…"

She winced at the memory. She placed her hand over the spot, as if she could ward off the old hurt and protect the new life there now.

"I can't imagine how tough that must have been for you." His fingers sifted through the ends of her hair, smoothing some of the strands that hung down her back. His other hand fell away from her cheek to cover hers where it rested on her lap.

The tenderness of the touch made her breath catch.

"I fell into a dark place afterward." She hadn't been able to pull herself out of the sadness, so she'd scheduled an appointment with a counselor. Which had been a blessing because she'd needed the support all the more when Jack checked out on her. "Then my husband served me with divorce papers two weeks later."

"Bastard."

She knew Jack had tired of putting so much effort into what he thought should be easy, but she hadn't realized until he left her how expendable she'd been.

"That about sums it up," she agreed. "In the end, the miscarriage hurt more than the dissolution of my marriage. It took some time before I was able to focus on myself again. Getting this job with Marcel was the best possible affirmation that I'd made the right choice to return to my dreams."

"All the more reason not to turn your back on it now." Letting go of her, Roman moved his plate closer so they could finish their meal side by side.

She missed his touch, even if she understood his need to reestablish boundaries. Or at least, she thought that was what he was doing. Apparently he had more discipline about their attraction than she did if he could stay away for two months. She might have asked for space this most recent time, but she'd regretted it a week later.

Even now, with the stress of an unexpected pregnancy and her total commitment to making good choices for her baby, she still craved Roman's kiss. His hands on her. She blinked through the haze of longing to consider his words.

"I understand why you think so. But I feel like I can't make any long-term decisions until I pass that twelve-week mark." She recrossed her legs under the table, grazing his calf in a way that she would have sworn was accidental.

Yet she couldn't deny she enjoyed the way his grip tightened on his fork and his body tensed.

"What did the obstetrician say about the miscarriage?" he asked after a moment. "Did she think you were at greater risk this time?"

"No. She reviewed my medical records before the appointment, and said everything was okay. She cleared me for...normal activity." She felt heat crawl up her face at the memory of that conversation.

Finished with her meal, she pushed the plate aside and took a drink of her water to drown some of the fire inside.

"You asked her about sex specifically?" His voice dropped to a deeper tone, pinpointing exactly the topic that had made her skin warm.

"I did." She suppressed a shiver, then forced herself to meet his gaze.

The answering heat she saw in his brown eyes sent her pulse into overdrive.

"Good." He gave a nod of satisfaction. "That's... good."

For a moment, she was mesmerized by the memory of what this man could do to her with a simple kiss. But then he shoved away from the table to clear their plates.

Right.

Because they were here to work out logistics for sharing a child. Or at least talk through what the next few weeks would look like. She'd told herself that this would be a business dinner, but she was already contemplating being in his arms again.

Or wrapping her legs around his hips.

She got up and began to help him, carrying the food back to the ultramodern kitchen. Clearly she needed something to keep her hands busy so she didn't wind up putting them all over Roman.

"I've got this, Sable." He took the dishes from her as she rounded the gray-and-white granite countertop. "'Normal activity' for you doesn't include cleanup when I'm around."

She didn't argue. Because how nice was that? Instead, she took a seat on the white leather barstool overlooking the kitchen as he worked. He wrapped the leftovers and stowed them in the refrigerator before pulling out a bottle of sparkling water and a container of raspberries. Then, finding two champagne flutes, he rinsed off a few berries to drop into the bottom of each glass before pouring the sparkling water over them.

"We're celebrating tonight," he reminded her, sliding a glass along the granite toward her. "Hearing that heartbeat today blew me away. So I'm going to propose a toast to our healthy baby."

He stood beside the barstool, his arm draped over

the back of the leather seat. He was close, but not touching her.

"I'll drink to that." She lifted her glass, touched at his thoughtfulness. "Cheers."

He tipped his flute to hers, and their glasses tinkled softly.

She watched the bubbles climbing the inside of the cut crystal glass, the column of his throat working as he took a drink.

For a moment, he seemed to sense her perusal because he set his glass aside and returned her steady look, causing her pulse to pick up speed.

"Now that I understand why you want to wait to make plans for the baby," he began, settling a hand on top of hers, "I'll try not to pressure you about moving in with me, at least for the next two weeks. But I'm going to continue to look for a place in New York so that it's ready if we need it. At the very least, I want to be here for the pregnancy and the remaining appointments."

She wanted to argue that it wasn't necessary. That she couldn't possibly move in with him since she wouldn't allow herself to rely on him that way. She needed to remain in control of her life and her future, even if that meant returning home to raise her baby in Baton Rouge.

Still, she appreciated his support. And she'd never forget the way he'd held her when she told him about the miscarriage. That moment…said a lot about him.

"Thank you," she finally managed, though she had to look away so as not to betray the confused tangle of feelings.

Then Roman, perhaps wanting to change the subject out of empathy for her, reached for his cell phone on the counter.

"I never had a chance to look at the photos from today," he explained, tapping the screen to life before scrolling.

All at once, the memory of the photo shoot returned. And in particular, the sexy vignettes she'd recreated from her night with Roman.

"Oh. Um." She wasn't sure exactly what had been posted online, so maybe the images weren't anything that Roman would link to her night with him. "I forgot about that."

She reached across the counter for the sparkling water bottle and refilled their glasses. Was it because she'd need to cool down after seeing the images? Or to hide her nervousness over whether Roman would recognize how she'd created her own visual ode to their time together?

Probably both.

She was already pouring the second glass when he made a strangled sound. Spilling a little water on the counter, she set the bottle aside to peer past where his strong arm was propped on the granite.

There, on the screen, a dark-haired model glanced over her shoulder toward a man only visible from behind. He was shirtless. She presented her back to him, two long ribbons framing her spine, and the man was tugging one free.

The shot was sizzling hot but didn't come close to capturing what those same moments had felt like when she'd lived them out with Roman two months ago. Blindly, she reached for the champagne flute, wishing she could stand under a cold shower of that raspberry-flavored water.

"Holy hell," Roman growled, his jaw flexing. His shoulder tensed. And his body heat became like a furnace beside her.

"Agreed." She slid his refilled glass toward him while she downed the contents of hers. "Although, in my defense, your brother urged me to do something sexier this time. So I couldn't help that this came to mind."

Straightening slowly from where he'd been leaning on the counter, Roman turned on her. He reached for her stool and spun it by the armrests so that she faced him fully. Then, arms bracketing her, he leaned closer.

"I did my best to give you space." His voice sounded gravelly.

"Thank you." She nodded, her heartbeat kicking hard inside her chest. "I know you have."

The leather upholstery creaked in his hard grip. He stepped between her knees, no quarter given because she was wearing a dress. The hem crept higher on her thighs. His gaze burned a hole through her.

"It's not easy to be impartial when I know you're thinking about that night as much as I am." His breath stirred her hair as he spoke close to her ear.

"I'm sure it isn't," she murmured, unable to argue with him when he could see the proof of her thoughts right there in those photos.

An ache of desire twisted low in her belly. She

shifted in her seat, her knee brushing his leg and sending a bolt of awareness through her. A whimper escaped her throat before she could swallow it back.

And then, after a scowl and a curse, Roman's lips covered hers.

Six

All evening long, Roman had done his damnedest to hold back. He'd had a game plan for putting her at ease. For ensuring she understood he wanted more than just sex. He wanted to be a part of his child's life.

Yet one look at the photo reenacting their night together had him hard as steel for Sable. And for his part, he didn't see why they shouldn't indulge in something that made them both feel good. But he guessed she hadn't reached that same conclusion based on the careful way she'd conducted herself with him since his return from LA.

Well, until now.

Because he wasn't alone in enjoying this kiss.

He stroked over the seam of her lips, demanding access. And she not only surrendered, she made hot demands of her own, her hands lifting to wrap around his neck, to pull him closer and take the kiss deeper.

And while he was game for both those things, but not at the cost of her retreating from him even more tomorrow.

Breaking the kiss with what felt like superhuman effort, he let his forehead fall to hers while they caught their breath.

"Sable." His gaze dropped to her lush lips still damp from his tongue and he had to close his eyes to keep from returning to that sweet spot for another taste.

"Mmm?" The sound she made in answer only tempted him more.

Her fingers were still locked behind his neck and, as he opened his eyes again, his attention shifted to the way her raised arms lifted her breasts toward him. The buttons holding together her white dress practically called to his hand to unfasten them. To free her body so he could worship her curves properly.

"Two months ago when we were together, I told you I'd stay away so things could cool off between us." How many times had he regretted that offer? But at the time, he wasn't sure how else to counterbalance the fact that she was technically his employee. He hadn't wanted their night together to be tainted by that.

"I remember," she said on a breathy exhale, her knees shifting around his legs, reminding him of how thoroughly he'd invaded her personal space. "You were as good as your word."

He couldn't quite read her tone, and damn it, they needed to be sure they understood each other now.

"We're relocating this conversation to the couch where I can look you in the eye." Shuffling back a step, he tucked one arm under her knees and slid the other under her arms, lifting her off the barstool to carry her into the living room.

"Oh." She let out a startled gasp, steadying herself with a hand on his shoulder. "Really? I'm pregnant, Roman, not bedridden. I can handle walking."

"It might not be wise to discuss beds right now. Not when I want you in mine this badly." He couldn't help looking down at where his hand wrapped around her thigh, and imagining how fast he could undress her so that he could touch even more of her.

She felt good against him. Like she belonged there.

But he shut down that thought fast. It was one thing to want her in his bed. It was something else altogether to consider a deeper connection. Because he wouldn't dishonor the vow he'd made to his wife that way.

Maybe that was why he settled her in the corner of the rolled-arm sofa and sat down beside her, instead of draping her over his lap the way he wanted. Still, he couldn't totally take his hands off her, either. He turned toward her, resting his right hand on her knee just below the hem of her dress.

"Okay." He let his fingers dip between her knees. But when she sucked in a rapid breath, he pulled back. "Clearly we need to revisit the parameters of our original deal. Things didn't cool off after two months. If anything, I want you more than ever."

"Same," she murmured. Her hazel eyes shot to his

after a moment, as if gauging his reaction. "That is, I agree about the heat level. Still…hot."

The sticky drawl of her words pulled at him as she wrapped a dark curl around her finger. With another woman, Roman might have thought the move was a deliberate flirtation. But Sable looked down, and the way she worked her lower lip with her teeth made her seem nervous. Uneasy.

And that, he couldn't abide.

"Hey." He cupped her jaw and turned her face toward him. "We don't have to act on it just because it's there. I'm going to be right there with you through this pregnancy whether you want to share my bed again or not. You know that, don't you?"

"I do." She nodded as if she'd understood that all along, but it unsettled him that some of her tension seemed to slide off her shoulders with his reassurance. "It's just the chemistry is so strong, I almost can't think when you're near me. What if a return to intimacy makes it all the more difficult to be objective about what happens next? And the stakes are higher than ever now, so I don't want to make a bad judgment call."

"I'm man enough to admit that while I don't *like* that answer, I respect the hell out of you for it." He appreciated her honesty, too. Because the attraction had the power to flatten both of them, which would be easy to prove with one kiss.

"You do?" Letting go of the lock of hair, she glanced up at him, her intelligent eyes tracking his.

"Hell yes. You're being protective of our future rela-

tionship as parents. I want you to trust your instincts."
Even though his body was already threatening a mutiny at the prospect of not being with her tonight. "The only answer is that we wait."

Hell, even saying the words out loud hurt.

"We wait," she repeated on a breathy sigh, sounding about as enthusiastic about the plan as he felt, which made him smile.

And gave him an idea. Because he didn't want to leave her unsatisfied. Not when she craved something from him that he could provide.

"Just because we hold off on sex doesn't mean I need to leave you unfulfilled." He allowed his fingers to unfurl again, tracing a circle just inside her knee.

Her breath caught. He was close enough to hear that tiny, staggered inhalation, and he liked what it told him.

"W-what do you mean?" She tipped her head back a fraction, her dark hair sliding sideways with the movement. The soft swish of silky locks against the leather made him want to wrap the dark length of hair around his hand. To tug her head back for another kiss.

"I think you know." He glided his fingers higher, beneath the dress's hem. "But I'm glad to be more explicit. Especially if hearing the things I want to do to you will add to your pleasure."

Her pulse throbbed harder, a reaction he could feel against his thumb on the inside of her thigh.

"Touching each other is an intimacy all its own," she said carefully, even while her pupils dilated.

"It's a middle ground," he countered, stilling his hand until he was certain of what she wanted to happen next. "I can take the edge off for you, and we keep our clothes on."

He could tell she liked the idea by the way her gaze fell to his mouth, her breath coming faster.

"What about you?" Her fingers grazed the buttons on his shirt, and his brain promptly supplied other uses for her touch.

"This isn't about me." He was resolute on that point, more than happy to delay his gratification in favor of hers. "I'm not the one going through pregnancy. It's only fair I do something for you while you carry the greater physical burden."

The corners of her full lips kicked up. "You make a compelling case."

He allowed his fingers to press lightly into her skin where he still touched her. The room was utterly still except for the dull ticking of a clock on the fireplace mantel. "And I didn't even use my most persuasive arguments."

She pressed her legs together, squeezing his hand lightly between her thighs. Her white dress took on a blue cast from the city lights filtering through the window behind her.

"Then by all means." She breathed the words over his mouth, arching her back to get closer. "Keep convincing me."

Hell. Yes.

Hunger for her surged through him when she gave him the green light. He needed to see her eyes blaze with passion, to hear her lips chant his name. She might prevent him from providing for her in other ways, but in this, he would never fail.

Sable shivered at the look in Roman's dark eyes.

It was knowing and primally male. A seasoned warrior sizing up the castle he was about to lay siege to. Was it wrong that she wanted to revel in being the object of that lust, just for a few stolen moments? All while keeping her clothes on?

She was maintaining some boundaries, after all. There would be no deeper intimacy tonight. Just Roman taking her body to levels of pleasure she'd only ever experienced with him.

And, oh God, it already felt so good to have his palm splayed over her thigh, his fingers drifting closer to where she desperately needed him. His wide shoulders loomed over hers as he leaned closer to kiss her.

"I hardly know where to taste you first," he said against her lips, the words vibrating up her spine since they sat so close. "Here." He sucked her lower lip into his mouth before letting it slide free again. "Or here." He licked his way down her throat, the warm suction of his mouth pulling a moan from her. "I just know you taste so good everywhere."

His fingers grazed the edge of her panties beneath her dress, one knuckle stroking up her center over the silk barrier as he spoke.

"Roman." She shuddered at the feel of him there, desire turning into a sharp, empty ache. "Please."

"I need you closer to me first." He scooped her up

and moved her to his lap, spreading his legs wide to cradle her while her head rested against his shoulder. "I want to feel you against me when you find your pleasure."

She wasn't about to argue since it felt amazing to be surrounded by so much male heat and strength. But the need to wriggle out of her clothes so he could touch more of her was growing fiercer by the second. And if she felt restrained, she could only imagine what a torment this must be for him. The proof of his need was a hot brand against her hip. It would be so easy to turn in his arms and straddle his hips to give them both what they craved.

"Is this better?" She arched up to kiss along his jaw. Lick the skin beneath his ear.

"Much. Now I have a front seat to see you come apart for me." He cupped her sex, stroking her with the heel of his hand and propelling her higher. "It's been too long since the last time. I've had months to think about all the ways I wanted to touch you if I ever got the chance again."

She wanted to focus on his words, but it was impossible with his fingers working her into a frenzy of sensation, gently pinching and kneading, stroking, and plucking. Her breath came too fast to catch and she tightened her grip on his shoulders.

"I missed you, too," she admitted, her defenses low while her need for him built. Besides, they were talking about sex. Right? "I missed this."

"I'm going to prove how well I can take care of you,

Sable," he whispered against her ear before nipping the flesh there. "You never need to go unsatisfied."

He slowed his touches beneath her dress and edged aside her underwear to plunge two fingers inside her. Her body stilled for an extended, breathless moment, her spine going taut. Then sensation rocked her, ripples of pleasure pulsing one after the other. Her feminine muscles shook and trembled with the force of her orgasm.

She might have screamed. She definitely called his name. More than once. The waves of release just kept coming, until she was wrung out and tucking her face into his shoulder to try to collect herself.

Slowly she became aware of Roman kissing the top of her head. Easing her underwear back into place.

All while his body remained rock-hard and in need of release.

"It seems unfair—" she began, but he bent to kiss her before she could complete the thought.

"Just...let me hold you a little longer." His tone sounded off, somehow, but she guessed that it was because he was still battling his own desire.

He didn't meet her gaze, though, so she found it difficult to gauge his mood, let alone pull herself back together.

Being together this way would only lead her to more feelings for the father of her child, and she wasn't ready for that.

And no matter what Roman said about wanting to provide for her throughout her pregnancy, she suspected that the events of the evening—the whole day, for that matter—rocked him, too.

"I should go." She shifted again, and this time he didn't stop her when she slid off his lap.

When she met his dark gaze, his expression was shuttered. So even looking right into his eyes, she couldn't get any read on him or what he might be thinking.

He had secrets, she realized. Or, at the very least, something he wasn't telling her. The idea pricked at her sharply, but she trusted the instinct.

"When will I see you again?" he asked, coming to his feet.

He didn't touch her this time, which had her emotional radar pinging all over the place.

She focused on his question, knowing she'd have to find a way to balance her feelings for Roman with practical concerns. The sooner she figured out how to do that, the better.

"Normally there are only two ultrasound appointments per pregnancy, but the obstetrician agreed to another one in two weeks." She retrieved her purse and slung the bag over one shoulder.

"I can't go another two weeks without seeing you." His brows drew together in concern. Or maybe confusion. "And I'll drive you home, Sable."

"That's not necessary." The sooner she resurrected boundaries, the better.

"I insist." He found his phone and keyed something in before pocketing it again. "A driver will meet us downstairs."

"Fine. I just need my coat." She moved toward the

door, feeling suddenly adrift and out of place in his
wealthy world.

Not just because she was an intern in his company
who was now expecting his child. But also because she
might need to leave New York in a few months' time,
while he was contemplating a second home here even
as he enjoyed a space like this one with the kind of view
that cost millions. How was she going to share a child
with someone like Roman, who could afford to order
his world however he chose?

"Sable." He wrapped an arm around her waist and
hauled her backward against him. "Don't shut me out.
We'll come up with a good plan for the future, but we
have to do it together. Right?"

He spoke the words against the top of her head, and
some of the tension drained from her shoulders at the
feel of his chest pressed to her. Which made no sense
since being physical with him also accounted for the
awkward turn things had taken between them. Hadn't
it?

"Once I pass the twelve-week mark, I'll be better
able to focus on the future." She was already attached
to this baby. Making premature plans with Roman could
only hurt more later if anything happened to endanger
the pregnancy now. Her heart had only just begun to
heal. She needed more time to shore up her boundaries.

"I understand." He turned her in his arms, his strong
hands gripping her shoulders for a moment before falling away. "So let's use the next two weeks to get to
know each other better. Feel more comfortable with

one another to pave the way for a good parenting relationship down the road."

She wanted to ask him why he'd checked out on her tonight after he touched her. Where had his thoughts flown in those moments when he wouldn't meet her gaze? But she wasn't ready to make herself vulnerable that way yet, to reveal the insecurity his inattention had stirred.

Besides, he'd been thoughtful and generous to her in many ways this evening. She wouldn't discount those efforts. She just needed to keep a careful rein on her feelings so she didn't end up reading more into the situation than what was really there.

"Okay. Two weeks to find our way," she agreed. She folded her arms across the front of body, suddenly feeling a need for more distance to regain her objectivity. "How do you suggest we implement this plan of yours?"

He stepped away to retrieve her lightweight trench coat, then settled it on her shoulders, all with minimal contact. Was he reading her signals? Or was he throwing off his own now that they'd reached the negotiation phase of the evening?

Exhaustion from the long, demanding day hit her all at once, bound up with the mental weariness from trying to decipher Roman.

"How much of New York have you seen since you've been here? We could play tourist for a day. Take in some sights." He grabbed a set of keys before escorting her to the door, then doubled back to the kitchen. "I almost forgot about the cake," he explained as he took out a small paper bag from one of the catering sacks that remained on the counter. "Never let it be said I sent you home without dessert."

"I wouldn't dream of it." Her cheeks warmed at the memory of how they'd spent the time after dinner instead. When he returned to her, paper bag in hand, she shoved aside the thought to focus on his earlier question. "And I'd love to play tourist for a day. I've been too busy working to see the sights."

Plus, if they were out sightseeing, they couldn't get sidetracked by the chemistry that was always simmering in the background, ready to boil over at the least provocation.

"In that case, can you keep your Saturday open?" he asked as he opened and held the door for her, readying himself to accompany her home.

"I can." That would leave her with three days to shore up her defenses before she saw him again. Three days of mental pep talks to ensure she kept their relationship more on a friendly level. Less passion-fueled.

"Perfect. I'll pick you up at noon and we'll make a day of it." His hand grazed her back as they stepped into the elevator cabin together, and just that small touch sent new shivers along her skin.

Who did she think she was kidding?

Three days wouldn't be nearly enough.

Seven

Friday evening, before her date with Roman the next day, Sable was already dreaming up excuses for canceling. She peeled off her earbuds as she trekked out of the Fulton Street subway station and headed toward Fort Greene Park, anxiety dogging her. She tried to think of something that Roman wouldn't see right through.

The truth was she didn't trust herself around all that potent sexuality, especially when it came wrapped up in so much concern for her. Well, for her *baby*. Maybe it was all the pregnancy hormones that made her swoon at the memory of Roman's obvious care for her health and the well-being of their child. But the fact that he wanted to be at her doctor appointments, that it mattered to him if she was eating healthy and sleeping well, and that he'd felt compelled to celebrate the ultrasound had all slid right past her defenses.

Add to that the way his touch could launch her body into the stratosphere? The man was her kryptonite. And she didn't have any more idea how to set boundaries now than she had two days ago when she'd come apart in his arms.

Her brownstone came into view as the lights of evening started to illuminate the darkening street. Sable's nerves twisted at the thought of letting him get any closer. Physically, sure, but even more so emotionally. She couldn't afford to lose her hard-won sense of self after the nightmare of her divorce following the miscarriage.

She was almost at her stoop when the blare of rock music hit her ears. A guitar solo wailed through an open window on the garden floor. There was a bedroom down there, but it had been vacated three weeks ago by a dancer who'd nailed down a spot as a Rockette and was now sharing an apartment with a few other performers in the theater district.

Had someone else moved in? Blair Wescott, the makeup artist and Mini-Me version of Cybil Deschamps, had already claimed the big bedroom on the third floor right below Sable.

She hurried up the steps to the entrance and let herself inside, more than ready to throw herself into any new roommate intrigue to take her mind off Roman and her situation. Whenever she wasn't thinking about how to build a secure future for her child, how to reconcile her professional dreams with her new reality, or when to tell Marcel she was expecting, she obsessed about Roman and what kind of relationship she should be building with him. She hadn't realized until she heard the music that she craved girl talk. Stat.

"Hello?" she called once she was inside the foyer. Her voice echoed hollowly in the entrance hallway as she peered into the great room. There wasn't a lot of furniture in the space.

Cybil had left them the basics—a couple of vintage couches and chairs to fill the huge great room with high ceilings—but there wasn't much in the way of rugs, paintings or decor. The original parquet floors shone dully in the light coming in from the street since no one had switched on any lamps up here. Laughter floated up the staircase from the garden level, audible in the momentary reprieve between rock songs.

"Hello?" she called again as she started downstairs, enticed by the scent of popcorn.

"It's my long-lost fourth floor roommate." Tana Blackstone appeared at the base of the staircase.

Petite and delicate, Tana had a fairy-like beauty with her glossy brown hair and heart-shaped face. But unless she was auditioning for a part, she took tough-girl fashion seriously. When she wasn't in leather and spikes, she draped herself in oversize flannel shirts, army-navy store finds, and combat boots. Her nods to femininity were dyed hair tips in an ever-changing rainbow of colors and glittery eye makeup.

Sable had to admire her commitment to an aesthetic. Today, Tana wore a T-shirt with a cartoon superhero, spiked leather bracelets, and jeans with more holes than fabric, which showed off spiderweb-patterned tights beneath. Her hair had green tips to match her eyeshadow and a tiny stud in her nose.

From behind Tana, their new roommate peeked her head around a wainscoted column that separated the kitchen from the hallway at the base of the stairs.

"We needed a Friday happy hour," Blair explained as she raised a martini glass containing a frosty-looking yellow drink layered on top of a red base. "Ready for a raspberry lemon drop?"

Tana waved Sable toward the all-white kitchen. "You have to try one. Blair is a grand wizard mixologist. These things look like works of art and they taste even better."

"Oh. Um." Sable would have given her right arm for one of those gorgeous drinks two months ago. She hesitated as she searched for a believable excuse. "I can't. I'm on a mega-strict cleanse."

"On a Friday?" Blair used one hand to hoist herself onto the marble counter next to the blender where she'd obviously been working. There were a few liquor bottles, and lemons and raspberries spilled over the edge of a cutting board.

Blair Westcott looked far more at ease today in a pair of purple leggings and a slouchy pink yoga top, her platinum blond hair in one long braid that swung over her shoulder. With her high-top sneakers and her face scrubbed clean, she looked more like a college co-ed than the sought-after makeup artist that Cybil Deschamps had personally chosen to work for her cosmetics company.

Spotting the bowl of popcorn on the counter near Blair, Sable scooped up a handful to nosh on.

Tana tapped the screen of her phone, lowering the volume on the head-banging music coming from the Bluetooth speaker balanced on the coffee maker. "We're drinking to my second callback for a soap opera role, which could be the difference between me getting to afford one more month in New York or—not."

Sable empathized more than Tana could know, considering how her own days in this expensive city were numbered now that she was expecting a baby. Unless she accepted Roman's offer.

Which she couldn't.

"You're going to get the part," Blair told Tana firmly. Then, she pointed her martini glass toward Sable and explained, "I ran lines with her before today's callback, and she's great."

Tana scoffed, but something in her expression showed her pleasure at the compliment.

Sable felt guilty that she'd offered her roommates so little of her time. Blair had only been living here for a few days and had already jumped in to help, while Sable barely knew what Tana did each day. Or maybe it wasn't guilt so much as simple regret that she hadn't taken the time to enjoy the camaraderie of things like Friday happy hours with these women who had the potential to be good friends. She'd been so invested in her job, spending all her extra time on creating content for Zayn social media, that she'd ignored her personal interests at a time when she might have really benefited from girlfriends.

Especially now, when this world was slipping away from her too quickly.

"I could at least have something nonalcoholic with you," she announced, stashing her bag on an open shelf of cookbooks below the breakfast bar that overlooked the dining room. "Second callbacks deserve celebrating."

"I made fresh lemonade," Blair said. "It's in the fridge."

"Wait until you see this," Tana added, darting past Sable to reach the refrigerator first so she could open the door for her. "Look."

The high-end appliance had been cleaned out and organized; the white interior was gleaming and the thinned-out offerings were now easy to see. In the middle of the tallest shelf sat a hand-painted glass pitcher filled with ice cubes and fresh lemon slices.

"As in you *made* lemonade? From scratch?" Sable lifted out the pitcher, exchanging looks with Tana, whose expression communicated equal enthusiasm for their new housemate.

"You know it's just three ingredients, right?" Blair opened a cupboard and located a hand-painted glass that matched the pitcher. "It's been fun exploring the kitchen. Cybil has everything in here."

Sable continued to stare into the refrigerator, suddenly ravenous at the sight of food and wishing she'd come up with a different excuse for not drinking. She hid a sigh as she poured her lemonade, returned the pitcher to the shelf, and closed the door.

Lifting her glass, she faced Blair and Tana. "To second callbacks."

"And staying in New York," Tana added as she raised hers, the silver skull on her leather wrist cuff glinting in the light from the Art Deco–style pendant lamp.

"And new friends." Blair slid off the counter to clink her glass with theirs. "I don't know about you all, but I'm far from home, and I appreciate the girl time. Cheers, *chicas*."

"Cheers." Sable's throat tightened; she agreed with the sentiment even if she wouldn't be able to enjoy it for long.

Didn't she owe it to herself and her child to have more of a network? Especially since she would be doing her portion of the childrearing alone. Sure, Roman wanted to share the duties with her, but that just meant handing off their baby to him so he could take his turn at parenting—alone. And when she got the child back, she'd have to navigate the decisions and responsibilities by herself, as well.

As the reality of that set in—along with hunger pangs for more than just popcorn—Sable decided she didn't want to keep her pregnancy a secret any longer. Was that unfair since she'd asked Roman to keep it quiet until the twelve-week appointment?

Yes. But he wasn't carrying the baby. He didn't have the same burdens she did, let alone the same anxieties. Even though he might share some of her fears about a miscarriage, he couldn't possibly know the devastation of losing a longed-for pregnancy.

It was on the tip of her tongue to confess the truth when the doorbell chimed.

"Did you order a pizza?" Sable asked, blurting out the only possibility that came to mind.

Tana was already jogging up the steps to answer the door. Blair was shaking her head when they heard voices at the front door—Tana's and a man's. It wasn't Roman. Sable would have known that particular tone anywhere. But she could see in Blair's face that the woman recognized who it was. Her cheeks went pink even as the rest of her skin paled. She swallowed reflexively.

A curious response.

"Blair?" Tana called down the steps. "Lucas Deschamps is here and he's asking for you."

Sable bit back a smile as Blair swore and then paced twice across the kitchen before heading upstairs.

Apparently Friday night happy hour was over. And maybe it was just as well, since now Sable could finally make herself some dinner. Soon, she'd tell her new friends about the baby.

But first, she had to get through her date with Roman tomorrow without things becoming heated. She hoped it would be easier now that she understood Roman was keeping a piece of himself locked away from her. More than once, she'd relived those moments when his expression had gone shuttered after they'd gotten intimate two nights ago. She'd had the sense he was hiding something from her, and the anxiety about what that might be had only grown in their time apart.

Maybe the memory of that feeling—the way he'd kept her at arm's length right after he'd taken her to sensual heights—would help her resist him tomorrow.

Besides, they were sightseeing. As long as they remained in public, there would be no chance of clothes coming off or boundaries coming down.

And her wounded feelings from two days ago would give her the extra defenses she needed around him.

"I wish I could take photos of your brother's designs with this as a backdrop," Sable commented as she strolled through the Cloisters museum, pausing briefly to admire the view of the Hudson River outside one of the doors. "Everything would look more elegant in this setting."

She made an expansive gesture with one arm, indicating the L-shaped arcade overlooking well-tended gardens planted with hundreds of species used for food, medicine or—according to the literature—magic in the Middle Ages.

Roman followed her, more captivated by the woman than the art and architecture. Spring bloomed outside the open arcade, with vibrant flowers and droning bees drunk on too much pollen. But the lush silhouette of Sable in a full yellow skirt and fitted white T-shirt drew his eye the most. The day had been relaxed and fun, with Sable taking as much pleasure from the architectural elements salvaged from medieval abbeys and churches as she did from the unicorn tapestries and the profusion of plant life. They'd played "I spy" with the huge tapestries, finding cats and frogs, hidden initials and dragonflies. She'd revealed a deep love of art that her husband apparently hadn't shared, making Roman all the more glad he'd brought her here for a day of sightseeing.

A day to get to know her better and—he hoped—start planning a workable future for raising a child together. So far, he'd been able to shove aside the ever-present attraction enough to put her at ease, and he was damned grateful she hadn't brought up the way their last date had morphed from dinner to him touching her. As much as he'd lobbied to give her that kind of release, and as much as he absolutely had wanted it, he hadn't bargained on the feelings that swamped him afterward. The need to pull her into his arms. To take her to bed for more than just sex. To hold her. Comfort her.

To lay his hand on the place where his child grew.

Those needs had rattled the hell out of him, reminding him there was risk involved every time he succumbed to the chemistry with Sable.

Now she glanced at him over her shoulder, making him realize he'd been lost in thought about what happened next.

"I'm glad you approve of this place," he finally answered, his hand moving automatically to the small of her back as they headed deeper into the unique building made up of reconstructed cloisters from medieval Europe. "The park is beautiful, too. I thought we'd take a walk on the paths whenever you're ready." He'd brought a picnic to share with her and left the hamper in the car while they toured the museum.

"Sounds good," she agreed, pausing inside the cool, shadowy interior where stone steps led down into a room they hadn't yet explored. "This must be the Gothic chapel. The colors of the stained glass are so pretty."

Roman followed, his gaze snagging on the tomb effigies laid out around the chapel, while Sable checked her phone for notes on the self-guided tour she'd downloaded for the day. He hadn't realized he'd halted his steps until she turned to look back at him.

"Are you coming?" She observed him, her head tilted to one side, dark hair sliding over her shoulder.

He couldn't imagine what she might see reflected on his face as the somber ambience of the chapel took hold of him, memories of another chapel weighing his feet like lead. He was standing beside a tomb featuring a sculpture of a woman in silent repose, her hands clasped just above her waist and her head resting forever on a pillow of cold limestone. And just like that he was catapulted back in time, to a casket he'd never wanted to stand beside.

Was it the atmosphere created by the stained glass and statues of saints around the chapel that brought back so vividly the day he'd laid his wife to rest? Or was it the effigy of the noblewoman in her gown and jewelry, a coin purse at her waist, that reminded him of Annette's family squabbling about which of her dresses to send to the funeral home? They'd fought about the outfit as if it mattered, as if it made any difference to the woman he'd loved, who was gone forever.

A bead of cold sweat rolled down his temple.

"Roman?" Sable's voice sounded far away now, and distorted as if she were speaking underwater.

He took in a breath to answer, but the feeling of

claustrophobia increased, as if the walls were pressing in and there was no air to spare. His fingers moved
to his throat, as if to loosen a collar or tie, or whatever
was making his airway feel constricted. But there was
nothing there.

Just skin gone clammy above the open neck of his
button-down.

"Excuse me." He thought he said the words aloud, but
couldn't be sure. He only knew he needed to get outside.

Away from the tombs and the dark, quiet chapel.

Now.

Bolting up the stairs, he crossed an arcade, passed
the tapestries room and followed exit signs to the east
side of the building. He went down a long ramp toward
a set of double doors and barreled through one of them,
craving sunshine and fresh air. A breath that wasn't
haunted by the past.

On the pavement out front, he dragged in one lung-
ful after another, waiting for his head to clear. For the
cold clamminess on his skin to disappear. He shoved a
weary hand into his hair and scraped his fingertips over
his scalp, willing some warmth to return to his body.

A moment later, he heard light footsteps approaching behind him. He didn't know how he knew it was
Sable when a hundred other people were there around
him, entering and exiting the museum or exploring
the park. Yet he knew without turning that she was
the one drawing near. The back of his neck prickled
with awareness.

And at this moment more than ever, it felt like disloyalty to his wife's memory. He briefly squeezed his

eyes shut in an effort to get his head together before he turned and faced her.

The tender concern in her hazel eyes slid right past his defenses, reminding him that Sable was a good person. None of his screwed-up feelings were her fault, and he owed her an explanation.

"Should we head home?" Sunlight streamed through her dark hair, burnishing the glossy locks to show subtle caramel strands. "I can drive if you don't feel well."

"I'm better," he assured her, taking her cool fingers in his. "Are you still up for that walk?"

He hoped it would help level him out. Calm his still racing heart. Plus, he really wanted to banish the shadows in Sable's eyes. Shadows he'd put there, when he'd been trying so hard to make the day all about her. But he knew he owed her an explanation, and he couldn't very well provide it here in front of the swarm of visitors.

"Are you sure?" She took a step closer to him, the yellow outer layer of her floaty skirt brushing against his calf as she moved. "I don't mind calling it a day."

"No. I'm fine." Squeezing her fingers gently in his, he lifted her hand to his lips and kissed the backs of her knuckles, trying like hell to turn his thoughts around. "Let's find a spot with a good river view."

After a moment she nodded, walking with him along the winding paths and stone steps of Fort Tryon Park, the highest point in Manhattan. They remained quiet while they passed through flower beds and crossed an access road, until they reached a low stone wall that separated the lane from the cliffs beyond.

His car was parked close by, but he wasn't ready to

retrieve the food yet. He needed to talk to Sable first. Scouting a good spot to sit and have some privacy, he followed the low wall until he found a flat rock on the other side. The promontory offered a good view of the Hudson River.

"Here. Do you mind if we have a seat for a few minutes?" He pointed out the place he had in mind.

"Sure. I might need a hand over the barrier." Her gaze flicked to him carefully, as if she was waiting for him to sprint away from her again.

Roman climbed the low stone wall first and then reached back for her, keeping her steady while she navigated the divider. She hopped down beside him, then took a seat on the smooth, flat rock. She folded her skirt around her and drew her knees up a little. She fixed her gaze on the water as a barge moved north, slowly passing the Palisades on the other side of the river. He joined her, sitting close to her but not touching.

"This is gorgeous. You'd never know we were in the city here." She withdrew her phone and snapped a couple of photos of the river and, south of them, the George Washington Bridge.

He wished he could lose himself in a conversation about the scenery. And, hell, he appreciated the way she gave him an out from talking about what had set him off back there. She had to know something was wrong and yet she was letting him have some space. But she deserved to know the truth.

"You must be wondering what happened in the chapel." His jaw felt tight. As if his body physically resisted telling the story. He scrubbed a hand over his face.

"I am. But if you'd rather not discuss it—"

"I need to." Of course, that wasn't entirely true. He started again. "That is. You should know."

He stared out at the water as he heard her set aside her phone. He felt rather than saw her tip her head toward him. Waiting. Listening.

"The tombs reminded me of someone I lost. It's been five years, so I hadn't really expected that strong a reaction." In some ways, Annette's death seemed so recent. But he'd been living without her for five years and three months.

He'd had the grief counseling. He'd thought he'd made his peace. But the baby news had stirred it up for him.

"I'm sorry," Sable offered quietly, slipping her hand over his to lay her palm on the back of his fingers.

"Thank you. It's been on my mind more recently because of the pregnancy. I think that's why the memories came back so strongly today." Even in the worst of his grief, he'd never had that claustrophobic feeling that had come over him today. That sense he couldn't breathe.

She went very still beside him. "Whom did you lose?"

He couldn't tell what she was thinking, but something in her tone made him glance over at her. She was pale. Worried.

Did she suspect what he was going to say? Even if she guessed he'd been married before, he wasn't sure why that would upset her. Not when they were only just getting to know each other, and she'd been so definite about not leaping into a more romantic relationship with him.

Knowing there was no way around it, he admitted what he hadn't shared with any other woman who'd passed through his life in the years since Annette's death.

"My wife." His gaze held Sable's. "I was married for fifteen months before she died during a failed heart transplant surgery."

Eight

Eight

Roman was a widower.

Sable allowed the revelation to sink in while the spring sun warmed her bare calves. Birds chirped in the trees overhead. Sunbeams glittered on the Hudson River below them. But the happy bloom of oblivious nature no longer gave the day the same glow that she'd felt earlier. Now she understood why Roman's skin had felt cold to the touch while they were inside the dim Gothic chapel.

He grieved for a woman he'd loved. A woman he clearly loved still.

"I'm—" *Stunned you never mentioned a previous marriage.* But this wasn't about her. She could see for herself how much he mourned his wife. "I'm so sorry, Roman."

She didn't trust herself to say much more until she'd wrapped her head around this new disclosure. Her hand remained on top of his, and she stared down at it now, feeling self-conscious about the gesture. Feeling like an intruder in his grief when she wasn't the woman who held his heart. Giving his hand a last squeeze, she let go and tucked her palms between her knees.

"I should have told you about Annette before. I almost did when we talked about your ex. But we ended up talking about the miscarriage and my thoughts shifted to the baby. And worry about you." The raw honesty of the words pulled at her, forcing her out of her own thoughts to focus on him.

"Tell me about her." She needed to know more. After that night she'd had dinner with him, she'd sensed he'd been holding back from her—keeping secrets. Now she understood this was it.

If he'd been holding his marriage close and not sharing with her, she suspected there was a reason for that. And it wasn't that he just hadn't found a way to introduce the topic.

Beside her, Roman draped his wrists over his knees, shoulders dropping.

"We met when she was still in college. I'd already graduated, but I went back to campus to speak at the invitation of one of my finance professors. Annette was one of his star students, on track for a big career after interning at a prestigious equity firm. She asked to speak with me about the industry and we—" He broke off, shaking his head as if he didn't want to reveal intimate details.

Sable's throat burned. She wouldn't allow herself to feel jealousy for a dead woman. But the sight of Roman's obvious all-encompassing love for someone else hurt far more than it should have. What room would he have left in his emotions for anyone else?

"You said she needed a heart transplant?" she ventured, trying to give him a way out of whatever he was remembering right now.

Nodding, he took a long breath. "She was born with a heart problem that required a transplant when she was just two years old. Transplanted organs have a shelf life, and although she'd done well with hers, she understood that there would come a time she'd need another one." His head dipped as he paused, lines carving into his forehead while he seemed to gather his thoughts. "She took antirejection medicine her whole life. Took great care of herself, and had such an amazing outlook."

The unevenness of his voice touched Sable, chastising her for the earlier flash of jealousy she'd experienced. She tipped her head to his shoulder, needing to give him some kind of comfort while she waited for him to continue.

"After the wedding, she had problems almost immediately. But I was traveling quite a bit those first few months, and she had a new job, so I didn't know about the signs." He sounded harsh. Almost angry. Did he blame himself somehow for her health issues? "When I found out about them, I insisted she see her doctor, and we cut short a delayed honeymoon trip to the Seychelles that we took six months after we married. We flew home and her cardiologist put her on a transplant list right away."

Her head still on his shoulder, Sable threaded her arm through his, her gaze tracking a speedboat slicing through the river spread out below them. She breathed in Roman's scent, which brought to mind woodsmoke and pine.

"Did it take all that time to obtain a heart?" She didn't know anything about organ transplants, but if they were together for fifteen months, that would mean it took nine months to find a donor.

"No. She was scheduled for a transplant six months later, but there was a problem with the donated organ and her doctor couldn't use it. So she went on the list again." His voice dropped. "When the next one arrived three months later, it seemed like a good fit. But—" He broke off before finishing in a rush. "Her body rejected it."

"How unfair for her. For you, too. And her family. What a traumatic way to lose a loved one."

"There are no good ways," he muttered dryly, his muscles still strung tight with tension where Sable touched him.

She lifted her head to see his face, and blinked at the stark pain in his brown eyes. Her fingers pressed into his forearm, and she wished she could take away some of the hurt with her touch. But she knew instinctively she wasn't going to make a dent in those feelings.

"Still, you had every reason to think you'd bring her home after surgery. She was young and vital. If she kept the first heart for over twenty years, you surely thought you'd have more time with her once she received the second."

He wrenched his gaze away from hers, shaking his head slowly, as if it weighed heavily on his shoulders.

"The risks are high every time. We both knew that. But— I would have given anything for even one more year. One more month." The trace of bitterness in his tone, of love, was unmistakable.

And it sharpened her understanding of her place in Roman's life. She might be the mother of his child, but it was clear that another woman still held his love. The realization sank home, like a cold weight deep in the pit of her belly.

Not that it should matter, since she'd been insistent on keeping him at arm's length to protect herself. Turned out she needn't have worried when Roman had no intention of a deeper relationship than shared parenting with her anyhow.

"And you think the news of this pregnancy brought the grief close to the surface?" She knew it was foolish of her to ask when her emotions were already unsteady.

Major understatement.

She *ached* with knowing how deep his love and loyalty ran to his late wife, and how far she'd always been from experiencing a love like that. She certainly hadn't had that with Jack. And she'd never have a chance to experience it with Roman.

"Annette wanted children," he said simply, in a way that made it clear he would have moved heaven and earth to fulfill her wishes. "We agreed we would contact an adoption agency on our first anniversary. Then we delayed it, thinking there would be time after her surgery."

Sable withdrew her arm from his, unsure she could offer comfort right now when she was feeling a hole open up inside her. "I can see why this pregnancy would bring a lot of mixed feelings for you, Roman."

"It doesn't," he said fiercely, his hands clamping on her shoulders as he shifted positions, seating himself in front of her so he could look her in the eye. "There are no mixed feelings about this baby. I will love this child and so will you." He waited a moment, as if allowing her to absorb the weight of that. Then, more gently, he stroked her hair from her face, combing it behind her ear. "I already do."

Her eyes stung. The silence stretched between them until she didn't trust herself to speak for the emotions bubbling up inside her. So she nodded a little frantically in agreement. "Okay," she managed in a raspy whisper as she tried not to cry. "Yes."

Roman took her in with an intense look in his dark eyes, making her wonder what he saw in her expression. She hoped he could only glean her love of their child and not the misplaced envy for his love, which she couldn't have for herself. It was foolish. She was foolish.

"Hormones," she finally said, as a couple of tears slipped free even as she attempted to laugh. "It must be the pregnancy hormones."

Whatever he saw in her face, it seemed to push him to make a decision. He gave a thoughtful nod before he spoke.

"Come on." He stood, took her hands and hauled her

to her feet. "I've heard there's a surefire cure for that. But first I need to know, what's your favorite flavor of ice cream?"

In the week since he'd last spent time with Sable at the Cloisters, Roman's mood had plummeted, getting worse and worse on a daily basis.

Every frustrating hour of that time weighed heavily on his shoulders, a weight he dragged around whether he was seeing properties with his Realtor, taking conference calls with his office in Los Angeles, or reviewing the books for the fashion house in Marcel's cramped back office at Zayn Designs.

Like now.

Parked behind his temporary desk, scrolling through his brother's business expenses on the computer, he could hear the easy rapport between Marcel and his assistants—Sable included—filtering through the open door. It made no sense that Roman felt a surge of jealousy every time Marcel teased a laugh out of Sable, the musical sound stirring equal parts gratitude for her happiness and possessiveness that he hadn't been the man to cause it. The caveman instincts were utterly new to him and unique to his relationship with Sable. He told himself it was because she was carrying his child.

There could be no other reason to account for the tangled-up reactions he hadn't even experienced with Annette, a woman he loved more than life.

Scowling, he ignored the latest round of laughter floating over the strains of a Duke Ellington song. The theme of the day seemed to be jazz and big band music.

Roman had no idea what they were working on in the design studio now that it was past five o'clock on a Friday, but it sounded a whole lot more fun than reviewing endless columns of poorly organized numbers, many of which struck him as unnecessary expenditures.

"Sotheby's Auction House?" Roman called through the door, needing clarification on a staggeringly costly purchase.

"Original artwork for the flagship store," Marcel shouted back, before his voice returned to a normal pitch as he gave instructions to someone about adding more beadwork to a gown.

Roman's head pounded at the response, since Marcel didn't even have a property purchased for his store, let alone a finalized business plan for a dedicated retail space. Roman wanted Zayn Designs to be a global success—needed for it to be since he'd invested much of his personal savings into financing the venture—but his brother refused half of Roman's business advice. It made him question why he bothered remaining in New York when Marcel ignored his counsel and Sable found excuses to avoid him ever since his revelation about Annette.

Had Sable been spooked by the fact that he'd been married before? He failed to see how that affected their relationship. Sable had been married to someone else before they met, too, so if anything, it put them on more equal footing. But what else could account for the radio silence all week? It had been tough as hell to leave her at her apartment door without so much as a kiss good-night after their day together, but he'd forced himself to do so. He'd hoped that by respecting her boundaries, taking a break from the ever-present chemistry, he'd get her to trust him more.

But damned if he didn't feel more alienated from her than ever.

Closing the laptop with a muttered curse, Roman threw the plan to keep his distance out the window and charged out of the office into the studio. He needed to see Sable.

Now. Tonight.

When he reached the open workspace, however, his feet stalled as he took in the scene in front of him.

A slender model, who couldn't have been much older than fifteen, stood on the raised dais in front of a bank of windows. She wore a flame-red gown with a highly structured, asymmetrical design. One shoulder was bare, the other supported a decorative flourish that came to an exaggerated point beside her left ear. At the young woman's feet, Marcel and Sable sat together on the platform, heads bent together as they examined the dress's hem, comparing it to fabric swatches in Sable's hand.

Beside his tall, powerfully built brother, Sable looked absurdly feminine, with her soft curves encased in a pink cotton dress. Her wavy dark hair almost tipped onto Marcel's shoulder as she tilted her head to view a swatch from another angle. And damned if the sight of her so close to his sibling didn't make Roman feel short of breath.

It didn't matter that his brother was gay. Or that Roman cared about both of them. He just knew he wanted her close to him instead. Wanted it with a fierceness that put an edge in his voice.

"Sable."

They both turned toward him. He could feel his brother's scrutiny and guessed that Marcel saw more than Roman meant to reveal. But his focus was all for the woman beside his brother. Her color rose slightly at Roman's regard, and whatever she saw in his face caused her smile to falter. Emotion flickered in her hazel gaze. Annoyance? Awareness?

Too late, he remembered that his brother was unaware of their relationship. But there was no calling back Sable's name from Roman's lips now. He withdrew his phone to text his car service so there would be a ride waiting for them downstairs.

"I can finish up here," Marcel said, his attention shifting to Sable as he grabbed a tablet from the floor at the model's feet. "You've worked late every night this week, Sable. We can pick up with up my notes on accessories on Monday."

She frowned, her gaze darting between the two brothers before returning to the designer. "Are you sure? What about the fitting?"

"I'm almost done. And Cara can help me with the last dress." Marcel waved over one of the women at his drafting table who'd been looking at sketches.

The petite Black woman with long braids piled on her head rushed to his side and sank down beside him.

Sable passed her colleague the fabric swatches before she moved toward Roman, her pink skirt swishing with the subtle sway of her hips. Now he could read the frustration in her expression. A simmering emotion that bordered on anger.

"Yes?" She bit out the word while retrieving her handbag from a low couch.

Seeing her bend over the seat back, her curves pressing the fabric of her skirt, didn't do a thing to ease his need to have her next to him. His hands itched for the feel of her, for the chance to slide up her legs and explore the softness beneath her dress.

"I'd like to speak to you. Privately." His low voice was pure gravel, a direct result of the onslaught of hunger for her that he'd shoved to the back burner all week.

Hell, it had been longer than that, since he hadn't even touched her the last time they'd been together. The fascination with her only grew when he tried to ignore it.

Her jaw worked, revealing her resistance to how he'd called her away from her work, but she gave a short nod. He guessed she simply didn't want to discuss anything more with him while they had an audience. Now he had to hope she didn't bolt when they reached the street.

"Have a good weekend, you two," Marcel called over his shoulder, his tone so casual an observer might miss the undertone in his voice that let Roman know he hadn't missed the byplay.

That he'd expect answers about what was going on between his brother and his stylist intern.

Well, damn.

With their relationship effectively outed, Roman couldn't resist resting his hand at the small of Sable's back as they moved toward the elevator. He felt her tense, and nearly withdrew the touch.

But it was a good thing he didn't because then he would have missed her shiver. A swift, sweet undulation of her spine that called to the heat simmering hotter in his veins. He wasn't alone in this hunger.

Far from it.

When they entered the elevator, there was already an older woman inside, preventing conversation and giving Roman more time to work out what happened next. He hadn't formulated a plan ahead of time, which was unlike him. But he now knew this much—Sable might be avoiding him, but that didn't mean she wasn't aching with the same need he felt. And all at once, he hated that he'd left her alone all week. He could have fulfilled that need for both of them.

One way or another they needed to navigate a relationship, and the chemistry between them wasn't just going to disappear. He'd tried staying away from her enough times to know that for certain.

When they reached street level, he guided her out of the elevator and toward the waiting luxury SUV, a glossy black Escalade that he'd retained for the month. Seeing his intention, she halted outside the vehicle.

"I thought you wanted to talk," she said in her unhurried Southern cadence even though her eyes still snapped with frustration. She pouted, only making her full, bee-stung lips more irresistible.

"We can speak in the car." He let go of her to open the door, gesturing her inside.

She didn't move. "I was going to head home," she explained, wariness replacing her annoyance.

"Haven't you avoided me long enough?" He hooked his hand over the top of the door, prepared to debate this for the chance to spend time with her. "The clock is ticking on those nine months, Sable. We've got a lot to work out, including how we're going to share parenting when you dodge my texts and don't return my calls."

She pursed her lips. "You only called one time," she shot back, though she seemed to let her guard down because she stepped inside the Escalade, sliding across the back seat. "And I knew I'd see you at work, so I didn't see the need to ring you."

He followed her into the vehicle, taking the seat beside her and closing the door. The driver was impassive behind the partition but pulled away from the curb almost immediately; Roman had texted him their destination earlier.

"Right. Because you've been so chatty when I see you at the studio," he reminded her dryly. "You wanted to keep our relationship private, and I tried to respect that—"

"Until today." Folding her arms, she flashed him a look.

"Until today," he agreed easily, hoping she understood why. "When you gave me no easy option for speaking to you without drawing attention to the fact that we know each other outside of work."

For a moment, she didn't answer. She looked out the window as they headed north. Away from the route that would have taken them to her home in Brooklyn.

"Where are we going?" She turned toward him again, her hazel eyes wide, her pulse thrumming rapidly at the base of her neck.

He wanted to stroke that spot. Lick it. Taste it.

But only if her staccato heartbeat was a sign of excitement. He hoped like hell it was.

"I want to feed you dinner," he explained, lifting the hand that rested in her lap and bringing it to his lips. She watched him with rapt attention, her lips parting slightly as he skimmed a kiss along the pulse in her wrist. "I happen to know you worked right through lunch today, so you need to eat now. I'd prefer to cook for you myself, but if you want to go somewhere else we can."

The car stopped for a red light, jolting them slightly, giving him an excuse to wrap his arm around her and pull her toward him. He could feel her breath shudder through her before she released it in a long sigh and nodded.

"Okay. I'll go home with you, Roman. Just for dinner, though."

His own tension eased a fraction at her words. He wanted her to stay well past dinner, but for now, having her with him was enough. He stroked a hand over the back of her dark hair and told himself to be grateful for small victories, even if it might kill him to leave her at her own door tonight without a kiss.

Nine

"Where did you learn to cook like that?" Sable asked an hour later, sipping herbal tea from a sleek white mug as she sat on the sofa in Roman's temporary apartment.

They'd finished the frittata he'd whipped up in a flash after arriving, and she'd been more than a little impressed at his efficiency in the kitchen. She'd tried to help—before and after the meal—but he'd had his own cooking rhythm and insisted he wanted her to relax. Even now, he made short work of loading the dishwasher since he'd cleaned up after himself as he cooked.

Her gaze followed him as he moved around the kitchen with a red dish towel slung over the shoulder of his white dress shirt. The strong, shadowed jaw and hint of olive skin at the base of his throat where his collar remained unbuttoned called to her fingers to stroke him there.

"Marcel and I spent a lot of time with our grandparents while we were growing up. My grandfather made his own fortune, and the equity firm I now oversee is his life's work." He started the dishwasher and then shut off the recessed lights in the kitchen, leaving on two pendants over the breakfast bar. "But my grandmother never lost her connection to simpler things, and she insisted Marcel and I learn how to prepare all her favorite dishes. Mostly traditional Lebanese dishes, but the frittata was something she liked to make for breakfast."

He joined her in the living room, taking a seat on the couch beside her. Feeling his heat so close vividly reminded her of what had happened between them the last time they'd shared this couch. She felt herself blush and ducked her head toward her ginger tea to hide her face. Knowing she should leave once she finished her drink.

But it had been too long since they'd touched each other. Longer still since they'd indulged an even deeper urge. Right now, she felt very aware of every week without him. Pulling her thoughts from the physical, she refocused on Roman's words to ground herself while she recovered her defenses. She knew his parents were celebrated academics who traveled extensively, but she hadn't realized that they'd left Roman and Marcel with their grandparents.

"I don't think your brother has many positive memories of your grandparents," she observed carefully, remembering a cutting comment Marcel had made about his judgmental grandfather in particular.

"With good reason." Roman's dark eyes veered to hers, his tone dust-dry. "Our parents were supportive when Marcel came out as gay at sixteen, but our paternal grandparents were…not. Their behavior drove a wedge into the family that never healed."

That was the impression she'd gotten. Only it was much worse than Roman made it sound. It wasn't her business. And yet, she felt a surge of loyalty for Marcel. She respected his talent and applauded his tireless humanitarian efforts for marginalized people. How dare his own family withdraw love and support from him during such a vulnerable moment in his life?

"Yet you remained close to them in spite of that?" Tensing, she set the mug of ginger tea aside. "Became your grandfather's protégé?"

"I wouldn't categorize the relationship as close, but I also didn't slash them out of my life. They'll never learn tolerance, let alone acceptance, if they're surrounded solely by people who think like they do."

She recognized some validity in his point, but she still didn't like thinking of Roman benefiting from the same family that had shunned Marcel.

Roman shifted on the couch beside her so that he could see her more fully. "Plus, as tempting as it might be to cut all ties with people who hurt my brother, that would have meant seeing our birthright sold off to strangers. Not just mine, but *his*, too. I wouldn't have minded for my own sake, but I'd be damned if I'd see Marcel wounded emotionally and then robbed financially, too." His scowl deepened for a moment before he let out a breath. "He deserved better than that. The stability of the equity firm gave us the capital we needed to build Zayn Designs. You see his talent. He deserves all the help I can give him."

Hearing the obvious pride in his voice soothed some of her ruffled defensiveness. "He's brilliant. Sometimes I have to pinch myself that I get to work so closely with someone who is destined to become a giant in the fashion industry."

"He will be. But first and foremost, he's my brother, and I need to tell him about the baby. Especially after the way we left together this afternoon." Roman's arm stretched along the back of the sofa so that he could twine his fingers in the ends of her hair. A gentle but potent gesture for the awareness it stirred. "I'm not going to deny that I like the idea of people knowing that you're carrying my child."

She met his dark gaze as she heard the hint of possessiveness in his voice. It shouldn't make her senses sizzle like that if they weren't going to have a relationship beyond shared parenting. But that didn't stop the desire from knotting in her belly, or keep her scalp from tingling as he smoothed a lock of hair between his fingers.

"I'm aware that we're reaching the point where I said we could start making plans." She sounded breathless and uncertain, but it was only because his touch made her ache for something she shouldn't want. Forcing herself to take a long breath in an attempt to relax herself, she continued with new steadiness. "The more I read about miscarriages at twelve weeks, the more reassured I am that we've already heard the heartbeat. It's a good sign I never had the first time I was pregnant. Should we tell your brother about the baby together?"

"I think his first reaction will be anger with me, so it might be best for me to speak to him alone until he moves past that." He searched her face, as if making sure she was okay with what he was suggesting. "I'll leave it to you to arrange for a less demanding work schedule."

She wanted to argue with him, to insist she could maintain her workload in order to squeeze all the joy out of what would most likely be her final days in a field she loved. But she knew he only wanted to do what was best for the baby, and so did she. Which meant safeguarding her energy and her health. No doubt she'd been putting in long hours for months, and she needed to be better about respecting her body's limitations.

"All right. That sounds fair," she agreed after a moment, sitting forward on the couch to pick up the mug of tea again.

Her hair fell from his grasp as she leaned forward, breaking their connection.

"Thank you. This is good progress." His strong jaw flexed and relaxed over and over again in the pause afterward, until he finally went on. "Have you given any more thought to moving in with me once I secure an apartment in New York?"

She swallowed hard against the indecision that welled inside her. "Roman—"

He plowed right over the rest of her words, laying out his case. "I've already looked at some spaces, and have a few four-bedrooms in mind that might work well.

There's one available in this building, but I wasn't sure how you felt about being that close to my parents once they return to town."

"Four bedrooms?" She couldn't even imagine what something like that cost in Manhattan. The building they were in was one of the most expensive in the city.

"We'd need a third for a nursery, and I thought a fourth would be wise so that we'd have an option for live-in help."

She was already shaking her head at the thought of residing in such close proximity to Roman. Just seeing him this evening felt fraught with tension as she battled her own urges. What would it be like to see him daily, in a private, intimate setting like a home where he might walk around the house without a shirt on?

Roman frowned, stroking along her arm. "Don't dismiss the idea until we see what it's like to have a newborn. You might be glad for a part-time nanny—"

"No." She shook her head more, pulling herself to her feet with the need to excise the jittery, anxious energy running through her. "I'm not arguing about the idea of live-in help. I'm saying no to living together. It won't work, Roman."

She took a lap around the windows of the curved great room, staying close to the perimeter where she could look out at the view of the city instead of the compelling man on the sofa. Her heels tapped softly over the hardwood.

She felt Roman's gaze follow her.

"It won't work to be in the same physical space as our child, so that there are at least two of us to answer the baby's needs, if not three? It's an exhausting business for the first year, Sable. This way we wouldn't be shuttling the baby around the city. Think how much safer and healthier it is for the child to be in one place." He hadn't moved from his spot on the sofa, giving her space to process what he was saying.

"You make it sound so reasonable. So easy." She reached the dining table in her pacing route and paused to look at him, his strong profile backlit by the skyline view behind him. "But since I could never afford my share of that lifestyle, I wouldn't feel at home—"

"You're bringing a child into the world. I think that more than evens out what we're offering." The deep sound of sincerity in his voice exerted a magnetic pull on her, drawing her inexorably toward this man.

"A child you never asked for or expected," she reminded him, folding her arms to try and shield herself from that pull.

"Neither did you, but here we are, and we both want the same thing. To be a part of this baby's life. To know the joys of being a parent." He rose to his feet, and her heart thudded harder with each footstep he took toward her. He stopped mere inches from her, his fingers reaching up to stroke over her cheek. "I told you about losing my wife. I thought the chance to be a father died with her since I'll never marry again."

Sable's breath caught sharply at the stark admission of his love for another woman. But she stifled the gasp, biting her lip to hold it back while his thumb caressed the soft place under her chin. When he spoke again, his voice was as persuasive as that touch.

"You're giving me something far more precious than any piece of real estate."

Despite all her efforts to reinforce her defenses around this man, Sable felt them melt into a puddle. Or maybe she was the one doing the melting. Everything inside her went soft and warm under the combined spell of his words and his light stroke over her skin.

"I never thought about it that way." Was it crazy of her to consider it when the need for him overwhelmed everything else? "Can I let you know at the ultrasound appointment? When I'm not so—"

She should make the decision when she was clear-headed. When she wasn't anticipating the feel of Roman's mouth on hers. The ultrasound was just three days away. Time enough for her to commit to where to go next.

His silken caress paused as he tilted her chin up to look at her. "When you're not so what?"

They were standing close enough now that each time she dragged in a breath, her breasts grazed his chest. The feel of him, hot and solid against her, tantalized her.

"When I'm not under the influence of your touch? Of your hands that I want all over me?" She blurted the truth in a rush.

She'd thought he might kiss her then, crush his lips to hers and end this conversation that had her hormones and emotions swinging wildly. But he only tipped his forehead to hers, wrapping his hand around the back of her neck to encourage her gaze.

His eyes were so dark she could hardly see the brown ring around the rims.

"Okay. But keep in mind that we've already tried staying apart, Sable. We've done that, and it's only brought us right here, breathing each other in, dying to tear each other's clothes off so I can get inside you."

Roman watched Sable, half expecting her to contradict him.

He'd told her what he wanted, after recognizing all her cues that suggested she hungered for the same thing.

But pointing out that they both wanted this was a double-edged sword. For reasons he didn't fully comprehend, she had been avoiding the physical attraction. Even when the need was a red flush in her cheeks, a pulse throbbing double time at the base of her throat, and the rocking of her hips toward his, she was hesitant.

So he held himself very still, watching while her hazel eyes smoked with awareness. Her gaze traveled over him as if she was already imagining him without the barrier of clothing. Heat streaked up his spine.

"Last time we were here," he reminded her, still hoping to draw words from her that would give them both what they craved, "you wondered if intimacy would make it difficult to be objective about what happens next. Do you remember?"

"I do. I still don't have an answer to that." There was a husky quality to her voice that turned him inside out, even as he feared she would retreat from him again.

"All the more reason I need to know what you want to happen tonight." He was already strung tight, and the conversation made it worse. "Should I touch you, so we both feel better? Or take you home now in the hope of…" he ground his teeth in frustration, before forcing himself to finish the thought "…objectivity?"

Her lashes lowered, shutting him out while she seemed to weigh his words. He steeled himself for her answer. For another night without her in his bed.

When she peered up at him again, a determined glint in her eyes told him she'd made her decision.

"I want to stay." She licked her lips, then hauled in a deep breath before admitting in a lower voice, "I need you."

The words leveled him.

No, *she* leveled him.

Right then, he vowed to do everything in his power to make sure she didn't regret sharing that moment of vulnerability. Because damn, hearing the raw truth fed something inside him that he hadn't even realized was starved to hear it.

He wrapped his hands around her waist, pulling her close so her soft curves molded to him. Something about her smelled lemony and sweet. Her hair, maybe. Or her skin. He wanted that fragrance all over him.

"I need you, too," he assured her, stroking up her back to find the zipper of her pink crepe dress. "I've dreamed about touching you every night since that first time." Lowering the zipper, he parted the fabric slowly while he looked into her eyes. "Every. Single. Night."

A shiver trembled through her as the material began to slip off her shoulders.

"My skin—all of me—is so sensitive now." Her lashes fluttered against her cheek. "Just having the dress brush against my body teases me."

Head thrown back, lips parted, she looked like a fantasy with her dress ready to slide off her exquisite curves, glossy dark hair spilling down her back. But with the city lights flooding through the floor-to-ceiling windows, he felt exposed. He wasn't willing to share the sight of this incredible woman with anyone who happened to glance into the apartment's living room.

"I'm going to take care of that. Come with me." Not giving her a chance to answer, he lifted her higher against him, so her feet dangled a few inches from the floor.

He kissed her as he carried her through the apartment to the guest bedroom he'd claimed as his own. The blinds were already lowered, the only light coming from a high-tech chandelier that he dialed to the lowest setting as he set Sable on her feet, never breaking the kiss.

Her fingers worked the buttons of his shirt while he walked her backward toward the low platform bed that dominated the space. He tugged her already loosened dress down and off her body, catching the slippery pink crepe in one hand as she stepped out of it. He draped it over a tan leather chaise that served as the room's only other furniture, then peeled his shirt off the rest of the way. He could see that her gaze was avid even in the half-light, following his every movement.

It felt like forever since he'd touched her, and he couldn't wait another second. Flicking open the clasp of the pink satin bra that hugged her breasts, he took the soft weights in his hands, bringing each to his mouth in turn to kiss, lick and suck. Her back arched, fingers combing restlessly through his hair, holding him where she needed him as her hungry moans fueled a fire already scorching him.

"Please, please, please," she chanted, hips rocking so they pressed tighter to his.

Damn near blinding him with lust.

He hooked a finger in her pink satin panties, dragging them down and off her hips until she was fully naked. It was a sexy vision he knew he would replay often in his mind. But right now, he needed to make her feel good, to take the edge off all the hunger that had mounted over these last weeks.

Lowering himself to sit on the edge of the mattress, he drew Sable down on top of him so she straddled his hips. With a gasp, she rocked against him while he withdrew his wallet from his pants to retrieve the condom he kept there. She stilled his hand before he could open it, however.

"I'm clean," she whispered against his ear. "And already pregnant."

The thought of touching her that way—with zero barrier between them—took hold fast, creating a sharp hunger for something he would have never allowed himself to consider in other circumstances.

"I'm clean, too. You're the only woman I've been with since I was last tested." And then, of course, they'd used a condom.

Even though it hadn't protected her from getting pregnant.

"It's up to you." She let go of his hand, allowing him to decide whether or not to skip the protection. "But I wanted you to know I'm okay with not using anything."

Dropping the condom on the bed, he moved his hand to his fly. She joined her efforts to his, and they freed him a moment later, her fingers circling him. Stroking him.

Just that light touch had him seeing stars every time he blinked. Or maybe it was knowing that he was going to be inside her with nothing to dull the sensation of all that feminine heat.

Gripping her thighs, he lifted her so she was poised over him. Then he lowered her slowly, easing his way inside her until they both groaned at the contact.

She clamped her legs tight around his waist, holding him there while she pressed herself close against him. He licked a path up her neck, the lemon scent of her skin intensifying with the heat of his kiss. She shuddered, the roll of her hips reminding him of her new, height-ened sensitivity. Testing that sensitivity, he molded a breast in his hand, running his thumb back and forth over the taut peak. When her breath caught, he trans-ferred his lips to her nipple, drawing it into his mouth. He used his thumb to trace her feminine folds, circling the tight bud between her legs.

She arched her back so hard he almost stopped, but then the tremors swept through her, her sex pulsing around him with lush squeezes. It would have been so easy to let her release spur his. But he helped her ride out the sensation, giving her a moment to recover her-self before he flipped her underneath him.

She blinked up at him with dazed, passion-filled eyes, her bee-stung lips fuller than ever. Hunger for her surged all over again, the need to claim her a fierce mandate, as if it were written in his DNA.

Holding her hips, he buried himself deep inside her. Over and over. Color rose in her cheeks, and her mouth worked soundlessly before she bit her lower lip. Roman quickly moved to kiss her, gently nipping and sucking on the fullness of her lower lip.

Her fingernails sank into his shoulders, and something about that light sting, as primitive a claim as his own, was what sent him over the edge. The force of his body's response was overpowering, and his hold on her tightened. He couldn't get close enough, and he would have sworn in that moment she felt the same way, with her limbs wound around his neck and his waist, her breasts molded to his chest.

Their shouts mingled, breaths huffing harshly in sync.

His heart hammered in his chest like it needed out, but his senses slowly returned. Closing his eyes, he rolled to his side, bringing Sable with him. He tucked her close to his chest and drew a corner of the lightweight duvet over her, covering her from shoulder to knee. As their pulses slowed, he brushed her dark hair from her face, combing lightly through the strands with his fingers.

She made a satisfied hum in her throat, a sound he wasn't even sure she was aware of as she cuddled closer. Something about that soft note of contentment crawled into his consciousness, taunting him with all he could never give her.

Did it matter that he wanted to provide for their child and give her a home when he couldn't offer her the love and commitment he'd shared with his wife? Four bedrooms in one of the city's most coveted apartments didn't seem like much compared to the daily joys of a partner who could offer her love and commitment.

If he couldn't give her that, was it even fair of him to ask her to move in with him?

A chill crept over him at the thought that he was being selfish to try to convince her to stay in New York for his convenience. So that he could know his child and help to raise him or her.

He hated to think what she would be missing out on. Especially since she hadn't been as fortunate as him in her first marriage. She hadn't known the kind of deep and abiding love he'd shared with Annette, so it would be all the more cruel of him to expect her to live with him when he knew he couldn't give her those things.

Her soft, even breaths slowed, falling into the cadence of sleep. And Roman was grateful that she wasn't awake to witness the churn of emotions he wrestled with now. Because whether or not it was fair of him to ask her to move in with him, he still wanted to. Needed to have his child and heir in close proximity.

His only hope was that Sable savored her independence as much as he needed his. Maybe then, they could live together and raise a child together without anyone getting hurt.

Any other alternative was unacceptable. He'd already lost too much to lay his heart on the line again.

Ten

Standing in front of her bedroom closet two days later, Sable still had no idea whether she should say yes to moving in with Roman or not. She stared at the calendar on her phone, where a reminder had just popped up about the twelve-week ultrasound appointment scheduled for the next day. She'd told Roman she'd get back to him with an answer by then, but she was still just as confused as ever.

Maybe more so since the unforgettable night she'd spent in his bed.

With a sigh, she tugged a few Zayn Designs sample dresses from the closet and began to pull the protective bags off the hangers. She was preparing for an impromptu social media photo shoot with her housemates. Blair and Tana had agreed to the idea as a creative group project, and Sable hoped it would give her an opportunity to tell her friends the news that she needed to move out of the house.

Was she giving up on her dream of being a celebrity stylist too easily if she opted to go back home to Baton Rouge to have her baby? Or was it a smart move to relocate where she would have a more affordable lifestyle as well as the love and support of her family during a time of tremendous change? It might be easier to decide if her feelings for Roman weren't so complicated. But the more time they spent together, the more she found to like about him.

His obvious concern for the baby was extremely compelling, of course. But there were other things that called to her, like the way he put her in charge of where she wanted their relationship to go, never taking advantage of her obvious attraction to him. She liked that he championed her career dreams, reminding her of her goals outside of motherhood. As much as she craved the chance to be a parent, she recognized that her yearning was tangled up with her past. It was so difficult not to fear for this pregnancy every moment of every day. She was grateful to Roman for challenging her to look beyond this pregnancy to ensure she put a value on her work.

The notes of an electric violin solo grew louder outside her bedroom door, warning her that music lover Tana was approaching.

"You're next in the makeup chair," Tana called as she reached the fourth floor of their Brooklyn brownstone. A moment later, the petite actress stepped across

Sable's threshold dressed in black booty shorts and a worn T-shirt with a rainbow outlined in rhinestones. She wore red clip-in braids today, but her understated makeup showed off flawless skin. "Blair already did my face, but I drew the line at letting her touch my hair. Do you mind if I leave my braids in for the photo?"

"Of course not." Standing, Sable passed her the hangers with Marcel's dresses before grabbing a pair of silver sandals for herself. "I like the idea of a photo of us all because we'd each look so different in the clothes."

Tana arched an eyebrow at her before heading toward the door to go downstairs. "So it's fine that Blair will look like a *Vogue* cover while I rock more of a 'Tinker Bell on an acid trip' vibe?"

Following Tana to the parlor, Sable laughed, grateful for the distraction from her worries about what to tell Roman and where to raise her baby. "Personally, I'd call it music festival glam. But that's the beauty of using real people in social media images for the brand. Followers with all different aesthetics can see how the clothes could work for them."

They reached the parlor floor where Blair had two fishing tackle boxes open on a wooden sideboard between two windows overlooking the backyard. She had dragged one of the living room chairs to the window for better light. Blair was currently studying what looked like smudges of lipstick in various colors on the backs of her hands.

"Cool. But don't stop there," Tana cautioned as she passed a cream-colored sheath dress to Blair. "You need more diversity in the Zayn Designs feed. You've done a good job with skin tones, but what about showcasing more kinds of figures? And people who are differently abled?"

"You're right." Sable appreciated the feedback and tapped a note into her phone as she sat in the makeup chair by the window. "That's important to Marcel, too. I'll remind him we need samples in more sizes. And thank you both for doing this."

"Are you kidding?" Blair said, digging in one of the tackle boxes and pulling out a sleek black case containing a compact. "This is like grown-up playtime for me."

"Even though you do this every day for work?" Sable asked, curious to know more about her friends before life pulled them apart.

Blair nodded as she swirled a brush through the powder inside the compact and then patted it onto Sable's cheek. "I got into makeup because I always liked sprucing up my friends and making them feel pretty. But in the last few years, pursuing it as a profession, I don't have as many opportunities to do faces just for fun. It's nice not to have an exacting client breathing down my neck telling me to erase someone's freckles or fill in scars."

While Sable mused over that, Tana pulled her T-shirt off and slid one of the Zayn slip dresses over her head. As she wiggled the silk into place, she strode closer. "Is Lucas Deschamps one of those exacting bosses?"

Blair's mouth pulled into a frown before she answered, "Lucas and I have very different visions. He believes makeup should be like fashion, and you should introduce a new look each season with all of the brand supporting the look. I happen to like faces that tell a story, and think sometimes makeup should take a back seat to the face."

Sable and Tana exchanged a look at their friend's uncharacteristically grim tone.

"Maybe there's a middle ground in there somewhere," Tana suggested carefully before she pirouetted in her cream-colored slip dress. "And this is the most gorgeous outfit I've ever worn, by the way. You must get along well with your boss, Sable, for him to trust you with all these great clothes."

Blair glanced up from an eye shadow palette. "Was that your boss who picked you up outside the brownstone two weeks ago? I saw you get into an SUV with a really hot guy wearing shades that first day I toured the house with Cybil."

"A hot guy?" Tana leaned a hip on the makeup table. "Do tell."

This was it. The time had come to tell them about Roman and the baby. Nerves knocked around inside her, but she pressed ahead.

"That wasn't the designer. That was Roman Zayn, Marcel's brother." She felt her cheeks warm for no good reason. She wasn't embarrassed by their relationship. "He handles the business end of the fashion house."

"But has he handled *you*?" Tana asked while Blair squealed with delight at the question.

Sable struggled to find the right way to admit their relationship without making it sound completely inappropriate. "Any and all handling was mutual."

Blair stopped working on Sable's face to gape at her. "I knew there was a hot vibe there when I saw you two together. I knew it."

"Is he the reason for the prenatal vitamins you left in the kitchen cupboard?" Tana pressed.

"Oh no." Sable dropped her head into her hands. "Did I honestly do that?"

So much for trying to find a tactful way to share the news. Clearly her pregnancy brain was broadcasting the news for her without her knowing.

"Seriously?" Blair knelt in front of her, forehead knit in concern as she rested a hand on Sable's knee. "Are you really…expecting?"

Deep breath. Her life would change forever once she said the words.

"Yes. I'm twelve weeks along. And it's a good thing. It's just that it was totally unexpected and I'm having to make a lot of decisions about what to do next." She'd done a half-hearted search for apartments in Baton Rouge, but she couldn't see herself back there, raising her baby alone while her ex-husband lived nearby with his new wife and growing family.

Blair sat on her heels, brushing aside her blond ponytail. "What kinds of decisions? Can we help?"

Briefly, she outlined the pros and cons of Roman's proposal that she move in with him versus returning to Louisiana. The biggest drawback of life in Baton Rouge, of course, would be watching her career dreams go up in smoke.

Tana twirled one of her red clip-in braids around her finger. "Why wouldn't you just stay here? I like babies." She glanced over at Blair. "Chances are good that Blair likes babies."

Blair nodded vigorously in the affirmative at this statement. "We'll help you. That way you can finish your internship, and go back to work when you're ready. On your own terms."

Touched beyond measure at their kindness, Sable blinked away happy tears at the vision of remaining in the apartment. "As amazing as that sounds, I'm pretty sure Cybil will want me to leave the apartment if I'm not actively pursuing a career in one of the creative fields—"

"But you are," Tana argued, folding her arms, and speaking with a new fierceness. "The whole idea behind this apartment house was to support single women trying to get ahead in artistic careers. Well, guess what? Pregnancy is part of a woman's life, and we're going to support you through that until you can return to your work. If Cybil doesn't like that, she can kick all of us to the curb."

Tana's impassioned speech was such a surprise there was a moment of silence afterward. But Blair recovered first, giving it a slow clap that turned into full-fledged cheers and wolf whistles that made Tana roll her eyes.

As for Sable, she was so overcome by the generosity of her new friends that she hardly knew what to say.

"Thank you," she finally said, recovering her voice even though there was still a lump in her throat. "Without a doubt, that's the coolest, sweetest offer anyone has ever made me." She stood up and surprised Tana with a hug. Then, before she could offer one to Blair, Blair joined them for a group hug.

The gift of friends having her back—very literally

at the moment—provided her a much-needed confidence boost.

"Cybil won't object to this, by the way," Blair said as they broke apart. "She might use it as publicity when she goes to search for the next round of candidates when we move out—a way to show off girl power in action—but she wouldn't try to kick you out of the building just because you're pregnant."

"You don't think so?" Sable hadn't reread all the fine print on the contract she'd signed when she moved in, but had just assumed it would be a huge imposition on the other women in the house to have a baby take up residence.

But Tana and Blair seemed adamant. Excited, even.

"Not a chance." Blair gestured to the makeup chair, wordlessly inviting Sable to sit back down. "We spoke for a long time the day she gave me the tour of the house, and she reminisced about her days of living in the Barbizon Hotel. She made the closest friendships of her life there, and that's what she hoped to foster here, too. She'll think this is cool."

"What will Lucas think?" Tana pondered aloud, in a laughably obvious ploy to get a rise out of Blair.

Blair took the bait without a second thought. "Like everything else in life, he'll probably think he could do it better, faster and more efficiently," she snapped. "But clearly, no one cares what he thinks."

"Clearly." Tana winked at Sable before her expression turned serious. "The bigger question is what Roman will say once he knows he's lost his leverage to get you to move in with him."

Leverage?

Her friend's more cynical view of Roman's motives troubled her. Sable had viewed his offer as generous. But even he had reminded her that by having his child, she was bringing more to the equation than he was. Was it possible that he was trying to use his wealth and power to maneuver her into a position that suited him best?

Certainly. But she couldn't fault him when he didn't have to make the offer to begin with. He could have simply sent her child support and walked away. She fully believed that he wanted to be a part of this baby's life.

And a small part of her even felt a twinge of guilt that he wouldn't have as much time with their infant if she accepted the offer to remain in the brownstone. But bottom line, she needed to make a decision that wasn't just good for the baby, but for herself, too.

"I don't know what Roman will say," Sable finally mused aloud, after Tana had moved off to set up the backdrop for the group photo.

Blair heard her, though, and paused between coats of mascara to look into Sable's eyes.

"If he's a good man, he'll put the mother of his child first," Blair told her firmly. "He'll understand that you need to live where you're most comfortable."

Sable agreed in theory. But she still felt a knot in her chest at the thought of telling Roman her potential new plan. Because no matter how much sense it made, she recognized how the separation from his baby would hurt him.

She would be lying if she pretended that it wouldn't

affect her, too. But that was what happened when you developed feelings for someone—their pain was yours.

And that was when she understood the truth. Despite her best intentions, she was falling for Roman. Hard. What a sad, hurtful moment to realize how close she was to loving a man who could never return those feelings.

Seated in the courtyard of a vacant Broome Street storefront the next day, Roman stole a glance at his watch to make sure he budgeted himself enough time to get uptown for Sable's ultrasound appointment. His brother and their Realtor were still inside the building, reviewing the space and making notes on how it could work for a Zayn Designs flagship store.

Roman had set up the showing since he'd been tracking Manhattan real estate closely over the last two weeks, and he'd seen the SoHo location come on the market the night before. And while he absolutely wanted to secure a prime storefront for Zayn Designs, his motive might have also been driven by a need to get back in his brother's good graces after Marcel's reaction to the news that Sable was expecting Roman's baby.

Scrolling through his phone while he waited for Marcel to finish up, Roman heard Marcel's damning words in his head.

Of all the women in this city, you had to take up with the best stylist I have? A woman who has single-handedly tripled the Zayn social media outreach when that wasn't even in her job description?

Roman hadn't been aware of the impact she'd had on the brand. Not that it would have made a difference since his attraction to Sable wasn't something he could have ignored. But Marcel had taken it as a personal affront that Roman had initiated a relationship with someone in their employ. Even worse, Marcel had anticipated what a baby would mean for Sable's hours on the job, even though Roman hadn't asked him to consider lightening her schedule. Marcel had warned Roman that he would need Sable to meet her work obligations.

The argument had only grown more heated from there. Thankfully, Sable had been scheduled for a job off-site on a two-day shoot with an Italian magazine spotlighting new American designers, so she hadn't been subjected to the tension in the Zayn studio.

"Roman." Marcel stepped out into the courtyard through the back door of the vacant shop. Hands shoved in the pockets of black jeans, he stopped just outside the double doors, crossing one loafer in front of the other as he leaned against the doorframe. "The Realtor asked us to lock up when we leave. He had another appointment. I know you do, too."

A hint of bitterness shaded Marcel's words at the reference to the ultrasound appointment.

Leaning back in his chair, Roman observed his brother warily. He had no wish to revisit the arguments of the day before. "What do you think of the space?"

"It's ideal. I'm sure it will get snapped up in a hurry, probably for the full asking price." Marcel's eye roamed over the courtyard surrounded by low brick walls. The surrounding buildings were taller with even higher fences, but that didn't detract from the patch of open sky overhead.

"We can at least make an offer. I'll text the Realtor to get the ball rolling." Roman thumbed in a number on his phone and hit Send.

Marcel nodded his approval, but continued in a stern tone. "I want you to know that I'm going to offer Sable the apartment at the studio."

Roman's gaze flew to his brother's. "What?"

He had to have misheard. Misunderstood. Surely Marcel wouldn't undermine Roman's efforts to build a relationship with his child by enticing Sable into an alternative housing situation.

"I don't use that apartment very often, so it won't be an inconvenience to have her there. And I can't abide the possibility that she'd leave New York before the internship ends just because she can't afford to stay. She's too valuable to me and to the brand."

Resentment burst inside Roman like a firework. "Screw the brand, Marcel. Don't you think she's far more valuable to me as the mother of my child?"

His brother arched an eyebrow. "If that's the case, I would think you'd be all the more grateful for the chance to keep her in the city instead of watching her jet off a thousand miles away to raise your baby without you."

Just the thought of that happening made him ill. Would she really consider such a drastic move simply to avoid living with him? He remembered how she'd felt in his arms three nights ago, how she'd trusted him with her body and her pleasure. Surely he hadn't been alone in the sense that they were right together? They didn't need to tangle up their emotions when they had a smart plan that was mutually beneficial for their future.

"Sable isn't going to leave New York." He'd been confident she'd see the wisdom of living together. And she was supposed to give him an answer this afternoon at the appointment. "She's going to move in with me because she wants to do what's best for our child."

"What about what's best for her?" Marcel gave him a narrow look. "She was already married to one selfish jackass who couldn't look beyond his own needs to ensure her happiness. She doesn't need another."

Roman hung onto his temper with both hands, unwilling to cross swords with his brother again. "How is it selfish to offer her a real home here, with space for her and her child, and a man by her side who's as invested in caring for the baby as she would be?"

"Wealth doesn't solve every problem, Roman. Trust me when I tell you that it doesn't even begin to make up for a lack of love." The words lingered in the air between them, so thick with old hurts it became obvious that there was more on Marcel's mind than just concern for Sable.

Was this his brother's way of telling him that he resented Roman's continued dealings with their grandfather? The thought rocked him, forcing him to question how he'd spent the last decade.

"Are you suggesting I should have walked away from Zayn Equity? Even when that income has financed every aspect of the fashion house?" A helicopter flew over the building, casting a brief shadow on them both.

Marcel blew out a long breath. "Forget it."

"I damned well won't." Roman shot to his feet, needing answers. "If I'd known you viewed my work with the equity firm as disloyal to you for even a second, I would have never taken a role there. And if you still do, I'll submit my resignation this afternoon."

Marcel studied him for a moment. Then, perhaps recognizing that Roman meant every word, he shook his head. "No. I might have seen it that way a few times over the years on days Granddad has been particularly brutal in his disregard for me. But I understand your reasons, and appreciate that your work has ensured we had the capital to start Zayn Designs."

"Yet you don't believe I have Sable's best interests at heart." Roman knew without looking at his watch that he needed to leave now if he wanted to make it to the ultrasound appointment on time.

He pulled open the door to return to the storefront so they could lock up behind them.

Marcel followed him inside before he spoke again. "I think you're too concerned with not having your heart broken again to recognize that you're going to push away an incredible woman if you don't get your act together."

Marcel had it all wrong. It wasn't concern for his heart that kept Roman from Sable, but his promise to Annette. Bottom line, that didn't make a difference when the outcome was still that Roman kept Sable at arm's length.

They could kiss, touch and turn each other inside out with shared passion. They could even raise a child together. But none of that changed the truth that he'd promised his heart to another.

He just hoped it didn't push away Sable for good.

Eleven

As she lay on the exam table in the imaging room, Sable kept her eyes on the screen projecting a black-and-white image of their baby. A tech in purple scrubs rolled the transducer over Sable's belly, sometimes increasing the pressure to enhance the picture or take a particular measurement. Ten minutes into the scan, all the signs were normal, with the tech pointing out the developmental cues she was looking for as she worked.

Sable relaxed enough to glance over at Roman on the other side of the exam table, his gaze rapt as he watched the screen. She'd sensed tension in him today when they'd met in the outer office, but he had side-stepped her questions, insisting they could talk later.

As if she wasn't already nervous enough about telling him she was considering remaining in the Brooklyn brownstone with her friends. Certainly, he would understand. But she knew he would be disappointed because he seemed to genuinely want this baby as much as she did. His sense that this would be his only chance to be a parent was sure to give him a good relationship with the child. But it made it more difficult to distinguish his concern for his heir from his feelings for her.

As of now? She could only assume she didn't figure into his future in any role beyond mother of his child. And the sooner they both accepted as much, the easier it would be to forge a new relationship based on shared parental concerns instead of shared passion.

To support that goal, she really needed to end their physical relationship.

"How are you doing?" Roman asked, his gaze suddenly focused on her.

Even that simple concern made her heart flutter. Especially since it was accompanied by a warm squeeze of her hand. He stroked the backs of her knuckles with his thumb, and used his free hand to smooth her hair from her forehead.

And that quickly, his touch threatened her resolve. How much easier would it be to simply let him take charge of the housing? To rely on him to help her prepare for the new arrival, and to share in the caregiving? But she knew where that kind of relationship would lead. Right back to the feelings of worthlessness she'd battled when Jack had left her.

It was one thing to rely on a man who was supposed to love you. But Roman had been very clear that he wouldn't be that man.

"I'm fine," she assured him, even though she was far from it.

Even though she could already tell how deeply she would miss his touch. Their relationship had rushed forward with heated intensity, the pregnancy only adding to the bond. She ached at the thought of losing that connection, but the longer she let herself feel this way about him, the harder it would be to walk away. And she couldn't imagine how she'd ever know or trust his real motivation for having her in his life.

"I can't believe how much the baby is moving." His gaze briefly flicked back to the screen before returning to her, a hint of wonder in the dark depths of his eyes. "You don't feel that?"

She shook her head, smiling at the sight of the squirming little figure on the screen. "Not even a little. I think I read most first-time mothers don't feel the baby move until week sixteen or later."

"That's going to be an incredible moment for you when you do." He lowered his head to brush a kiss across her temple, voice dropping for her ears alone. "I hope I'm touching you when it happens."

A pleasurable shiver stole over her, quickly followed by a genuine chill as she remembered the conversation they needed to have after the appointment. The thought made it difficult to focus on the rest of the ultrasound, although she tuned in enough to savor the news that her baby was growing normally and continued to thrive, a blessing she could still barely believe was really happening.

Twenty minutes later, after putting back on the floral

pencil skirt and red puff-sleeve blouse she'd worn for what she suspected would be the last time during her pregnancy, Sable accepted the arm Roman offered her as he accompanied her down the elevator and outside.

"How should we celebrate a successful and healthy twelve weeks?" he asked as they stepped out into the late-afternoon sunshine. "Dinner? Shopping for cribs? It's not too early to think about what you want in a nursery."

His enthusiasm for the baby pierced her heart. For a moment, she allowed herself to imagine what it would be like to share those milestones with Roman at her side. How different today would be if she could simply say yes. She could imagine Roman comparing car seat features with her by day, then delivering toe-curling orgasms by night. But commitment to their child—even when combined with commitment to her pleasure—wasn't the same as love for *her*.

And the sooner her traitorous body got the message, the better off she'd be.

"We're close to the park." She pointed toward the Seventy-Second Street entrance, remembering the cherry trees she'd used as a backdrop for some photos the month before. "Do you mind if we walk around a little? I've been cooped up indoors all day."

"Sure." He agreed easily enough, but she didn't miss the flash of wariness in his dark eyes before he escorted her across Fifth Avenue and into Central Park.

They made small talk for a few minutes, discussing what parts of the park they'd seen. Since Sable was new to New York City and Roman spent more of his time on the West Coast, they still had a lot to explore.

The Cherry Hill Fountain was in sight when she asked him about his home in Los Angeles. Even though she needed to break their romantic connection, she still wanted to know about Roman's family and his home since their child would undoubtedly spend time there. Without her.

Sable's heart squeezed.

"My place is in Malibu now, so I can be near the water." He hooked his arm around her waist as they passed a group of schoolkids, all dressed in matching T-shirts, touring the park. "My grandparents lived in Anaheim when Marcel and I were growing up. Our parents had a little place in Westwood, close to the university, but we didn't spend much time there since they traveled so much."

"Malibu?" She didn't know her West Coast geography very well, but she had a vision of crashing surf and beautiful sunsets. How welcome would she be there once she told Roman that she didn't want to live together? Would he stop wooing her?

"It's a long way from the city—in miles and in mindset. I keep an apartment downtown in case I need to be in the office on back-to-back days, but for the most part, I work from home." He guided them toward a vacant bench near the fountain with its wide granite pool.

A group of joggers and a bicyclist swooped around the circular concourse, but other than that they were alone. A few couples and families played on Cherry Hill overlooking Bow Bridge and the Ramble. The view was so pretty and rural she could almost forget they were in uptown Manhattan.

But she couldn't afford to forget why they were here. She'd purposely chosen a public place to explain to him why they couldn't continue a romantic entanglement. She hoped the outdoor venue would serve as a reminder that she shouldn't kiss and touch him anymore.

"That sounds nice," she admitted as she took a seat on the wrought iron bench, musing on his life on the other side of the country. A life she'd never be a part of, even though her child would be.

"I hope you'll take advantage of it once you're ready to resume working." He sat close to her, his arm draped over the bench behind her back, his palm a warm weight on her shoulder. "It would be ideal for your work as a celebrity stylist since you'd have a couple of home bases you could work from."

His thoughtful concern for her future twisted in her chest, making it hard to breathe.

She needed to tell him about her new plans. Delaying would only make things more complicated. Would only put her heart at greater risk.

"That's kind of you to suggest," she began carefully, closing her eyes for a moment as she drew in a steadying breath. Then, she forced herself to meet his dark gaze. "But I've given it a lot of consideration, and I really think it's better that we keep our households separate."

In the aftermath of her declaration, the sounds of squealing children playing Frisbee and the rhythmic thump of a jogger's sneakers hitting the pavement seemed out of sync. Off-kilter. Roman stared at her, his forehead wrinkled as he took in the words.

His hand on her shoulder tensed. "Meaning you don't want to move into a shared apartment with me? Or are you still contemplating a return to Louisiana?"

Concern laced his voice. Tension. She needed to rip the Band-Aid off this painful conversation.

"My housemates offered to help me with the baby. They insist I can still live in the brownstone so I can finish my internship." She felt a burst of pride that her friends had extended the offer. She wasn't alone. She needed to remind herself of that as her heart ached over giving up moving in with Roman.

"And you would rather your friends care for our child when you're not around than me? The child's father?" He spoke with slow deliberateness that made her realize how very still he'd gone. Pain flashed in his eyes.

Empathy tugged at her, warning her this wouldn't be easy for him to accept.

"We'll still share custody of course—"

"Without question." The brusque words reminded her how much he wanted this child. The protective instinct ran deep for them both.

She shifted on the bench to face him, taking another approach. "But I need people around me to support *me*, Roman."

"And you think I wouldn't do that?" He spread his arms wide, a gesture that somehow emphasized how ludicrous he found the suggestion.

"I'm sure you would try, but I need more than support, okay?" She hadn't wanted to spell it out so baldly, afraid of how desperate it made her seem. But she knew he'd never give her what she needed most, and she was equally sure he understood that it wasn't within his capability to give. "If I don't have the love of my family to help me as a single parent, I at least need the love of friends."

"Love." His arms fell back to his sides, his shoulders drooping as if under an enormous weight.

And didn't that speak volumes about how hopeless it was for her to ever imagine him giving her that valuable commodity?

Her chest hurt. Her eyes stung. And her heart broke.

"It nearly killed me to realize that I married a man who chose me only because I checked the right boxes for the kind of life he wanted. And when I stopped checking an important box—the baby-making requirement—I was as disposable as yesterday's news." She'd fought back, though, and recovered a new life for herself.

She wouldn't sacrifice that now. For herself. And to model strength for her child.

"Please don't compare me to a man who couldn't appreciate you for all you have to offer, Sable." The anguish in his voice—in his eyes—was real. "I told you that you shouldn't shortchange your dreams. I would make sure you had the resources you need to return to your work. Hell, I just told you to come to Malibu once you're ready—"

"And I'm so grateful for that. You were the one who made me see that I couldn't go back to Baton Rouge just because I craved the love of my family during a challenging time. You helped me see the consequences of compromising too much of myself, and I can't thank you enough for making me see that." She was a stronger woman for knowing him.

His hand clenched and unclenched where it rested on his knee, and his voice sounded hollow when he spoke again. "But that doesn't mean you want to live with me. Even knowing we'll both see our child less this way."

Her chest ached at the thought, a heavy sorrow weighing her down that they couldn't be the family she'd dreamed of having. But she was doing the best she could.

She spoke a last, futile hope out loud before she could think better of it. "If I thought there was any chance that love might grow between us one day—"

At the dark look in his eyes, the rest of the words dried up. Her hopes withered along with them.

"My brother was right," he said finally, scrubbing a hand over his face. "Marcel said that wealth doesn't make up for a lack of love. Apparently, a portfolio is all I've got to offer anyone."

They must have walked out of the park soon afterward, but Sable didn't remember much from the rest of their time together. Roman had a car pick them up outside the park, and he saw her safely back to the brownstone where he said something about a contract that would formalize a custody arrangement.

When he dropped her off, she stared up at the apartment building that had once represented all her hopes and dreams of a new life. Now it would be the haven she would return to, when she brought her baby home from the hospital. Alone. Tears threatened as the image blurred in front of her eyes.

She didn't look back as she walked up the front steps. Not after the way Roman had shut down at the mention of love between them. His reaction had told her more clearly than any words that she'd been wise to break things off between them before she was irretrievably in love with him. Except, from the way hurt cracked her insides now, Sable knew she'd been too late.

She loved Roman.

And he'd all but admitted there wasn't a chance in hell he'd ever love her back.

Drained, Roman returned to his parents' vacant New York apartment for the last time to clear out his things, knowing he couldn't remain in Manhattan when Sable didn't want him in her life.

He called his Realtor to put his search for an apartment on hold since there was no rush to set up his place. He would still get something to facilitate seeing his child, of course, and living in the same city as Sable made the most sense. All that damn money gave him options. But he wouldn't be her unwelcome shadow for the next twenty-eight weeks, even though he already missed her.

And not just in his bed.

He already missed holding her hand. Hearing about her day. And he missed the chance to feel his child move in her belly, along with a whole host of moments he wouldn't get to be a part of now.

It had been five years and three months since he'd felt

this empty and alone. A thought which had him opening his laptop at the kitchen counter, seeking a hidden
file that he rarely let himself open.

Inside the file were old photos. Pictures of his life
with Annette back when he'd been a different man. A
better man, who had more to offer than a fat bank account.

He'd forgotten how blue her eyes were. Maybe because Sable's were hazel and that was the color he saw
in his dreams now. Was that so wrong? So disloyal?

His vow to love Annette forever hadn't just been
some wishful youth's romantic thinking at her death-
bed. He'd promised it to her in desperation, as part of
a plea to convince her to stay strong in her heart surgery, as if he could animate her exhausted body with
his own fierce will. Maybe it had been a youth's wishful thinking after all.

Scanning more photos, he paused on one from their
trip to the Seychelles. He recognized the beach they'd
visited on the north shore of Praslin Island—a long
stretch of soft, blond sand and crystal-blue water. Annette was alone in the photo, laughing as she slung an
arm around a palm tree. As he enlarged the image, the
T-shirt she wore caught his eye, a simple white T-shirt
with black block letters containing an Emily Dickin-
son quote: "That it will never come again is what makes
life so sweet."

The words hit him like a freight train. Especially seeing them on the woman he loved who would be dead
just nine months after the photo was taken.

Cursing, he shoved the photo away from him, unable

to look at it. But memories flowed over him anyhow, moments he hadn't thought about in years.

He remembered her buying the shirt. He even remembered talking about why she liked the quote since, at the time, a new transplant hadn't even been on their radar. She'd been in great health, and she was the most vital, vibrant woman he'd ever met at the time they married.

Yet she was always aware of that quote, she'd told him. It was why she lived every day with so much love and joy. She knew life could be taken from her at any moment, and she refused to waste a second of the time she had.

Hot tears burned his eyes and his throat as he forced himself to open his laptop again and look at the image. To look at her, and really see her. Not just the woman he'd loved, but an inspirational figure. A woman who had deep, meaningful insight into life, insight he'd been unable to fully appreciate because he'd just mindlessly wanted that love and joy to last forever.

Shame washed over him like a rogue wave. Not for loving her—never that. But for not *listening* to her. For not honoring the gifts she'd tried to give him.

His whole universe shifted. Or maybe just his view of it changed. But in that moment he had startling clarity for what he had to do next. He had a lot of work to do, and life was too precious for him to waste another second in the narrow wasteland of his grief.

First and foremost, he would write a letter to his grandfather relinquishing his position as CEO of Zayn Equity. He'd read between the lines with his brother, and no matter what Marcel said, Roman could see that maintaining the connection to their grandfather's business hurt his brother. If they got disinherited, Roman would move around his assets and find a way to still finance Zayn Designs until it was operating firmly in the black.

He shot to his feet to retrieve his phone. On his way across the living room, he texted the Realtor again to sweeten the offer on the Broome Street storefront. One way or another, Marcel would have a good launchpad for the flagship store.

Full of hope and determination, Roman racked his brain for a way to show Sable he'd been wrong about what he had to offer her. There was more than wealth, damn it.

There had to be, since he'd have less of it at his disposal now that he was about to cut ties with the equity firm.

He wasn't sure how long he sat there, thinking and planning, but the dawn was approaching when he got a text from a number he didn't recognize.

This is Blair, Sable's roommate. I'm taking her to the hospital. She started bleeding—

The words blurred until he couldn't even see them. His brain hammered, not just with fear for his child, but for Sable, until a single thought drowned out all the rest.

He had to be at her side, no matter what.

Twelve

Sable felt cold everywhere.

Shivering under the bleach-scented blanket an emergency room nurse had given her, she listened as Blair explained her symptoms for the second time since they'd arrived. The first time had been to the admitting nurse. Now Blair repeated the story for an attending doctor who said he'd already called for an obstetrician. Sable had been assigned a room and a bed almost immediately, the hurried movement of the ER staffers telling her they took her condition seriously.

How could she be losing her baby when she'd just seen it moving in an ultrasound twelve hours ago? After crying herself to sleep over the breakup with Roman, she'd awoken to cramps and bleeding a little after 3:00 a.m. She'd almost fainted when she realized what was happening, the trauma of it making her knees turn to jelly so that she stumbled against the sink and shouted for her friends.

Tana had called an Uber, insisting it would be faster than an ambulance. Then she'd personally directed the driver to the drop-off entrance while Blair held Sable's hand and told her everything would be okay.

Even though nothing was okay.

A minute or two after the attending physician stepped away from the exam room, a commotion sounded outside the door, and Sable hoped the specialist had arrived. As she pushed up in the bed, the door swung open to admit....

Roman.

Wrong though it might be, she couldn't help the rush of relief at seeing him. No one else knew how worried she'd been. She hadn't confided in Blair and Tana about the other miscarriage. In spite of all the hurt and heartache she felt with Roman, she knew without question he would understand. Empathize.

"I got here as fast as I could." Striding closer, he wove his way around a rolling table and dodged a scowling Tana.

"How did you know where to find me?"

"Your roommate texted me." He glanced at Blair, who was standing beside the bed. "Thank you."

He sat down at Sable's other side, dropping onto the bed, strong arms offering her a comfort she desperately needed.

She couldn't have possibly denied herself that consolation. She tipped her head against his solid, warm chest, knowing he was feeling the same wrenching sense of loss that had devastated her ever since she caught sight of the blood.

Tana hovered at the foot of the bed, looking ready to intervene if necessary. But Blair murmured to her quietly, and tried to lead her out of the room.

"We'll be in the cafeteria," Tana called over her shoulder, her expression still wary. "I can be right back here in less than two minutes if you need anything."

Sable nodded through her tears, then closed her eyes to cry quietly against Roman. He rubbed her back as she melted into his warmth.

After a minute, he spoke, voice rumbling in his chest beneath her ear. "Are you in pain?"

Her heart hurt so much that it took a moment for her to process how the rest of her body felt. "Not right now. I woke up with cramping, but that's…" The reality of the loss struck her like a blow. "The pain is gone now."

"What did the doctor say?" Roman tipped her chin up to look in her eyes.

He looked stressed. Harried. But the tender concern she saw in his gaze was so compassionate and kind that she had to remind herself it wasn't for her so much as their baby.

"He called in a specialist. I'm waiting for an OB now." She swiped her wrist under her eyes and tried to straighten when she saw that she'd left a wet spot on his blue dress shirt. "Sorry to cry all over you."

He shook his head, as if to dismiss her apology. He smoothed his thumb along her temple, wiping away more tear tracks. "I'm the one who's sorry. I'm so damned sorry you're bearing this, Sable. The pain. The fear. I hate thinking about you waking up alone and hurting. I can't imagine how scared you were."

His regrets were so focused on her that she met his dark gaze again, trying to gauge what he was thinking.

"I know you love this baby as much as I do—" she began. But she couldn't finish.

"And I still do." He wrapped her in his arms and squeezed her, the scent and feel of him reminding her of all the times she'd been close to him. The times that had made her fall in love with him. He pressed a kiss into her hair. "But there's no reason to think you've already miscarried, is there? There's still a chance they'll say the baby is fine."

A fresh wave of sadness made her pull away, the hygienic pillowcase behind her back crinkling as she moved. "I don't think you should get your hopes up—"

"This isn't about my hopes, Sable." He gripped her shoulders, steadying her as if he could impress the words on her. "I just want you to be healthy and well. I know how much the last miscarriage devastated you, and I'd do anything to ensure you never feel that kind of hurt again."

The sentiment behind the heartfelt words was reflected in his eyes. Or was that wishful thinking on her part, born out of a need to be loved by him?

While she wondered about it, a loudspeaker nearby crackled to life with a code message, the speaker's voice urgent. Outside the ER room, she could hear a rush of footsteps as medical professionals scrambled to answer the summons. After a moment, she recalled Roman's words.

Along with her sense that he might have cared more for her than she'd realized.

"But you really wanted this baby," she reminded him, unwilling to get tangled up in her love for Roman. He'd already made it clear he wouldn't return her feelings. "I know your hopes were high, too. I could see it in your eyes both times I had the ultrasounds."

"Being a father was a gift I didn't think I'd ever have." He reached behind her to adjust the pillows before coaxing her to lie back against the raised bed. Then he smoothed her hair from her face, his dark gaze roaming over her features. "You stirred that hope in me, Sable. Not just because you're pregnant. You made me feel deeply again. Being with you made me long for a life I thought I'd turned my back on forever."

Her heart skipped a beat, the tempo feeling as off-kilter as she did. "But at the park yesterday, when we talked about the future—"

"I'm so ashamed of myself for not recognizing that I loved you before now, Sable, but I—"

"What?" Her question was barely a breath of sound, but he must have heard it because he squeezed her hands in his.

And repeated the words she feared she'd dreamed.

"I love you, Sable. I didn't allow myself to acknowledge it because I told myself that I was dead inside after Annette died." The bleak sorrow she remembered from the day at the Cloisters was there in his eyes again, but it was tempered with a different look now. Regret. "I'm so sorry I refused to see what was right in front of my eyes all along. But after I went home yesterday—"

The door to the exam room burst open, and in the next instant, a tall Latina woman in a lab coat was striding straight to the bed. "Ms. Cordero, I'm Dr. Incarnacion." Behind the doctor, a nurse rolled in a cart with a small machine. "I read your doctor's notes from your ultrasound earlier today, and based on the baby's activity at that time, I hope you're just experiencing some first trimester cervical bleeding. I brought the fetal Doppler with me so we can listen to the baby's heartbeat to learn more."

The woman's calm demeanor steadied her, even though she could see the nurse was working quickly to set up the Doppler machine. Vaguely, she heard Roman introduce himself while the doctor dragged a stool to the foot of the bed to perform her own exam.

Sable's thoughts were still half on her interrupted conversation with Roman. He'd said he loved her. The certainty in his voice still hummed inside her, a resonant echo that gave her new courage for facing whatever came next, even though she didn't fully understand what had changed his mind.

Hearing he loved her—knowing she hadn't given her heart unwisely—healed something inside her. Helped her let go of the past that had weighed on her shoulders for too long.

The need to take comfort from that love made her thread her fingers through his while they waited for the doctor's prognosis.

"Are you okay?" Roman shifted so he faced her fully,

his dark eyes filled with concern that she now understood wasn't just about their baby after all.

And for a moment, she thought that maybe she could be okay. Even if she wasn't able to carry this tiny life to full term, the caring etched in the lines around Roman's eyes told her that she wouldn't be alone in the aftermath. He wouldn't leave her if she didn't have this baby.

Because this man's love was deep and true, and he didn't give it lightly.

Before she could answer him, however, the Doppler machine broadcast the sound of a strong, rapid heartbeat. With the volume cranked up high, that steady and insistent pulsing filled the whole room.

Filled all the spaces of her heart that weren't already taken up by Roman.

Relief flooded Roman.

Not just because he already loved the child Sable carried. But because he'd been scared out of his mind over what the loss of another baby would do to the woman who meant more to him than anything.

The joy he saw in her hazel eyes now was the most beautiful thing he'd ever seen, making him all the more committed to moving heaven and earth to keep that expression there as often as it was in his power to do so. And, far from feeling disloyal to his dead wife, he breathed in a deep certainty that he was—at long last—at peace with her loss. Annette would have wanted him to be happy and live fully. He'd always known that on a rational level. It had been his own need to prove his devotion to her that had kept him from admitting what he felt for Sable.

What he had now was every bit as deep and intense. Now that he'd embraced those feelings, he finally honored Annette's love of life better than he'd been able to over the last five unhappy years.

Still holding Sable's hands, Roman lifted each to his lips in turn, kissing the backs of them while the doctor assured them their baby was thriving and that the bleeding was likely from the internal exam performed earlier yesterday. Nevertheless, Roman quizzed the physician about signs to look for in the days ahead, even asking if he should purchase their own fetal heart monitor for at-home use if it could give Sable peace of mind.

"It's very rare that I recommend them for in-home use," the doctor explained while she washed and dried her hands at the sink off to one side of the exam room. "The risk of side effects is minuscule in the hands of a trained technician, but unless they're medically needed, I don't recommend my patients use them. You can certainly check with her physician, however."

Roman made a mental note to do just that. And to read as much as possible about keeping Sable safe.

For now, he just hoped he would have the chance to show her how much he loved her and wanted her in his life. Their conversation had been interrupted earlier, even if it was for the very best of news.

"Is it safe to take her home?" he asked while Sable texted the friends who'd brought her to the emergency room.

Friends he needed to thank profusely. Both for their fast thinking and their vigilance in watching over her.

"Yes. Just make sure she gets adequate rest." The

woman turned to the laptop a nurse slid in front of her, and she began typing notes on the keyboard. "She should check in with her doctor tomorrow, and I'll send her records from this visit. But I would be surprised if they need to see her before the next regularly scheduled appointment. Your baby looks very healthy."

With that, the woman and the nurse departed, leaving Sable to dress.

And leaving Roman unsure how to proceed.

Should he let her leave with her friends and ask to see her once she was better rested? If he didn't think it might upset her, he would ask her to return home with him now where he could watch over her personally.

Damn, but he regretted not being able to finish their talk earlier. Would she even believe him now? Believe that he loved her for her own sake and not just as the carrier of his child? He ached at all the words still left unsaid. And he hated that it had taken him this long to realize how devastated he would be to lose this woman.

"Sable." The word was cracked and raw, just like his emotions.

She glanced up at him, pausing in the act of tugging a plastic bag of her belongings from a shelf near the hospital bed. Her expression fell as she saw his face, which no doubt reflected the fear taking hold of him.

But the door to the room flew open again, this time admitting her girlfriends—the tall, elegant blonde, and the petite dynamo with rainbow-colored hair who'd tried to keep him from entering the room when he first got there.

The women swooped in with arms outstretched, folding Sable into hugs between them with so much love that it made him remember how slow he'd been to offer his own.

With regret burning a hole in him, he backed up a step.

"Can I come by tomorrow? After you've had a chance to rest?" It hurt to walk away. But it was his fault that he'd thrown every barrier imaginable in the way of loving her.

"Of course." She nodded, and although she still smiled, she looked a little puzzled at his retreat.

Or was that sheer hopefulness on his part?

"Until tomorrow, then." He turned his attention to her friends. "Ladies, I can't thank you enough for taking care of her. Will you be okay getting her home? I can give you a ride—"

"We're fine," the dynamo assured him, pale gray eyes turning steely as she looked his way. "She's in the best possible hands."

The emphasis on *the best* let him know where he ranked in the woman's eyes.

But since dawn would be breaking any minute, he wasn't going to argue with her. Bottom line, Sable needed her sleep as per doctor's orders.

Still, he was surprised the rainbow-haired pixie followed him to the door to see him out of the room while Sable's other friend helped her into a pair of sweatpants.

"If you're not going to bring your A game to wooing Sable tomorrow, don't bother showing up at the brownstone," the friend warned him in a low voice as he stepped out into the corridor.

Roman's respect for her climbed another notch.

"I'll be there," he assured her. "I'm going to lay the whole world at her feet."

The woman's eyes took his measure for a long moment, her somber gray gaze unwavering, but in the end, she cracked a smile that transformed her whole face. "Good luck, then, Daddy-to-be. You've got your work cut out for you."

Thirteen

Feet propped on pillows, Sable reclined on a patio lounger in the garden behind the brownstone later that day when she heard a man's voice inside the house.

Roman?

Her hopes soared unchecked after his declaration of love at the hospital. And even though she wasn't entirely sure why he'd given her over to the care of her friends so readily after sharing that he loved her, she trusted him to know his own heart. She understood him well enough to know those words hadn't been said lightly.

She'd thought about him to the point of distraction ever since she'd awoken a little past noon, well rested and no longer bleeding. She'd phoned her doctor's office right after waking, but her OB hadn't deemed it necessary for her to come in, assuring her that she could continue with her normal activity.

After showering and checking in with her mother via text, Sable had come downstairs to be greeted by a flurry of admonishments from Blair and Tana, who'd insisted on serving her a late breakfast in the courtyard where they'd toted blankets and pillows to make her comfortable.

All in all, she'd been thoroughly spoiled. The only thing missing was Roman.

Until now.

He emerged from the house dressed in dark pants and loafers, the sleeves of his pale gray Henley shirt rolled up in a way that showed off his forearms. She hadn't seen him dressed casually very often and today he appeared...delectable. He was clean-shaven in a way that told her he'd showered recently; she'd noticed before how a shadow of scruff covered his jaw within hours of a shave. Thinking about it made her want to trail her lips over his cheek to test the smoothness for herself.

"You look beautiful," he told her in lieu of a greeting, the serious undertone of the words making her think he'd been perusing her as intently as she'd been checking him out.

The thought made her hopes—already fizzy and light—lift off even higher. Behind him, she noticed shadows move in the windows of the dining room on the garden level of the brownstone. She smiled to think that her friends were keeping tabs on her. No doubt they felt a little protective after the way she'd cried her eyes out the day before when she'd returned from the Central Park outing with Roman.

But things had shifted dramatically between them at the hospital. Over the late breakfast with her friends this morning, she'd told Tana and Blair about Roman's declaration of love. Blair had squealed with unchecked approval. Tana had told her that anyone could throw around words like "love," but only special people backed up the idea with actions.

If anything, the words only underscored for Sable that she'd already seen so many acts that spoke of love. Of Roman's need to care for her and provide for her, his insistence that she think about a future beyond motherhood to ensure her happiness.

"Thank you. I feel much better." She watched as Roman drew a second padded patio lounger closer over the gray-and-white striped outdoor rug and seated himself on the edge of the chair to face her. Now that he was closer, she noticed the shadows under his eyes. "You look tired. Did you have trouble sleeping?"

Birds chirped in the ornamental trees planted around the courtyard, the nearby buildings dulling the sounds of traffic from DeKalb Avenue along Fort Greene Park.

"I'm okay. Better now that I can see for myself you've recovered nicely since I saw you at the hospital." His expression was troubled. "I've spent all the time since then thinking about how to convince you—"

He broke off, shaking his head as if frustrated.

"What? How to convince me of what?" Alarmed that he seemed worried, she shifted on her bed of pillows so she could take his hand.

"I'm going about this all wrong." He stared down at the place where her fingers gripped his. He stroked his thumb over hers, capturing it beneath his. "I came here today with a car and driver waiting out front, thinking I'd give you a tour of all the best options for you to consider for a home." He huffed out a long breath.

"Really?" Curious, she wondered if he still wanted her input on a place for himself. She liked the idea of him having his own place in New York with room for their child.

And maybe, one day, room for her, too. Suddenly, that was a very real possibility now that he had feelings for her.

"Yes. And we can still do that." He gave a clipped nod, but his gaze remained anxious. "But now that I see you, all I can think about is how to make you believe that I love you, Sable. Even if the worst had happened last night, I would still be right here today, asking you for another chance to prove how much you mean to me. For another chance to make you happy."

Her heart swelled. She sat up enough to cup his jaw with her free hand, testing the smoothness of his jaw with her fingers.

"You *are* making me happy, just by being here and caring about what I need." She felt his love and concern wrap around her as tangibly as a hug. Her whole marriage had never given her as much security as she felt just from Roman's one declaration of love. "And how could I doubt that you love me after you told me as much? I know too well you would have never said the words unless you meant them. Look how well you loved the last woman who held your heart."

His heavy shoulders relaxed a fraction, some of the concern in his eyes dissolving. He clasped a hand around hers where she cupped his face, and he turned his lips into her palm to kiss it.

Pleasure shivered over her skin. Joy shimmered in her soul.

"I didn't know if you would trust what I said when I was so adamant about keeping that torch for her." His voice was pitched low, the words rough-edged as if he hadn't ever planned to share them. "But she would have never wanted me to grieve that way. She spelled it out for me, actually, before she went into surgery that last time. She wanted me to promise I'd find happiness no matter what happened. But I was so adamant about ignoring what she said, so certain she'd come through."

Needing to offer him comfort, Sable slid from her lounger to climb into his lap. "It must have been so painful for you."

Strong arms held her tighter. "I thought I was being strong for her by discounting what she said. It turned out, she was the strong one. I just wasn't ready to hear what she said until yesterday. I came home from the park, and the memories of what she said—of everything that was important to her—just came flooding over me and I knew how deeply I'd messed up with you. I felt like she was right there telling me not to be an idiot. To go get you and our child and live our dreams."

Sable kissed his cheek. His lips. She shed a few

happy tears in between kisses, unspeakably grateful to have his loyal, passionate heart to call her own.

"You have me, Roman," she promised, pausing the trail of kisses long enough to meet his dark eyes. "You have my body, and my heart, and all my love. You've had them ever since you undressed me that night in the studio, even though I kept trying to tell myself it was just physical." A smile curved her mouth, the happiness inside her bubbling over. "My heart knew better the whole time."

"After how stubborn and blind I've been, I'm not sure I deserve you." Frowning, he traced the fullness of her lower lip with his thumb. "I resigned my position as head of the equity firm, by the way. So on top of being stubborn and blind, I'm most likely disinherited. But I wanted to show Marcel my love and support in no uncertain terms. You were right about that."

"Good for you." A different kind of pleasure filled her. "Does that mean you want to relocate to New York full-time?" It hadn't occurred to her until now that he had worked hard to help other people—guiding the business end of Marcel's company, taking the reins for his grandfather and caring for his wife when her health failed. But who worked to bring comfort and ease to Roman's life?

She could do that for him. She welcomed the chance to be there for him the way he wanted to be there for her. A partnership. Something she'd never had before.

Something that was now possible because of this amazing man who'd taken her life by storm.

"I'm keeping a toehold in Los Angeles for when

you're ready to move your celebrity stylist business to the West Coast." Leaning back in the lounger with her still in his lap, he shifted position so they reclined together, her leg straddling his in a way that stirred a new heat. "Besides, I might have clients who'll want to come with me if I decide to do any private investing. For the next year, though, I'm going to put all my focus on helping Marcel launch a storefront. I found out this morning our bid was accepted on a property on Broome Street."

"Get out!" Excitement stirred at the thought of a flagship store happening so quickly for Zayn Designs. She levered herself up on her elbow, propping herself on his broad chest. "Can we see it?"

"I do have that car waiting to take you house hunting," he reminded her. His hand resting on her waist ventured lower, curling around her hip. Squeezing her curves. "There's a brownstone near Prospect Park that just came on the market if you want to stay in Brooklyn, for that matter."

Wow. He really meant what he said. He'd been planning.

The idea of being close to her friends tempted her, but the warmth of his palm refocused her attention on the proximity of his hard body. She arched her back in a way that lifted her breasts closer to his mouth while pressing the juncture of her legs against his thigh.

"How long will your driver wait?" she inquired, her fingers tracing his collarbone just inside the lightweight cotton of his shirt.

Roman's eyes flamed. He gripped her more securely

in a way that caused her to rub against him. "Long enough for you to give me a tour of your bedroom."

An empty ache inside her made her wriggle impatiently. "You read my mind. I've been wanting to show it to you."

"And what do you know, I've been dying to make you feel good."

Sable kissed him, long and deep, tongues tangling until they were both breathless. She tried to pull away enough to stand up, but he tugged her off her feet and carried her through the garden toward the back door.

"We're going to make *each other* feel good," she clarified when she recovered the power to speak.

"And then, we're going to make each other happy for a long, long time to come." He stared down at her with dark eyes full of promise, a future written there that made her a little giddy and a whole lot satisfied.

She didn't bother trying to reply, though. Winding her arms around his neck, she lost herself in the kiss and the certainty they were going to make all their dreams come true.

Epilogue

Ten months later

Tucking his four-month-old daughter into the crook of one arm, Roman pushed open the double doors to Zayn Designs with the other, eager to deliver his sweetly fretful little charge to her mama.

Not that he minded settling Leyla down when she fussed. He took it as a personal endorsement of his parenting skills that he could distract his baby girl even better than the nanny, who would arrive at the new store within the hour to take Leyla home.

"You're here!" Sable's happy voice greeted him even before he saw her in the small crowd of after-party guests Marcel had invited for the grand opening.

Dressed in a silk slip dress that hugged her newly

voluptuous curves, she waved Roman over to a corner near a freestanding bar, where she was flanked by Marcel and Cybil Deschamps.

After eight months of construction and two more months of interior design, Zayn Designs had opened for business today. And while Sable had long ago completed her internship for the company, Marcel had recently enticed her back part-time as an assistant to the creative director. The opportunity had come just in time for New York Fashion Week in February, when Leyla was two months old.

By now, Leyla was used to her mother's schedule, and Roman didn't mind ferrying his daughter around when she needed to be breastfed. Having the chance to sit with the two people he loved most in the world was the best part of his day.

"Hello, beautiful girl." He greeted his wife with a kiss before saying hello to Marcel and Cybil. "How's it going?"

Cybil, decked out in the Zayn Designs brand to support the store, wrapped an arm around Sable's shoulders. "Sable is making waves with her social media photos from the grand opening. She already got Zayn some celebrity endorsements and reposts."

As Sable lifted Leyla from his arms, the baby seemed to remember she was famished and let out a wail. Murmuring her excuses, Sable started for the back room. Roman began to follow her when his brother fell into step beside him.

"It's pretty convenient how you can make her cry on cue to get your wife alone," Marcel observed before clamping a hand on Roman's arm and bringing him to a halt in a quiet corner of the store. "We got calls from around the globe today, Roman. Orders from London, Paris and Milan. A few from Singapore and Dubai. One of the Dubai customers asked if she could invest in a storefront over there to facilitate our getting into the market."

Marcel's excitement was palpable as he stood there surrounded by the results of his hard work. A champagne bottle popped behind the bar as the caterers passed drinks to the guests hand-selected for the after-party. The lighting highlighted the clothes like fine art against the walls, which were also covered with paintings that Marcel had personally chosen. Everything about the restrained elegance of the space reflected his brother's keen eye and good taste, and it did Roman's heart proud to see Marcel's efforts rewarded and embraced.

"Wow. That's incredible." Impressed, Roman clapped him on the shoulder. "Congratulations, Marcel. You deserve every accolade that's coming your way, and more. You've done great work here."

"Me?" Marcel shook his head, dark hair falling in one eye. "*We* did great work. The Zayn brothers. With the help of one very talented newcomer to the clan."

Roman grinned at the way he included Sable in the family. Roman had convinced her to marry him in a courthouse ceremony last fall before Leyla was born, but they had plans to exchange vows on the beach in Malibu over the summer in a ceremony with their closest friends and family. Sable had been to the Malibu house with him twice. She'd fallen in love with the ocean views and looked forward to spending more time there soon.

"I don't know about Dubai, but I'll look into it. Next up is Los Angeles, then Miami." He had a solid business plan in place, but if sales were as strong as Marcel hinted, maybe they'd accelerate the timeline. Capitalize on the momentum.

He hadn't gone back to Zayn Equity, even when his grandfather had suggested a family meeting to iron out their differences. Roman had recognized that he enjoyed working with his brother far more, and he appreciated the additional time it allowed him to spend with his wife and daughter.

Ever since he'd promised his love to Sable, he'd been on a mission to enjoy life and the good things that came his way. And life was very, very good.

"Of course." Marcel nodded, content to give Roman free rein to handle the business the same way Roman gave his brother control of the creative end. "I hope you know Sable can head home whenever she wants. The party won't run late. I'm just glad to have seen you both tonight to celebrate the success."

"The nanny will be here shortly to take Leyla home," Roman assured him, his gaze darting to the door to the back room where Sable was feeding the baby. "Sable and I both want to stay a while to celebrate the first of many new milestones."

"Good." Marcel lifted a champagne glass in a silent toast. "Find me before you leave so we can have a real drink."

Agreeing to that plan, Roman opened the door to the small employee break room at the back of the shop. He didn't see Sable, but heard her call from down the hall.

"Roman? I'm back here."

Following the sound of her voice, he reached the storage area where Marcel had left a new sofa that hadn't worked in the store's interior design. Surrounded by rolling racks of clothes, Sable was tucked into a corner of the white leather, a layette blanket covering half her dress. She'd tugged off a strap to free one breast, and cradled their baby close.

"I'm so glad you brought her." Sable smiled up at him, maternal contentment glowing in her lovely face. "My breasts were killing me."

"They're killing me, too," he assured her, taking the seat beside her so he could wrap his arm around her as securely as she held their little girl. "You're more gorgeous every day."

"Mmm." She tipped her head against his chest, nuzzling into him. "So are you. Seeing you carry my baby around is the sexiest thing ever."

"One of many reasons I like being a dad." He pressed a kiss into the top of her hair. "I see that hungry gleam in your eye whenever I show off my parenting prowess."

He cupped her elbow just beneath the spot where Leyla's head rested. Already the little girl's eyes were closing, her rosebud lips loosening from Sable's nipple.

"This day has been so perfect," she said on a soft sigh, trailing her fingers over Leyla's cheek. "The store is a success. My baby is happy and healthy. I'm wildly in love. And soon I'll get to go home with you and show you how much."

Roman shifted her in his arms just enough so that he could look down into her hazel eyes. She was his temptress. His lover. His wife. He'd never imagined his life could be this full, his heart this complete.

"If it's even half how much I love you, I'm the luckiest man alive."

* * * * *

COMING SOON!

We really hope you enjoyed reading this book.
If you're looking for more romance, be sure to
head to the shops when new books are
available on

Thursday 10th June

To see which titles are coming soon, please visit
millsandboon.co.uk/nextmonth

LET'S TALK
Romance

For exclusive extracts, competitions
and special offers, find us online:

- facebook.com/millsandboon
- @MillsandBoon
- @MillsandBoonUK

Get in touch on 01413 063232

For all the latest titles coming soon, visit
millsandboon.co.uk/nextmonth

MILLS & BOON

THE HEART OF ROMANCE

A ROMANCE FOR EVERY READER

ODERN
Prepare to be swept off your feet by sophisticated, sexy and seductive heroes, in some of the world's most glamourous and romantic locations, where power and passion collide.

STORICAL
Escape with historical heroes from time gone by. Whether your passion is for wicked Regency Rakes, muscled Vikings or rugged Highlanders, awaken the romance of the past.

EDICAL
Set your pulse racing with dedicated, delectable doctors in the high-pressure world of medicine, where emotions run high and passion, comfort and love are the best medicine.

ue Love
Celebrate true love with tender stories of heartfelt romance, from the rush of falling in love to the joy a new baby can bring, and a focus on the emotional heart of a relationship.

Desire
Indulge in secrets and scandal, intense drama and plenty of sizzling hot action with powerful and passionate heroes who have it all: wealth, status, good looks…everything but the right woman.

EROES
Experience all the excitement of a gripping thriller, with an intense romance at its heart. Resourceful, true-to-life women and strong, fearless men face danger and desire - a killer combination!

To see which titles are coming soon, please visit

millsandboon.co.uk/nextmonth

JOIN US ON SOCIAL MEDIA!

Stay up to date with our latest releases, author news and gossip, special offers and discounts, and all the behind-the-scenes action from Mills & Boon...

 millsandboon

 millsandboonuk

 millsandboon

It might just be true love...

MILLS & BOON

HEROES

At Your Service

Experience all the excitement of a gripping thriller, with an intense romance at its heart. Resourceful, true-to-life women and strong, fearless men face danger and desire - a killer combination!

MILLS & BOON
True Love

Romance from the Heart

Celebrate true love with tender stories of
heartfelt romance, from the rush of falling
in love to the joy a new baby can bring,
and a focus on the emotional
heart of a relationship.

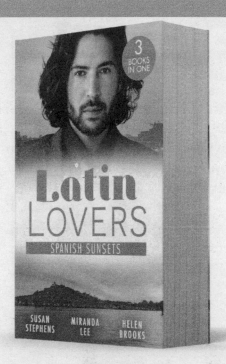